He would guard his secret at all cost....

Kyros turned his head to see Thera by Hester, rummaging through his saddle bag. He sprang to his feet and ran to her.

"Wait!" he called and grabbed her hand away just as she was about to discover his secret. He held onto her wrist and she looked up to him with those Olympian blue eyes.

"What's the matter?" She shook her hand loose and was about to dig back into the bag when Kyros spun her around toward him. He had to distract her.

His lips brushed against hers ever so lightly and when he pulled away, he realized he wanted to do it again.

He lowered his mouth to hers and this time, gave her a lingering kiss. One that turned into a deep kiss on both their parts. She tasted like a cross between honey and ambrosia—like the nectar of the gods ...

It was a long time since he'd had a woman. No woman wanted him once she knew his secret....

Kyros' Secret

By

Elizabeth Rose

New Leaf ✧ Illinois

A New Leaf Book
Published by WigWam Publishing Co.
P.O. Box 6992
Villa Park, IL 60181
http://www.newleafbooks.net

Copyright © 2000 by Elizabeth Rose Krejcik
Library of Congress Catalogue Card Number: 00-105336
ISBN: 1-930076-03-7

Front cover photography copyright © 2000 by Elizabeth Rose Krejcik
Cover design copyright © by Teresa Basile

Printed in the U.S.A.

To my good friends and cover models, Leland Burbank and Leslie Metcalf. Always remember, we create our own reality. Dreams really do come true. This one's for you!

ONE

Thera, Goddess of Sensations, closed her eyes and pulled back the bowstring slowly. Killing a rabbit should be an easy task, but she knew it would hurt her more than it would the poor creature she hunted. She didn't need to see her prey, for her hearing was so acute she'd learned to pinpoint the animal's hiding place by the sound of its frightened breathing.

"Go ahead, Thera," came her father's voice from behind her. "Kill the senseless thing just like I've instructed you."

Thera felt the lump in her throat as she swallowed dryly. It wasn't easy being the daughter of Ares, the blood-thirsty god of war. And she knew in her heart she could never be the warrior he wanted her to be.

The tip of her arrow dropped a little as she felt the coppery taste of the rabbit's unshed blood in her own mouth. It was times like this that made her curse her powers of the senses which graced her as a goddess—her only attribute in being born the second twin of Ares and Aphrodite.

"Raise your arrow and finish the job, you coward!" Ares' voice wasn't more than a hot whisper in her ear, but it rattled her brain as much as it did her nerves.

Her finger twitched on the taut string, as she wanted nothing more than to please her father, but at the same time being the daughter of the goddess of love, she found it hard to kill a defenseless creature.

"I can't."

"You will."

"I won't!" She opened her eyes but kept the bowstring taut and the arrow aimed.

She felt her father's gaze burning a hole through her and felt his anger mixed with shame.

"You're worthless, Thera. You're the cursed second-born twin and you know you really shouldn't be a goddess at all. You're weak. No god will take you to his bed knowing you act more like a mortal than the immortal goddess you are.

He was goading her, appealing to the war-like blood he'd spawned in her veins. She felt the rage choking her as her loving instincts fought the forces of dormant hatred within. She wasn't like her sister, Harmonia, who'd learned to balance the forces of war and love. No, she wasn't as pretty or as strong as her mother's favorite child. She knew the gods laughed at Ares behind his back for fathering a weak-willed daughter such as herself. And this only made her father more determined to sway her to fight in his army and live by his war-like ways.

"I won't kill just for the sport of it." She lowered her bow and turned to look at her father. Dressed in black leather from head to toe, his well-groomed body seemed almost contradictory to the destruction and havoc he usually caused. His black hair fell in waves, slicked back from his chiseled face. His full lips curled up in a slight half-smile, exposing a mouth of perfect white teeth.

Thera felt a chill run through her as his dark eyes bore into her. She respected Ares as a god but feared him and felt uncomfortable by his presence. He had used the gift of eternal youth well. His appearance made him look not much older than her own age of twenty-seven years. She groaned inwardly, knowing at birth, Zeus, her grandfather had bestowed upon her these same gifts of eternal youth and immortality. Now, not even death could take her away from the sensations and the turmoil that battled within her soul.

Ares held out his leather-clad arm and an enormous raven appeared from nowhere. Thera recognized her father's latest pet, smiling inwardly as she thought of how much it meant to him.

"You're not killing for sport, daughter." He ran his finger over the raven's feathered head. "I want the rabbit for my supper."

The raven cackled a throaty laugh in mockery, which only brought more unwanted feelings rising to the surface inside Thera.

She looked past her own short leather skirt to her booted feet, not wanting to fall under her father's hypnotizing eyes.

"You don't need me to hunt," she reminded him. "With the shake of a finger you have all the food you need."

"Ah, but you're so right, Thera." Ares held the raven up and admired it as he talked. "I don't need you to hunt … I just need you to kill."

The rabbit darted past them and disappeared into the brush. Thera took a deep breath, feeling its relief and walked over to the empty spot.

"Just once is all you need to kill and then the rage and glory of war will be imbedded upon your soul. Just once is all you need to feel the triumph of power over your mother's weak blood that flows through your veins."

Thera felt her mother's presence even before she turned to look. Materializing out of thin air came Aphrodite, the Goddess of Love, and Thera's twin sister, Harmonia.

"Since when is the power of love weak, Ares?" Aphrodite's thin, white gown clung to her voluptuous breasts and flowed down her body as she spoke. Harmonia stood next to her looking more like her mother's twin than Thera's.

Thera had her father's course black hair, while Harmonia inherited the fine gold silken hair of their mother. Thera was built tall and lean like her father, while Harmonia was petite, yet curvaceous and feminine in all ways.

"Aphrodite, you're not welcome here," snapped Ares, placing his pet on his shoulder.

"That's not what you said the night our daughters were conceived," she reminded him. "As a matter of fact, I remember you saying how strong love was that night."

The raven croaked a protest, and Harmonia glared at it with disgust. "Let's leave this filthy place and go back to our chambers," she begged her mother.

"I'll go with you." Thera broke in, truly wanting to leave the forest though she usually loved to spend her days in nature. Today just wasn't one of those days.

"You'll stay until you've killed," warned her father. "After that, you're free to go."

"I'll not stay and watch this," Harmonia said and disappeared from sight. Thera didn't regret her departure.

"You really think Thera is going to be the one to start your next war between—"

"Silence!" Ares interrupted Aphrodite. "This is none of your concern."

"A war? Between who?" asked Thera.

"You haven't told the poor thing, have you?" Aphrodite laughed and started to disappear.

"Mother wait for me." Thera tried to move toward Aphrodite, but Ares raised his hand and without touching her, sent her sailing back against the trunk of a tree.

"You'll kill before you leave my sight. Is that clear?"

Thera watched as her mother's wispy form faded in and out. The woman's laughing voice echoed the carelessness in her heart. Aphrodite was the Goddess of Love, but conceit was another trait that should have been noted. She thought of herself as too beautiful to even be seen with her plain daughter. Thera knew without a doubt her mother didn't want her any more than her father did. Aphrodite's laugh may have been directed towards Ares, but in a way she knew it was also directed toward herself.

Thera got to her feet and started toward her mother. This time, Ares just raised his elbow and an unseen force pushed her face-down to the ground.

"You pathetic child," came her mother's voice. "You're a goddess, now start acting like one and use your own powers and quit groveling at your father's feet."

Thera had only used her powers once or twice in her whole life. She didn't like the way they made her feel. She knew it could be dangerous to get too used to her abilities. Power had been the downfall of many a god and goddess. She knew her emotions weren't stable enough to know when to use her powers and still be able to stop if she had to.

"Kill, Thera, or I'll be forced to punish you!"

Thera felt the bolt of energy coming straight for her back and thanked her sensations. She rolled out of the way just as a tree split and caught afire.

"Leave the girl alone, Ares." Aphrodite protested until Ares looked her way and raised his hand. "You're on your own, Thera," she called as she left. "Act like a goddess or you'll have to learn the hard way."

Thera's heartbeat quickened. Her mother's form disappeared and Ares turned back towards her.

"You see, Thera, no one's going to protect you. Now pick up your bow and let's get on with our little lesson."

"I want to leave."

"You'll kill first."

"I won't." Thera's eyes drifted to the bow and arrow lying next to her hand. She felt the disgust of her mother and the bitterness of her father.

Her own fear melded together with these emotions and her mind began to think that to kill one small rabbit wouldn't be so bad after all.

Ares chuckled, obviously knowing her thoughts. "Pick up your bow, Thera. Today you'll become a warrior."

The raven flapped his wings upon Ares' shoulder and its dark eyes focused on her own bright blue ones.

"I just have to kill once and then I'll be free to go?" asked Thera.

"That's what I said, wasn't it?" Ares ran his hand over his short beard.

"And you'll never bother me about killing again?"

"Never. Now do it, for you know you really want to."

Anger pushed its way through Thera's veins. She shivered as the war-like side of her suddenly seemed to come to life. She never wanted to kill before, but now she felt she did. One arrow was all it would take. One death and she'd be able to leave this whole situation. She'd show her father she could be strong. She'd show her mother she wasn't as worthless as everyone thought she was. She'd play Ares' little game and then it'd all be over.

"There's a deer just beyond the trees, Thera." Her father crossed his arms and waited.

Thera didn't need to ask where. She could feel its presence. She picked up her bow and cocked the arrow. The deer was eating grass in a clearing just up ahead, not even aware of their presence. One clean shot and it wouldn't even know what happened.

She glanced over her shoulder and caught her father's triumphant grin. His huge black raven was perched upon his shoulder, just waiting to dive in and scavenge the meat as soon as she'd made her kill.

Thera pulled back the bowstring quietly and lined up her shot. The deer raised its head for a second.

"Kill it!" came her father's hoarse whisper. "Kill the senseless thing already!"

"I will, Father," Thera answered, feeling like she was in a trance. "I will kill for the first time in my life."

"And you'll enjoy it," Ares reassured her. His laughter burned her ears while the cawing of his raven pierced her heart.

Thera spun on her heel and released the bowstring. The arrow made its way to its victim. The animal fell to the ground, dead on contact.

Thera lowered her bow and gloated at her father. "I killed, Father. And you're right, I do feel good about it."

Ares' face darkened and his eyes bore fire. He looked to the ground and let out a curse. "You'll pay for this, you little fool. You'll not get away with what you've done!"

Thera felt his sadness but did not regret her action.

"I killed for you, Father."

"You are a damn fool, Thera," answered Ares. "You never should have killed my favorite raven."

Kyros stretched out on the lush grass, his hands behind his head as he stared up at Mount Olympus. Home of the gods and goddesses. Palace of the fierce and feared rulers. Kyros' own late father, King Mezentius had never favored the gods, even though it endangered his life not to. Kyros carried on his father's dislike and had just cause for his feelings. After what Ares had done to them, it was no wonder his father died from nothing more than sorrow.

Kyros heard the sound of hoofbeats and jumped to his feet, grabbing his sword from the ground in preparation.

"Kyros?" called a voice from behind some brush. "Are you here?"

He took a deep breath and replaced his sword.

"Yes, Chiron. I'm here."

He watched as his close friend, the old Centaur Chiron trotted out from behind a bush. From waist up the old man was human like himself; from waist down he was nothing more than a horse. With a swish of his tail, Chiron came forward, his bow and arrow flung over one shoulder.

"You're late." Kyros greeted his old friend with an embrace. "I feared my brother may have found you and brought you back to the castle to use you as this evening's entertainment."

"No, my good friend. Pittheus may have succeeded your father as king of Trozen, but he'll never be a good enough warrior to capture me."

"It's time for the Centaurs and the people of Trozen to unite."

"You're a dreamer, Kyros. It'll never happen."

"My father had this dream," Kyros reminded him, "and almost succeeded in uniting the people of Trozen and the Centaur race."

"Yes," agreed Chiron. "And because of his foolishness, Ares punished him, or have you forgotten? After all, you were the one who really paid the price."

"I think you know the answer to that," said Kyros. "Ares' curse upon me is probably the reason for my father's death. He died of a broken heart and I couldn't even be there to comfort him when he passed on."

"Your father was a good man," said Chiron, "but now that he's left this world, the union between Centaurs and Trozens will never happen. Pittheus will see to that."

"If only I were king of Trozen, I'd—"

"You're not, Kyros. And as long as your brother lives, the Centaurs will never walk the same ground as the people of your father's kingdom."

A twig snapped and Kyros and Chiron raised their weapons as they turned toward the sound. A young Centaur emerged from the bushes shyly.

"Nemos!" scolded Chiron. "Haven't I told you never to bother me here in the glen?"

Kyros motioned for the boy to come forward. He was familiar with the names of the Centaurs but had only made contact with Chiron. The Centaurs were leery of humans and tried to avoid them at all costs.

"Come here, Nemos. You don't need to be afraid." Kyros extended his hand but Nemos made a wide circle around him and stood next to Chiron.

"I've been raised by Chiron and am not afraid of anyone," said Nemos.

Kyros admired the young boy's bravado but knew it wasn't so. And for good cause, he had to admit. Since Kyros' older brother Pittheus inherited the kingdom, Centaurs were caught for sport. However, they'd always been let loose afterwards, and none to this point had yet been killed. Only Chiron's instructing the Centaurs to forget the issue had stopped the Centaurs from striking back and causing an all-out war.

"I overheard some of the others talking." Nemos eyed Kyros cautiously. "They say that Ares is stirring up trouble again."

"What kind of trouble, boy?" Chiron put his hand on Nemos' shoulder.

"He plans on sending his daughter down from Mount Olympus to marry the new king of Trozen."

Kyros chuckled at the thought. "I'm sure Pittheus will love the idea of marrying a goddess. Especially Harmonia. That's one goddess that could please any man with just a smile."

"Not her," said Nemos. "The other daughter."

"I wasn't aware Ares had another daughter." Kyros frowned and looked to Chiron for reassurance.

"He does," verified Chiron, "though he's basically kept her hidden. She's the twin of Harmonia … and nothing but trouble. If Ares is sending her to marry your brother, there must be something amiss."

"That's not all I heard," said the boy. "I overheard some of the Centaurs saying that Ares has made a deal with Rodas."

"Rodas," Kyros repeated. "Isn't he the rambunctious Centaur who's been trying to talk the other Centaurs into pillaging Trozen?"

"He is." Chiron's voice was solemn and yet a bit anxious. "What else do you know, Nemos? Tell me everything before it's too late."

"All I know is that Rodas is supposed to meet with Ares and his daughter outside the temple of Aphrodite. When Rodas was heading out I heard him mumbling something about the girl bearing his child."

"Damn him to Tartarus!" Chiron grabbed an arrow and his bow from his back and turned to go.

"Wait, Chiron." Kyros ran to catch up to him, sword at the ready. "What do you think is going on?"

The old man stopped and lowered his bow. "It's happened, Kyros. Ares has found a way to bring war between the Centaurs and the people of Trozen. And when he's finished, not a single Centaur will live to tell about it."

"Father, where are we going?" Thera glanced over her shoulder at her father's three henchmen who followed them. Oddly enough, they were on horses while she and Ares were on foot. Her bow and arrow were mounted on her back, though she had no intention of using them to hunt a poor defenseless animal again.

Ares didn't answer, just dragged her along behind him. In the distance, Thera could see the temple of her mother, Aphrodite. No one would be there this late in the day. Usually by sunset, all who'd come to worship had gone on to the safety of their homes.

"You're still angry because Hades refused to bring your raven back from the dead, aren't you?" she asked her father.

That got his attention. He stopped so suddenly that Thera went crashing into him. The smell of leather surrounded her and she felt her father's anger though he tried to hide it.

"I thrive on war and my brother Hades thrives on the dead I send him. He's upset I haven't sent more his way lately. For this, he's decided to keep my raven. But don't worry, Daughter, for it doesn't bother me at all. I'm sure Hades will return my pet all in good time."

"You mean after you've started another war?"

Ares chuckled and ran his hand over his beard. "No, Thera. I mean after *you've* started a war."

Thera took a deep breath and let it out slowly as she digested her father's words.

"I would never start a war between anyone and you know it."

"No, Thera, you wouldn't. That's why I've decided to help you out. You see, you've got the war-like abilities in your blood. And now that you've killed my raven, you'll find yourself wanting to kill even more. First you'll feel pity, then disgust. Next you'll feel anger and then hatred. Soon that hatred will blind you and you'll want nothing more than to kill. And you'll kill all right, even those you may have once thought you loved."

"What are you saying?" Thera was shocked at the thought. Never could she kill the animals of the forest she loved so well. The henchmen caught up to them, and Ares nodded for them to wait in the distance. As Thera watched them leave, she realized one of them brought along an extra horse.

She backed away from Ares and eyed him suspiciously. "You plan on sending me away, don't you?"

"You're to marry the king of Trozen."

"What? You're sending me to marry a mortal?"

"You'll no longer be immortal, Thera. I've talked to the other gods and we've decided to take back your immortality along with your gift of eternal youth."

"Zeus gave me those gifts, not you."

"He's agreed to it. But because of him you'll maintain your power of the senses."

"And my other powers as well?"

"No, Thera. You'll live like a human, but you'll only have your power of the senses. Nothing else."

Thera almost welcomed the change but decided not to show it. "Sounds more like a curse than a gift. Are you telling me the truth about Zeus?"

The sound of hoofbeats grasped her attention. She turned her head to see a rugged-looking Centaur standing just beyond the temple. His gamy aroma filled her nostrils and her blood stirred restlessly in her veins.

"Who's he?" she asked.

"He's going to be the father of your child."

Thera looked at Ares in disbelief. She knew that Centaurs only mated with the sea nymphs. If a Centaur were to mate with a human woman, as she would now be, she would die giving birth. She'd also bring mixed blood and probably war to the all-male Centaur race.

"You said nothing about the king of Trozen being a Centaur." Thera felt the Centaur's lust as he eyed her up and down.

"The king isn't a Centaur."

"Then why did you say—" Thera suddenly understood it all too clearly. Her father planned on using the Centaur to impregnate her before sending her to the castle. When a Centaur child was born to the king, a war would take place between the people of Trozen and the Centaur race. And she would be the cause of the war whether she liked it or not. Ares would have his war after all.

"I'll not lie with him."

"Centaurs don't need to lie down to accomplish the act," Ares told her with a devilish grin. With a flick of his head, he motioned for the Centaur to join them.

"No!" Thera raised her hand and shook her head. An invisible wall stopped the Centaur from coming any closer. She still had her powers, or at least for the time being.

The Centaur looked at Ares and growled, "I thought you said she'd be willing."

"So I lied," answered Ares. "But don't worry, I'll give you a little help. I'll use my powers to induce her with your seed. Then we can get on with the plan."

Ares raised his hand and sent a bolt of lightning toward his daughter and the Centaur simultaneously.

Kyros made his way through the clearing just as the beam of lightning left Ares' hand and headed toward Rodas. He'd remembered Ares' beam crashing into him the day he was cursed. This time a Centaur was about to be punished by Ares, he was sure of it. He knew the life of hardships he himself had suffered because of this god. He had to save this Centaur from whatever it was that Ares had in store for him, for no one deserved the punishments and curses Ares dished out.

"Noooo!" he screamed, jumping in front of the Centaur and taking the beam square in the chest.

The shock of energy vibrated through him. He felt every hair on his body stand on end just as he had that awful day almost a year ago. He waited for the intense pain and severe cramps but they never came. This time, a lusty feeling engulfed him and he felt his manhood swell beneath his breeches. A bright light momentarily blinded him, the flash somehow taking control of his senses. His knees buckled beneath him and he fell to the ground. What should have been pain was replaced by sensual pleasure.

A wash of joy and elation engulfed his body. Vibrating. Hot. Sensuous. Pure bliss like he'd never felt before. For one pure moment he was one with all that ever was. He was the earth, the sky, fire, the sea. He felt alive, glowing—pleasure in the true sense of the word.

His vision cleared just as he climaxed, coming to a height he'd never experienced even in the throws of coupling with a lusty woman. He felt sated, fulfilled—satisfied to the very brim.

Still, while all this was taking place, he couldn't help but notice the dusk sky above him. The warmth left him immediately and a chill swept his body from head to toe. Nightfall was creeping in around him and there was nothing he could do to stop the dreaded transformation that always took over his body this time of day. From an emotional high to the lowest of lows. And all in one split second. His breathing was labored; a sweat beaded his brow, and he realized that the sun had set behind Mount Olympus.

He heard Ares curse and also the sound of a woman's scream; then the hoofbeats of Rodas as the Centaur made his way past him.

"You'll pay for this," Rodas threatened, rearing up and pawing the air with his front hooves directly above Kyros before galloping away.

Kyros' vision was still a bit blurred, but he saw the girl lying on the ground with her eyes closed. Dark hair tumbled past her shoulders and fanned out around her on the dusty earth. Her body was lean and straight. A quiver of arrows had fallen next to her; a bow was clutched in one hand. This must be Ares' daughter, he thought. The daughter Chiron told him about that was nothing but trouble.

Ares had left the scene in a rage, but his henchmen were headed in Kyros' direction.

"Kyros!" Chiron and Nemos appeared from the brush and the old Centaur reached down to give him a helping hand. Kyros allowed Chiron to pull him to a standing position. He stretched his stiff legs and pawed the earth beneath him in aggravation. Why did this have to happen now? He shook his head, trying to clear his vision as he turned back towards Chiron and young Nemos.

Nemos stared at him, wide-eyed and open mouthed. "He's ... he's..."

"Yes, boy," Chiron replied as he placed a hand on Nemos' shoulder. "Kyros is a Centaur like us ... for now."

"Then he's cursed?" asked Nemos in a faint voice.

"I am," Kyros spoke up. "And I have Ares to thank for it. Because of him I've been living a nightmare. Because of him I'm a man by day and a Centaur by night."

"We must leave here at once," said Chiron, guiding Kyros into the cover of the bushes before any of Ares' men came after them.

Kyros looked over his shoulder with blurred vision at Ares' soldiers pulling the girl to her feet. He wanted to stay, wanted to find out more about what just happened—about the girl. But he knew Chiron was right. If they were to stay, they'd only be captured by Ares and then there would be no chance for him to bring peace between the Trozens and the Centaurs. He had to go ... for now. But he would be back.

TWO

"Centaurs!"

Thera didn't need to actually see the wretched half-men, half-horse creatures to know they stalked her and her traveling companions. Her sixth sense, not to mention her nose, made her aware they were hiding somewhere in the thick shrub. She shifted her weight in the saddle and ran her hand across the back of her mare's head. One of the guards rode in front of her down the narrow path, the other two brought up the rear.

"Let's get these horses moving, Ganymede, unless you're up for taking on an army of Centaurs." She sniffed the air once more, certain she'd smelled the wild, gamy sweat of the Centaur warrior. She'd never been fond of the creatures and after what just happened she disliked them even more.

She couldn't remember much of how it happened, only the rugged Centaur that stood before her devouring her with his eyes. Probably an ally of her father. And definitely no good if he consented to mate with a human. It wasn't a Centaur's way. A Centaur had pride in his race and would never mate with anyone besides the beloved sea nymphs.

"How can you be sure, your Highness?" Ganymede sat taller upon his horse, scoping the sides of the narrow road with his eyes. A quick jerk of his dark, curly head, and he called to the men behind. "I don't see anything. Do you, Akil?"

Akil stifled a yawn, and let out a loud belch before answering. "Naw. No creatures back here. That is, unless you count Loxias." His large belly jiggled as a deep bellowing laugh lodged in his throat. "Loxias has been known to scare off a few virgins in his time."

"Bite your tongue, Akil." Loxias spit a stream of phlegm toward Akil, just missing him, but hitting Akil's war-horse instead. The animal threw back its head and reared up on two legs. Akil nearly fell off his horse from the unexpected jolt.

"Hades take you, Loxias! Your own spittle burns a fire into my animal hotter than the fires of Tartarus."

"Stop it, you fools," Thera warned. "Can't you see the horses are spooked? They've caught the scent of the Centaurs."

Ganymede stopped his horse, thereby halting the entire caravan in the process.

"I don't see the problem. My horse is calm." He turned his steed and came toward her slowly as if to demonstrate the animal's controlled behavior.

"That nag's not calm," Akil mumbled as he raised a wineskin to his lips. "She's dead."

Thera fumed as she listened to the raucous laughter of the fools that were supposed to escort her to Trozen. With warriors like these along for protection, she could almost count the moments left of her futile life. She'd have to lose them as quickly as possible.

"Believe me, they're here," she answered. "I can feel it in my veins."

"Not to mention other parts," sneered Ganymede and they all broke out laughing. "After all, one of those wretched things is going to be your child."

Thera's stomach lurched at his words. So it was true and not just some frightening nightmare as she hoped. She was pregnant and at the same time still a virgin. Turmoil rolled through her along with a strange sort of excitement.

"Your Highness ... I mean, Thera," Loxias corrected himself as he rode to her side. "Centaurs have never been seen in these parts before, plus they always stay near their hovel after dark. I suggest we stop for the night and get a little shut-eye."

"I agree." Akil swung a heavy leg over the side of his horse and dismounted with a thud. "I could go for something to eat."

Thera sat rigid in the saddle as she surmised the situation. The sun had just sunk into a red ocean of sky as it peeked a last futile ray through the tall trees. Nothing seemed amiss; actually everything seemed very calm. Maybe she was only jittery since her powers were reneged. Not that she'd ever even used her powers more than a few times, but she had been a goddess with nothing to fear. Now she had old age to look forward to if she ever lived that long. Now she was human and had to fear pain and death. She was afraid of just about everything at this moment. Just like that small, helpless rabbit hiding in the brush waiting for the steel tip of her arrow to pierce its heart. And just as the rabbit feared people, Thera feared the Centaur creatures that lurked behind trees in the night.

"All right," she agreed as Ganymede jumped off his own horse and held out a guiding hand for her to dismount. "I guess a good meal and a full night's rest will make everything look better in the morning."

She was just about to slide to the ground when a twig snapped in the forest, calling all their attention.

"I'm sure it's just a night animal," Ganymede reassured her.

Thera held tightly to the reins of her horse. The animal beneath her danced nervously, twitching its ears toward the sound.

"You're half-right, Ganymede." Thera took a deep breath and peered into the dusky sky toward the forest. "Half-animal, that is ... and half-man."

Kyros watched the small party from behind the cover of a large tree. His hooves ached from traveling over the rocky ground, trying to keep up with Chiron and Nemos as they showed him a shorter route to the clearing where they knew Thera and her guards would stop for the night.

Chiron held back a branch in one hand, his bow held tightly in the old nimble fingers of the other. Nemos crowded his own small body between the two, and Kyros found it comforting that the young boy would accept him so easily. If only the adults would be as open-minded and accepting as the innocence of a child. If only the Trozens and the Centaurs could live in peace and harmony side by side.

"They're going to be looking for food." Chiron's voice brought Kyros' thoughts back to the matter at hand.

Nemos looked up at Chiron with wide blue eyes. "That means they'll be coming into the forest to hunt."

"Not to mention, they'll be fair game for the Centaurs who reside here," added Kyros.

"Rodas is angry with Ares." Chiron talked without moving his gaze from the small group. "He'll alert the others that they're here."

"Will there be fighting tonight, Chiron?" asked Nemos.

Kyros listened to the boy's words and his hand caressed his own sword that hung awkwardly from a leather belt strapped around his chest. He should have been armed with a bow and arrow like the rest of the Centaurs, but instead he chose to wield his own sword. It was the sword his father gave him when he became a man. A sword he'd used often to ward off enemies. A weapon used for protection—a mere extension of his own arm as he saw it.

"There'll be no fighting if I can help it." Kyros turned away and Chiron let the branch loose quietly.

"You can't stop the Centaurs," Chiron remarked as Kyros paced the ground. "If Rodas tells the rest that Ares betrayed him, they'll be looking for a battle."

"Will they try to kill Ares' daughter?" asked Nemos.

"They won't," Kyros stated with conviction. "They fear Ares too much to taunt him. But they might try to scare her; or worse yet, capture her to somehow bargain with Ares. Don't you agree, old man?"

Chiron shook his head slowly and looked to the ground. "We've got to do something before it's too late."

"We may have more time than you think, Chiron." Kyros felt his tail swish in anticipation and cursed his inability to control his actions. "After all, it wasn't Ares that betrayed Rodas. It was me. I took the beam that was meant for him. He'll be after me before the idea ever hits him to go after Thera."

Kyros turned back to peer through the brush. The guards were making a fire and tending to the horses while Thera pulled bread and fruit from the saddle bags. Her back was toward him and all he could see was her long wavy black hair that traveled down to her tiny waist. Her long legs jutted out from beneath her short leather skirt and stopped in short black boots that were scuffed and dirty from travel.

His loins stirred as his mind relived the feeling of euphoria that had consumed him when Ares' bolt of lightning joined them for a mere fraction of time. It had been a long time since he'd had a woman and he'd almost forgotten how pleasurable it could be. For a second, he found his thoughts engulfing him: her body wrapped in his arms, their naked bodies joined as one.

She swung around suddenly and Kyros dove for cover behind a thicker clump of trees. When he dared to peek out, he saw her staring in his direction, her body stiff and her features rigid, almost as if she knew he was there. Almost as if she heard his thoughts or somehow felt the emotions of lust looming within him and brimming over the edge at just the sight of her.

"Kyros? Are you all right?" Chiron's voice came from the dark.

Kyros saw Thera's head tilt to the side. She seemed to be listening intently. The warm hues of firelight danced on her skin and illuminated a softness that he'd never expected to see from the warrior daughter of Ares. A goddess. A goddess who now carried his child, which he wasn't even sure was human. His tail swished once again and he gripped his sword tightly in his fist.

"I'm fine," he answered.

"I'm going back to the Centaur village to try to talk some sense into Rodas. Where will you be?"

"I'll be in the shadows watching over my unborn child." His gaze fell on the young Centaur Nemos and his heart went out to him. Would his child be a Centaur and raised in the forest hovels? Or would his child be human? Either way, the child would grow up hating his father who was neither species, yet both at once. The child was doomed to hardship in life even before it stepped foot or hoof upon this earth.

"Stay out of sight," warned Chiron. "You may just be a pawn in this whole game but you've already set the ball in motion." He disappeared into the night with Nemos right behind him.

Kyros turned his attention back toward Thera. She paced nervously with her arms crossed in front of her. Kyros felt a longing to comfort her but knew it'd be a mistake. He was a creature now. A creature she was sure to hate since her father's plan was in action. He had to stay away from her. He should just walk away and forget the whole issue if he was smart.

Kyros reached down to his open, royal purple vest and ripped it from his body. He had to get a closer look at the woman who was to bear his first and probably only child. He ripped the vest into a long strand and poked two holes in it with his sword. He then wrapped it around his eyes, letting the ends fall loose down the back of his long, wild hair. He'd be masked if they did see him, thereby saving his identity. He could be one of over a hundred Centaurs. She wouldn't know for sure.

He pulled his sword from his sheath and trotted closer toward the little party. He'd just have one quick look and then retreat deeper into the woods before they caught on that he was there.

THREE

Thera sat down by the fire and waited alongside Ganymede for Loxias and Akil to come back with meat for a meal. They'd left only minutes ago, but Thera knew they'd be back soon. They were too lazy to hunt in the dark, not to mention they went the wrong way.

"The boys will be back with dinner soon," reassured Ganymede.

"No they won't."

"You doubt my word?" Ganymede took a slug from the jug of ale and spit into the fire. The flame flared up a bit then receded.

"You're forgetting about my power of the senses. There are no animals where they went, but I did hear some movement near that clump of trees just beyond our camp."

"Well, go hunt then. I'm hungry."

"You're forgetting you're supposed to protect me."

"And you're forgetting you're not a goddess anymore, sweetie, so go do it yourself." He took another long draw from the bottle and lay back in the dirt putting his arm over his face and started to snore.

Thera felt the hunger aching in her belly and a wave of nausea overcome her. She wasn't sure if it was a human feeling or a pregnant feeling. Either way, her body was hungry and she found herself craving meat for the first time in her life. She had never eaten meat before, as the sensation of dead animals had been more then she could handle. She could always feel the animals' fear even after they were dead. But now she was different. She craved meat and nothing else would do to fulfill her powerful hunger.

She got to her feet and wandered over to her horse. She strapped a quiver of arrows to her back and grabbed her bow. The horse whinnied and Thera realized some animal lurked nearby. She should have taken the time to smell the air but her hunger got the best of her. She headed over to the clump of brush where she'd heard an animal just a short time ago.

Thera blocked the thought from her mind that Centaurs may be stirring about. Her hunger won over her fear and she found herself wanting to hunt for the first time in her life. Her father's raven was the only animal she'd ever killed and even the thought of eating it at the moment was appealing.

Such a hunger she had never known. An aching to fill her belly with rich, succulent meat that would satisfy the emptiness within. She heard a small rustle in the bushes and picked up the scent of deer nearby. Her ears pinpointed the exact area and the loud thumping of the poor creature's heart. It was a strong, heavy heartbeat—stronger than the average deer.

She closed her eyes to the blackness of the forest and felt the comfort of the new darkness that surrounded her now. It had always calmed her in the past to reach inside and still her thoughts. Now it only made things worse. She could hear the heartbeat of the animal coming closer. It seemed to grow in size with each breath she took.

She didn't feel the poor thing's fear, only its curiosity as the twigs snapped beneath its hooves and it entered the danger zone, unsuspecting it would soon be dead. Thera pitied the dumb creature. A pity so strong she knew it was of her father's doing—a feeling within her that he'd predicted. She kept her eyes closed and raised the bow toward the sound, her stomach winning over her emotions. She cocked the arrow and pulled back the string.

It was then she knew she'd made a mistake. She smelled the faint scent of Centaur and her eyes shot open. Standing right before her in the dark was a huge Centaur. His body towered before her and she wondered how she could be so out of touch with her sensations that she had thought he was a helpless deer.

Her heart thudded and for the first time she felt the taste of fear—her own fear—on her tongue. Her arm weakened on the bowstring and her grip slackened some. He was staring at her through a royal purple mask that covered his eyes. His long oaken hair fell wild past his shoulders, which brought her attention to his bare chest. Strong, sturdy, muscles and sinew cording his chest and thick arms. A sight that left her in awe. He had a large sword strapped across his chest instead of the usual Centaur weapon of bow and arrow, but it was dark and she couldn't see it well. She almost got caught up in the moment until her eyes settled on his lower half. Huge brown legs—four of them—took a step closer and she found herself backing away.

"Don't be frightened. I'm not going to hurt you." The Centaur's voice was a low husky whisper. The tone shot a warning through her body that this creature may want more than her life since her father had thought to introduce breeding with a goddess into their clan.

"Get away. Get away before I shoot you." She lifted her bow and prepared her arrow once again.

"I don't think you really want to do that." He grabbed the tip of her arrow and she felt her arm relax as he lowered her bow.

"What do you want from me?" she asked in a shaky voice.

"Only to look at you. Nothing more."

He reached out his hand and ran a finger across her cheek. She felt a shiver run down her spine and then the spark of the touch. It was warm, caring, an attribute she never thought a Centaur would carry. After all, Centaurs were wicked, evil warriors that often ended up on Ares' doorstep and willed their souls to him just to have a place in his army. Centaurs were deceitful, not to be trusted in the least. Still, she felt herself wanting to surrender to him, pitying him for the poor creature he was. With her eyes closed it was easy to forget the gentle caress was from a wretched beast and not from the hand of a lover.

Lover. Just the thought excited her, yet at the same time disgusted her to be thinking it about a Centaur. She jumped back and raised her bow again. What was the matter with her? After all, a Centaur had been the one who was responsible for her condition. Along with her father, of course. She couldn't trust this beast standing before her any more than she could throw him. She needed to get away—far away before something dreadful happened to her. Disgust filled her senses and turned her stomach. Disgust like she'd never felt before. Just like what Ares had told her would happen just from the fact she'd killed. It was his prediction in motion and she could do nothing to control it.

"Get away from me or I'll kill you."

The Centaur's brow raised and for a fraction of a second she thought he was going to grab his sword and challenge her. She watched his hand quiver a bit but he didn't move.

"I said to leave me alone you filthy beast. Your kind disgusts me." She couldn't believe she was feeling this way, but the words came and she didn't regret a one. She had always been leery of Centaurs but now the seed was planted deep within her. Not only the seed of a Centaur but the seed of hate. Her pity had buried it. Her disgust had watered it. And the anger she now felt toward her father, all Centaurs and especially herself, would be the heat that swelled the seed and brought to fruition the ugly head of hate.

The Centaur turned quickly and galloped off into the darkness, disappearing from her sight.

"Thera! Thera, where are you?" It was Ganymede, followed by the other two guards.

Thera dropped her bow and fell to her knees. A wave of relief washed over her that her human guards were coming to protect her. Never before had she needed protection, but then never had she been human either. She felt a knot in her stomach and then movement from inside her womb. The baby inside her stirred already. A god's doing that the child of war be born as early as possible. A hunger consumed her like never before, wrenching through her insides, twisting her empty stomach round and round. Her mind spun.

"I found her!" Ganymede ran to Thera's side and Loxias and Akil ran up behind him. Thera lifted her head from her hands and flinched at the sight of their bows in hand, but not even a single dead hare.

"I'm hungry." It came out more like an order than a comment. "I need food. Now."

"We've got food, Goddess," said Akil. "Back at the camp we've got bread and fruit."

"Damn you fools! I'm not a goddess anymore. But if I were I'd strike you down dead for being so incompetent." Thera ignored Akil's outstretched arm and grabbed her weapon and got to her feet. "I want meat. Something that'll fulfill my needs."

"We've no meat, Goddess." Akil caught her nasty stare at his use of that word again.

"Then I'll hunt for myself." She took a step into the forest and her knees wobbled. Her head spun and once again she fell to the ground. Unable to speak, she didn't argue when Ganymede hoisted her up and helped her back to camp.

"You need rest more than you do food, Thera." Ganymede helped her lie down by the fire. "Now go to sleep and we'll hunt again in the daylight."

Thera's body gave her no choice other than to obey. She closed her eyes and drifted off to a place somewhere between Tartarus and Olympus. A place where restless souls invaded a dreamer's visions. A place where she was being watched by the Centaur in the purple mask.

FOUR

The warm sun hit Thera's eyelids, forcing her to sit upright and momentarily forget where she was. For a moment she was back on the outskirts of Mount Olympus, traveling through the forest where every tree and rock were a part of her soul. As a child, she'd been raised by her aunt Persephone, the only one on Mount Olympus who'd taken pity on her after she'd been virtually abandoned by her own parents.

Persephone had a heart of gold and was to Thera her only family. She'd taught Thera the beauty of nature and helped her to love the fertility of the earth. Thera missed her deeply since Hades had claimed her for his wife and taken her as queen of the underworld years ago. Since then, Thera had lived in the forests of Mount Olympus as a child of nature. One with the earth, but still alone.

"Hungry, Goddess?"

Thera's eyes flew open to see Akil popping a grape into his mouth. He held up a chubby hand, dangling grapes in front of her nose as she lay on the cold ground.

"Give me those, you fool!" She shoved the grapes into her mouth as fast as she could and then tore a loaf of bread from his hand. The grapes exploded with essence within her mouth, only causing her tastebuds to water and her belly to crave more of the food that did nothing to satisfy her extreme hunger.

Loxias shuffled up with a jug of spirits in his hand and stared at her stomach. "Eating for two? Or is it three?"

She looked down to her stomach and was surprised to see how it had grown just overnight. When a goddess gave birth, it was almost instantaneous to the act of making love. A goddess never went through the trauma a pregnant human did. Human's took forever to carry and birth a baby. She'd seen pregnant humans from time to time when she ventured from the mountain. And Persephone had even taken her once to the bedside of a human giving birth—just for the experience.

Well, she knew it was nothing she'd ever want to experience and now pitied herself for being in such a position.

"Don't talk to me that way." Thera got to her feet and went to her horse to dig through the saddlebags, hoping to find something that would satisfy her. She noticed Ganymede's horse was gone as well as his bow and arrows. He'd be out hunting for food. Either that or scoping the land for Centaurs.

Akil came up behind her and patted her rounding stomach. "Eating like a horse. Wouldn't you say, Loxias?" He walked back to the fire, laughing, popping grapes into his mouth. Loxias belched loudly and laughed along with him.

A feeling of disgust settled over Thera. Two men who were supposed to guard and respect her were toying with her, and she didn't like it. She could feel Ares' war-like blood in her veins. This time, she dealt with anger.

She tried hard to fight it, but found herself weak. She really tried to ignore the men's jests, but every one of their comments brought to life the formerly dormant warrior instincts within her that had been awakened when she killed her father's raven.

"Got any good *tales* to tell this morning?" Akil jested to Loxias.

"Neigh," answered Loxias with a catch in his voice trying to sound like a horse.

Thera took a breath and released it. Angry, vengeful emotions were taking over and she was helpless to stop it. She cursed Ares silently for ever taunting her to kill and stir these feelings in the first place. She never should have done it. But since she had, Ares had a hold on her she couldn't break loose. His own anger grew within her and she didn't know how to stop it.

"Thera," called Akil. "Trot on over here and let us see your belly again."

"Yeah," added Loxias. "We want to see the baby kick. All four hooves, that is."

Anger boiled in Thera's veins and she grabbed her bow and an arrow from the saddle bags. The horses pulled at their reins sensing trouble. She felt like a prisoner to herself, watching her body's actions. She cocked the arrow in her bow and turned abruptly.

Horrified, she watched her fingers let loose with the bowstring. The arrow whizzed through the air and lodged itself into Loxias' chest. Akil jumped to his feet and stared at her with wide eyes, obviously not believing what she'd done. She couldn't believe it herself.

"You killed him!" Akil reached for his sword but Thera was already reloaded.

"No," she cried more to herself than to Akil. "No!" But her body didn't obey her mind's command. The arrow left her bow, and Akil fell dead on the ground next to Loxias.

Reality hit Thera like a boulder in the head. Her bow slipped from her fingers and fell to the ground. She fell to her knees in shock at the feelings that had overcome her. Feelings of hate and anger. Feelings she'd never had before and of which she didn't know how to control.

She'd killed. And not just a simple raven this time. She'd killed a man for the first time in her life. Not one man, but two. Her body trembled as she hid her face in her hands. A heat filled her pores that was hotter than the fires of Tartarus.

Now she knew hate. She knew what anger brought upon a person and she hated herself for doing what she did. She wept uncontrollably into her hands, wishing she was dead herself for killing the men who were sent to guard her.

"Not bad, Thera. I knew you could do it."

She heard Ares' voice and the slow clapping of his hands. She raised her face to see him leaning against a laurel tree.

"This is your fault!" Her voice came out stronger than she'd expected. "You did this to them, not me."

"Not so." Ares walked over to the dead men and pulled a grape out of Akil's hand. Popping it into his mouth he continued. "It was of your own accord these men are dead, Thera." He looked back at the men and nodded. "That should get Hades off my back for a while."

Thera pushed herself from the ground and on wobbly legs made her way towards Ares. "You're disgusting. You have no sympathy for even the dead."

Ares licked the grape juices from his fingers.

"There you go with pity and disgust again," he laughed. "You've already felt the anger and now you'll get the taste of hate. You'll learn to like it. Give it time."

"I have no taste for hate. And I have no desire to kill. It was by your doing that I killed them. I tried to stop the feelings but you held my control. Let me loose from your spell and leave me be."

Ares chuckled. "You should have learned to control these feelings like your sister and this wouldn't have happened. You've always been weak, Thera. Don't let anyone control you. It's a lesson you need to learn. Actually, I have you to thank for getting rid of these two fools. I would have done it myself earlier but I wanted to give you the pleasure."

Thera swallowed deeply and blinked once. She'd almost fallen for Ares' tactics again. He was goading her. He wanted her to anger and she wouldn't give him the chance. She still had her power of sensations and she'd use it to her advantage. She'd hide somewhere in the forest away from anyone she could possibly harm until after the baby was born. Maybe then she'd break free from Ares' little spell.

She left her weapon and mounted herself upon a horse. She'd get far away from Ares and his devious plot. She'd show him his games would no longer work on her.

"You can't hide from me, Thera."

"Maybe not. But I can stop myself from doing any more harm to innocent people." She took off into the woods without looking back.

Ares crossed his arms over his chest and shook his head. "It's not that easy," he mumbled as he watched her go. He glanced toward the dead men and they dissipated into thin air with a shake of his finger. They'd never been real men, only something he'd conjured up, but Thera didn't need to know that. They'd done what he hoped they would—brought her to the brink of hatred. Enough to actually kill. He was pleased with the way she was progressing. A little nudge from him was all she needed to come around to his way of thinking.

Since she thought she'd killed for real, her mind would be muddled and it'd be easier for her to make the real mistake. He'd push her as far as he could and eventually she'd be the warrior he wanted her to be. She had the war-like blood in her veins and he was only helping her get in touch with her real self. She ought to be thankful he cared enough to try to help her get in touch with her true nature.

Rodas stepped out from behind a tree along with several other Centaurs, having waited until Thera was out of sight.

"Is it time yet?" he asked Ares.

Ares answered without looking at him. "Give her until tomorrow. By then Kyros will have taken her under his wing and it'll save you the trouble of looking for him. Then you can bring them both to Pittheus and explain to the king that his beastly brother has stolen his bride."

"It was supposed to be *my* child, Ares. I want the baby who brings war and death upon the Trozens to be *my* son, as was promised."

Ares turned quickly and grabbed the Centaur around the neck. His fingers sank deeply into his flesh and he felt pleasure at seeing the creature squirm beneath his grip.

"Are you saying I'm not fair?"

"N...no." Rodas choked out the word. "Not at all, Ares."

"Good." He released his neck slowly. "Because I'd hate to think I'd have to kill you for simply annoying me. This little mishap could very well work to our advantage."

"But why can't you just undo the damage and we can start over?"

"It's not that easy, you fool." He looked in the direction Thera went, then pulled Rodas to the side so the rest of the Centaurs wouldn't hear their conversation.

"But you're a god! Surely you can undo your own curse," insisted the Centaur.

"If she were but a human ... it would be simple. But I can't interfere again."

"What is that supposed to mean?"

"It means I'll kill you if you tell her or anyone else what I'm about to say. Thera believes Zeus took back his gifts, but Zeus really knows nothing of my little lie. You see, Thera is so very naive. She believes my little story of her powers being stripped when, in fact, the girl is still a goddess."

FIVE

Kyros waited nervously beside Chiron and Nemos as the sun broke on the horizon—the start of a new day. He was anxious, frustrated, and wanted to get closer to Thera, but not in this form; not as a Centaur, but as a man.

With a swish of his tail he pawed the ground nervously, taking his sword from around his chest and handing it to Chiron as he waited for his transformation to start.

"So what exactly happened last night?" asked Chiron.

"I told you everything." Kyros watched the sun rise as he spoke. "I covered my face with the mask so she wouldn't know me and went to get a closer look. That's when she caught me. But as far as she knows, I'm just any other Centaur."

"Oh really?"

Kyros turned his head to see Chiron running his hand over the back of his father's blade. Nemos watched silently on, wanting to witness Kyros' change. The sun glimmered off his sword for a split second and reality hit him. He'd made a mistake. He'd worn his sword and she'd seen it. No other Centaur carried a sword, but a bow and arrows. He'd tried so hard to protect his identity and one foolish mistake may have given it away.

"Damn!"

Just as he spit out the oath, a ray of sun shone on him and his body doubled over. The pain seemed to be getting more intense. Or was it just that his memory was flooded with the elation he'd experienced when his seed was implanted in Ares' daughter? A true contrast.

He tasted blood inside his mouth and realized he'd been biting the inside of his cheek. He struggled with his breathing and looked back toward Chiron and Nemos.

The young boy was half hidden behind the old man, his eyes round and his mouth a gaping cavern. Chiron comforted him with a hand on his shoulder. Kyros couldn't help but think it was a mistake to let the boy see him this way.

His body convulsed and he fell to the ground. A humiliating experience to let anyone witness his transformation; but Chiron and Nemos were his friends. Chiron already knew all about it and the boy may as well learn just how ugly the truth was sooner or later. After all, someday Kyros' own son would be watching the same scene: his father, half-beast, half-man, lying before him convulsing in pain because of the god of war.

A chill crept over Kyros and he found himself leaving the world for a few brief minutes, just as he always did when he changed over. He wasn't sure if it was involuntary or brought upon by himself in order not to feel the last few sharp stabs of pain.

"It's over." Chiron's voice drifted over to him and he felt his body shiver. The scent of Centaur hung in the air and he wondered if this was the way he smelled to others while in his beastly form.

A sudden warmth covered him and he opened his eyes to see Nemos, gingerly placing a tunic wrap over his body.

Kyros struggled to sit up, all the while eyeing the boy. He saw curiosity in Nemos' eyes and a false courage that hid the fear within him. Kyros accepted the clothing and got to his feet, wrapping the garment about himself.

"Do I have you to thank for this garment?" he asked the boy.

"Aye," answered Nemos without giving any voluntary information where he'd attained it.

"I sent Nemos to the old weaver who lives in a hut outside your father's kingdom," added Chiron still clutching Kyros' sword. "She's a blind old hag and doesn't realize Nemos is not human; nor I for that matter. She supplies me with garments or tidbits if we need them and never asks questions. We hunt meat for her in exchange."

"Well, it's not a pair of breeches but it'll do."

"You'll look like the rest of the Trozens now and won't stand out." Chiron handed him his old pair of sandals. The laces had broken during his last transformation, but the old man managed to fix them. He also handed him a leather tie which Kyros used to tie back his long hair. "Next time remove your clothing during your transformation and I won't have to ask the old witch for more."

Kyros surveyed his wrap-around tunic which ended just above his knees. It was the style of the Greeks and though he felt practically naked, he knew Chiron was correct in saying he'd blend in better.

Kyros grabbed for his sword but Chiron didn't release it.

"You realize she'll know this is the sword of a king and not one of just a soldier."

"It's my father's sword, Chiron. It's all I have left to remember him by and I won't give it up."

"Your choice, Kyros."

Kyros stared at the old man for a minute, then strapped it around his waist. "I'll wear it while I'm in human form and hide it in your hovel when night falls. Though I'll be a weaponless Centaur—something I don't like in the least."

Nemos tugged at Chiron's ragged vest. "We can give him Phylo's bow and arrows to use. Can't we?"

"Phylo?" asked Kyros with a raised eyebrow as he donned his sandals and laced them up his legs.

"Phylo was my mentor," explained Chiron. "One of the greatest of Centaurs until he died in battle against Ares years ago."

Ares again. Just one more reason for Kyros to hate the god of war. Kyros got to his feet and brushed himself off. His legs were stiff and his back hurt but he was happy to be once again in human form.

"I'll take them," he replied. "And I trust Nemos here will watch over my father's sword while I'm in ... nonhuman form."

The boy's eyes opened wide and he looked first at the huge sword swinging from Kyros' hip and then back to the old Centaur, Chiron.

"Well, what do you say, boy?" asked Chiron. "It isn't every young lad that is bestowed with such an honorable job as watching over the future king's sword."

Kyros' gut wrenched at the words "future king." He knew now that with his curse he would never again be normal, let alone the future king of Trozen. He walked up and laid his hand on the boy's shoulder. "It's not to get into the wrong hands," he warned him. "And especially not the hands of my brother Pittheus. If Pittheus gets a hold of the sword I'll no longer have a reason to live. For 'tis said by the oracles that when the successor to my father sits upon the throne with this sword raised to Artemis, the moon goddess, on the feast day of Dionysus, then the fate of Trozen will be sealed for the next hundred years."

"I see," remarked Nemos nodding his head solemnly.

"That feast day nears," Chiron reminded the boy.

"And Pittheus is going to be eager to find it before then," explained Kyros. "Without the sword of Trozen, the people will never accept him as my father's successor. By right of the first born, Pittheus can claim the sword and make Trozen his."

"Hasn't he already done that?" asked Nemos eyeing the sword carefully.

Kyros laid his hand atop the sword, feeling the warmth of the sun already emanating from the large moonstone embedded in the hilt. A stone given to his father by the goddess Artemis years ago at her approval of his mission to unite the Centaurs with the human race.

"He doesn't have the people's loyalty yet." Kyros' voice was soft as he thought about the kingdom and the people's fate if his brother should truly rule. "He is the regent king until they find my father's sword. Because of this, I've had to stay hidden for nearly the past year."

Nemos looked up at him with bright blue eyes—the eyes of a boy who was willing to give his life for the better cause. It was at that moment Kyros knew Nemos would never be just a boy again. For his courage and his good heart had transformed him into something much stronger—a warrior.

"I'll watch your sword for you, Kyros, while you walk the earth at night as one of us. I'll do all I can to help you in uniting the Centaurs and the people of Trozen and bringing peace upon the land."

"You'll make a fine warrior," Kyros remarked, then looked to Chiron. "Chiron has taught you well."

Kyros found a friend in Nemos and could only hope his own son would someday accept him so easily. But with the daughter of the god of war for the child's mother, he doubted it sincerely and was saddened by the thought.

"Someone comes!" Chiron grabbed his bow from his back ready to fight or protect.

Kyros heard the twigs snapping in the forest a minute later and cursed himself for not noticing earlier. But then again, his senses weren't as sharp as a Centaur's when he was in human form. He motioned with his hand for Chiron to take Nemos to safety.

"I'll handle this," he whispered and took off into the dense thicket.

Thera plodded through the thicket, her ankles swelling from walking so long. She'd left her horse back by the turn of the river when the animal twisted its foot on rocky ground. She'd felt its pain and knew it would be torture for the poor animal to continue. So she'd thrown the heavy saddle bag over her own shoulder and started out on her own.

She had no idea where she was going and didn't really care. Just as long as it was far away from her father and she had time to think the whole thing through. Her stomach had grown since the night before and the infant within her kicked like a horse. A pain shot through her abdomen and she lowered the saddle bag and sat to rest on a nearby rock. She'd been following the river for awhile and knew it was time to stop and refresh herself.

Leaving the bag behind, she made her way down to the water. Kneeling down, she scooped up some water and drank heavily. The coolness on her hot skin seemed to turn to steam and rise before her very eyes. She loosened her bodice and splashed water on her neck and chest. The water soaked her clothes and clung to her skin. What she'd give to take a dip and soothe her aching body once and for all.

She listened intently and heard nothing but the birds. She didn't catch the scent of any Centaurs nearby and knew she'd be safe for the time being. Quickly she pulled off her clothing and laid it on the banks. She slipped into the river and swam halfway out, soaking up the energy from the fish and other beings that made it their home.

She felt safe here. At home with nature once again. She was happy and playful and for the moment forgot her troubles as she romped in the cool waters of the earth.

Kyros had his sword drawn when he stepped through the trees, not sure of what to expect. But what he saw was not an army of Ares' men but a beautiful woman floating in the water on her back with her eyes closed.

Her midnight hair floated out around her, touching and caressing her milky white skin. The girl hummed an alluring tune and Kyros couldn't help but remain quiet for a moment and listen instead of making his presence known. Such a voice was so entrancing he wondered at first if she was a siren. Singing, pleasing, luring him to his death as they'd been doing to poor sailors for centuries.

His eyes settled on her two full bare breasts poking their rosy buds through the water and reaching upward toward the bright warm sun. Like flowers waiting to bloom, the buds grew slightly as they warmed, and Kyros couldn't help but want to taste their sweet nectar.

She kicked her legs slightly and he noticed the nest of curls settled between her thighs. He felt himself thicken under his tunic and was ashamed of himself for spying on this maiden and thinking thoughts that were too crude for a woman of her beauty and obvious pureness.

Then he noticed the small mound of her stomach that rose above the water with each breath she took and realized she wasn't all that pure. Reality hit him like an avalanche. This was Ares' daughter. The girl who'd agreed to be impregnated by a Centaur so she could marry Pittheus and anger him when she bore him a Centaur child. A child that would bring war between the Trozens and the Centaur race.

All thoughts of pleasure left him as he felt himself anger. This woman was no better than her father. Using a poor Centaur and an unborn child to create a war. His child, he corrected himself. A child that he'd always longed for, but not in this way.

The child in her womb was conceived in a malicious nature. It was only a pawn that would lure so many to their deaths. This wasn't the way he wanted it to be and he knew somehow he had to stop it. He couldn't allow his own child to bring about the destruction of Trozen and the death of the Centaur race.

He knew now the only way to stop Ares' little scheme. It was a thought that horrified him, yet he knew it was the only way to save the Centaurs. The child—his child—could never be allowed to be born. Only by stopping its birth could Ares' plan be altered.

SIX

Thera floated on the calm waters, the only turbulent tide being the one that washed through her head. She was a murderer now, like it or not. She was no better than her father. She'd killed not one man, but two. She'd killed twice in one day and once the day before. What would happen tomorrow? Perhaps she'd kill off a Centaur? Maybe a whole family … maybe the whole race.

She felt the hot sun beating down on her, burning her virgin skin and wondered if that's the way it felt in Tartarus. After all, she was no longer an innocent. She was a warrior, a murderer, an executioner; and she hated herself for being all of them. She deserved to burn in Tartarus. And now that she was human she knew she would indeed die and wind up there. If it wasn't for the baby inside her she'd kill herself right now before she found herself angered again and killed someone else. But she couldn't. The baby was innocent through this whole mess. The baby was only a pawn in this whole game and didn't deserve to die.

She knew now she had to live in order to protect it. The poor child was going to be the symbol of war. Once this Centaur was born, he would be the icon for hate. Two races would feud and many would die. She was to blame for not using her powers to stop Ares when he thought to impregnate her in the first place. If only she had her powers now. Surely she'd be able to use them to her advantage in some way or another.

Thoughts filled her head of the Centaur's look of disgust when she refused him. But then she remembered the wonderful sensations that engulfed her when the beam left her father's hand and connected her with the Centaur. She felt guilty, ashamed and confused. She never should have enjoyed coupling with a creature she abhorred.

Her body tingled when she thought of how she rose to heights she'd never known were possible. It was almost as if she relived the incident.

The warm sun lapped at her thighs, rising higher and higher until she felt her core coming to life. She found herself with her hand between her thighs, touching, stroking, wanting the touch of a lover instead of a memory of something that should have never happened without physical contact of any kind. She'd been cheated in a sense. It was her first experience, and not the way she'd hoped it would have been.

She let out a small moan and tried hard to remember what happened before she blacked out. Her memories were becoming more vivid with each caress. She tried not to think of her beastly partner. Instead, she focused on the pleasure, the sensations—the wonderful sensations. And with her gift of feeling sensations, she knew she felt them more than a human would.

Her legs kicked to keep her afloat, the cool water rushing between them only exciting her further. She wanted to experience the ecstasy again but felt ashamed. She despised the Centaur for being so low as to go along with her father's plan. A part of her hated the Centaur for coming to her. Another part of her hated herself for enjoying the pleasurable feeling so much.

Then the face of the rugged Centaur changed in her mind and she remembered something she hadn't before. A man. Yes, now she could see it all so clearly. A handsome man with dark hair tied back behind his head. He was tall and agile, but the rest of his body seemed blurred to her. He was there. He ran toward the Centaur. She saw him in her mind as he sprung through the air toward the beam and ...

Thera jerked upright and got her footing on the bottom of the lake. She looked to the shore and saw that same man standing there, sword at the ready and staring right at her. At first she thought she'd somehow conjured up a vision, but when he slowly lowered the sword and replaced it in his scabbard she knew he was real.

The water was only waist high on her, and her breasts were exposed, but she did nothing to cover herself. She knew now he'd been watching her all along and she felt her face redden as he caught her in the act of trying to please herself.

"How long have you been standing there?" she asked.

"Long enough to know you ought to cover up before some man decides to have his way with you."

The idea at the moment sounded inviting, as she was still vibrating and in definite need of a man. She watched as he walked over to her clothing and held it up in front of him, purposely blocking his view.

She pitied herself for a moment, thinking she must be too homely even naked for this man to want to look at her. She made her way to the water's edge and took the bodice and skirt from him. His hand brushed against hers and a wave of excitement washed over her. His scent clung to her clothing—nature, life and a musky essence as well. She found herself attracted to it. She found herself attracted to him. She turned away and slipped the bodice over her head. When she bent over to put on her skirt, she caught him watching her, and he quickly looked the other way.

Her heart beat a bit faster and a smile painted her face. Maybe he didn't think she was so ugly after all. Maybe her twin sister, Harmonia, wasn't the only one who could turn a man's head. Of course, Thera had never known she, herself, had the ability. On Mount Olympus she'd stayed in the forests, alone most the time. And Persephone always kept her away from human males when the two of them came down from the mountain on the few occasions.

"I've seen you before," she spoke as she slipped on her boots. "I think I know who you are and why you're here."

Kyros felt the blood rushing to his brain. She knew he was a beast and yet she didn't seem scared. She had no idea of the horrible thought running through his brain to stop the child within her from being born or she wouldn't be smiling at him so sweetly and in an inviting way. She was beautiful when she smiled. White straight teeth against her silken goddess skin. She was so fragile, yet at the same time so dangerous. He thought of their unborn child and wondered if it would resemble her or perhaps him instead.

This is what he'd always longed for in life, yet it was wrong ... oh, so wrong. He wanted a woman to bear him an heir—to have a child he could call his own and teach the ways of the world. But not like this. Not in this way. He wanted to touch the mother of his child. Caress her, kiss her, make her one with him as they created a child of love—not of war.

He took in Thera's beauty. Simple, natural, refreshing. She was like a part of nature, blending into the wonders of the earth so well. He found himself remembering the sensations of their joining. And though he'd never even touched her, he felt he couldn't stop himself from wanting to do so now. Her presence filled the air around him. He raised his hand slightly, wanting to touch her face and stroke her cheek. He needed to run his fingers through her long dark hair. He wanted her close to him. Not only her, but also their unborn child.

He dropped his hand and turned away, cursing himself silently. He was possessed by madness. A desire so strong for peace between the Trozens and the Centaurs that he even considered killing to do it. How ironic. Killing to fight for peace. He hated himself for stooping to such an ill thought.

How in the name of Zeus could he even think for a moment he could harm this sweet, beauty of a woman or an innocent unborn child? And even if he could have convinced himself it was a just deed, he was forgetting she was a goddess. She had powers over him he could never combat. He didn't stand a chance against her from the start. She'd said she knew him, though he'd never even heard of her. Ares must have told her about him. The whole thing was probably planned to trap him into being the father of a baby who would bring so much death and destruction.

"You ... remember me?" He wanted to hear it from her own lips. How she knew of him and plotted against him. "You're saying you know who I am?"

He felt doomed already. He wanted to remain anonymous in both his forms, yet she was saying she knew all his secrets. Well, he was the son of a king. He was well known, so why shouldn't she know him? Unless she'd been living the life of a hermit, she'd know all about him and want nothing to do with him. Nothing, unless she was like her father, and would do anything to trap him into a plot that would ruin his dreams.

"Well, I don't actually know your name." She smiled and took a step closer. Her gaze settled on his sword and a bewildered look crossed her face, as if she was trying to recognize the sword but couldn't.

"You said you know who I am?" He paced to distract her.

"I do." She actually seemed happy about the whole thing. She had to be just as evil as her father to actually agree to mating with a Centaur in the first place. "You're the man who dove in front of Ares' beam."

"I am," he answered. She almost sounded as if she'd just discovered this fact.

"I knew it! I knew I wasn't dreaming."

Her face lit up and Kyros couldn't help but want to touch her again. Instead he kept his distance.

"You weren't dreaming," he reassured her. "I'm the father of your unborn child, as if you didn't know."

She grabbed his shoulders and pulled herself to him, placing a kiss directly on his mouth before letting go. She twirled in a circle, laughing all along.

"I'm so happy," she announced.

Kyros could see it was true. His lips tingled from her kiss and if he wasn't so angry at her he would have wanted her to do it again.

"And it's all because of you," she added.

"Because of me?" Didn't she mean because of her father and the success of their scheming plot for war and destruction?

"Because of you, I'm having a human baby!" She headed over to the saddlebag and flung it over her shoulder with such energy and enthusiasm that he wondered if being pregnant did this to a woman. Then he realized what she said and he felt his heart sink.

"What do you mean by that?" His voice was barely a whisper. She'd said human. Human baby, not Centaur baby. He felt his stomach tighten. Could it be possible? She really didn't know who he was after all?

"Because of you, I now have the will to live again. Because of your seed that is going to be our child, my father's plan will not succeed. And because of you, you wonderful man, not only the Trozens but the Centaurs will be safe from the war that would have destroyed them. Don't you see? Now that I know I'm not going to birth a Centaur baby, my world has changed. I won't have to start the war my father wants. The god of war has lost this one. I won't have to be a warrior in his army. I won't have to kill innocent people on his command and most of all, I won't die giving birth.

She heaved a big sigh and looked at him with those translucent blue eyes that held all the hope in the world. How he wanted to tell her she was right. How he wanted to believe it himself. But she still had half a chance her baby would be a Centaur. And that half a chance gnawed at his insides, eating away her innocent hope bit by bit without her knowing. She thought he was her savior when he was nothing more than an accessory to seal the fate of the people.

She obviously didn't know him or anything about her father's curse upon him. She looked so happy—so alive, so vibrant. She'd kissed him, for Zeus' sake. She liked him. She actually liked him for whom she thought he was and it felt good.

It felt so damned good to be looked at and respected again. It was so refreshing to find someone who didn't know his past and didn't cringe or keep their distance from him when they saw him. She liked him and had actually touched him—kissed him too. His lips still vibrated from her kiss. How good it would feel to be touched again by a woman. To be caressed, cared for—possibly loved someday. And he wanted this almost as much as he wanted to see peace between the Centaurs and the Trozens.

He knew he should tell her the truth, but couldn't bring himself to do so. Maybe the baby would be born human after all. Maybe he could wait and see before he spoiled her hopes and crushed his own dreams.

She smiled at him once again and he felt his body warm. He gripped the hilt of his sword several times, feeling the sweat beneath his palm.

"Thank you." She said it so gratefully he thought he was going to bust. She looked at him with the respect one would give to Zeus, when at the moment he felt like Hades himself. His jaw twitched as he swallowed the words of truth that lie on his tongue. If only she knew what she was really thanking him for.

"Save your thanks," he growled. He made his way up the hill and she followed. "If I would have known I was volunteering to make a baby with you when I jumped in front of that beam, I never would have done it."

SEVEN

Thera followed the man up the hill, not at all sure why he seemed so angry all of a sudden. She sensed confusion, aggravation on his end, though she couldn't decipher the reason behind it.

"My name is Thera." The bag weighted her down and she became winded following him so fast. "What is yours?"

He stopped for a second and looked at her. His eyes were dark and she wasn't sure what he was thinking. "What does it matter?" He turned around and continued up the hill.

"I was just wondering who the father of my child is, that's all." She sensed the man was disturbed about something. If she wasn't mistaken, he wasn't happy that she carried his child.

"I'm no one," he answered without turning to look at her.

"But surely that's not so. Everyone is someone."

"I'm no one that matters. You're better off not knowing."

When they reached the top of the hill, his horse awaited them. A welcome sight for a pregnant woman whose body ached. Maybe he'd give her a ride somewhere. Anywhere where she could get away from her father and think this whole thing through.

"If you don't want to tell me your name then just tell me where you come from."

He fiddled with his horse's saddle bag, then he turned his head slowly and stared at her for a second before answering.

"My name is Kyros." He looked at her almost as if he were expecting some kind of a reaction on her part. One which she couldn't give him since she'd never heard of him.

"Kyros," she repeated. "It's a nice name. And where are you from?"

He turned away and petted his horse on the nose.

"I'm from nowhere ... and everywhere. Where I'm from doesn't matter. It's where I'm going that truly counts."

She liked that answer for some reason. Instead of being angered that he was being so secretive, she saw him as a deep thinker. One who could change the world with his thoughts and probably his dreams as well.

"Well, Kyros from nowhere, where are you going then?"

Before he could answer, a war-like cry came from behind the bushes and the sound of trampling hooves across the earth brought to their attention that they were under attack by a small group of Centaurs. Thera screamed and dropped the saddlebag she carried. Kyros pulled his sword from the scabbard and held it up in the air.

"Get on the horse, Thera. Ride out of here as fast as you can."

She was moving before he'd stopped talking. Her boot was in the stirrup, but the horse was large and it was awkward mounting with her bulging stomach. An arrow whizzed by her head. She'd felt it coming and moved out of the way just in time, losing her balance and falling to the ground.

"Damn," she heard Kyros grind out. He grabbed her arm and hauled her to her feet. The Centaurs were closing in on them but Kyros did nothing to defend them.

"Do something!" she screamed and tried once again to mount the spooked horse but with little luck. She did all she could just to hold on to the reins to keep it from running. "Kill them!" How easily the words came from her mouth now. Kill. It was almost natural to her, now that she was a killer herself. She hated the way it felt, but fear was consuming her and she only wanted this all to end.

He flashed her a glance that said a thousand words: shock, appall that she'd ordered him to kill them—almost as if it had never even entered his mind. Here a group of angry Centaurs were shooting arrows all around them, and he seemed to dodge the damned things instead of defending her. Sure, he was outnumbered six to one but he was a warrior and should fight no matter what the odds. What good was that huge sword if he didn't know how to wield the thing? If she'd had her bow and arrows right now she'd show him how to handle the situation. But instead, she'd been so eager to leave the scene of her crime that she'd jumped on the horse and left her weapon behind.

He replaced his sword in the scabbard and she felt her heart sink. He wasn't going to fight for her. He wasn't going to protect her after all. He stepped in front of her and pulled himself into the saddle. Doom overcame her as she realized he was running and she'd be left to face the Centaurs by herself.

"You coward! You don't deserve that sword if you can't even use it."

He turned his skittish horse in a full circle and his muscled arm came down toward her. He was going to hit her, she thought, and now regretted calling him a coward. At the same time, she heard the hooves right behind her from one of the Centaurs. He was so close she could smell the gamy aroma and feel the anger that pumped through its veins. She knew who it was and jumped away just as he approached. Fire licked his eyes and he reached his hand out to grab her. It was the rugged Centaur who was supposed to mate with her. The one who had made the deal with her father.

She closed her eyes for a mere second, the huge arm grabbing her around her waist and lifting her up high. But when she opened her eyes, she realized it was Kyros who was lifting her in the air, not the Centaur. Kyros pulled her up into the saddle in front of him and shielded her in the warmth of his arms.

"Hold on to me," he commanded.

She gripped his arm that cradled her unborn child. His other arm held tight to the horse's reins. He urged the horse forward, dodging the flying arrows and maneuvering his way skillfully through the attacking Centaurs. He tried to outrun them, but it was too late. They were too close and there was nothing they could do to escape.

An outburst from the forest brought her attention to an old Centaur leading a group of about ten other of his kind. They burst through the forest and distracted the attackers long enough for them to escape.

It worked. The distraction saved their lives. Kyros didn't slow down until he was deep into the forest near a brook. Stopping the horse, he dismounted, taking the warmth of his protective hold with him.

"What happened?" Thera looked down at him. He scanned first the land and surroundings and then tied the horse to a tree.

"We were being attacked by Centaurs," came his calm answer.

"No doubt. I could see that." His reluctance to tell her more disturbed her. "Why didn't you fight back?"

The look on his face said it all. She saw the confusion in his eyes, felt his own anger at her words pumping through her very blood.

"Fighting isn't always the answer. But then again, I don't suppose the daughter of the god of war could understand such a thing."

He turned from her and stared out at the water. A raw feeling of emptiness engulfed her. That would have been her answer at one time. Before this all happened to her. But now the thought of running never even entered her mind. Her war-like abilities had been triggered ever since she'd killed her father's damned raven. She struggled with her inner thoughts, knowing Kyros was right for not wanting to hurt anyone, but still she couldn't help but feel he should have killed every last one of those Centaurs that wanted her own life.

"They could have killed us, you realize." She put one foot in the stirrup and swung her other one around to dismount.

"Well, they didn't. So don't worry about what I did or didn't do back there."

The horse moved and she lost her balance. She screamed and fell.

He was there instantly. His protective arms wrapped around her, keeping her from hitting the earth below. She felt so safe in his presence, yet she didn't know why. They almost died a few minutes ago and the man had done nothing to ward off their attackers. Yet, here he saved her from a short fall to the ground.

"You ought to be more careful." He gently set her feet on the ground, yet his arms lingered around her as he steadied her. "You might hurt the baby in a fall like you almost took."

The man didn't make any sense. He was worried about a little fall, yet when the arrows were whizzing by her head, he refused to use his sword to defend them.

"I'm not used to the awkwardness of being pregnant, yet."

She looked up into his soft, brown eyes and felt a hidden sadness behind the gaze. She wanted to ask him about it, but couldn't. She couldn't bring herself to say a word. His touch was strong, yet gentle. His body was warm and comforting as his hands rested on her shoulders for a mere second before he shook his head and stepped away.

"We'll rest now. I need to water my horse." His voice went cold; the warmth and kindness she'd just sensed diminished as he grabbed his horse's reins and led the animal to the water.

She, too, was thirsty and took the time to kneel down at the water's edge and drink. She splashed the cool water on her face trying to make sense of her sporadic emotions.

"So. You never told me where you were headed."

She looked up and realized he no longer stood by his horse. She heard a small rustle in the bushes and figured he was relieving himself.

"Kyros? Where are we going from here?"

When she didn't get an answer she became a bit unnerved. If it wasn't Kyros in the bushes, then who was it? And why didn't Kyros

answer her—wherever he was?

"Kyros?" She stepped toward the bush and screamed when she saw a pair of eyes staring back at her. It was a small Centaur. The young boy's eyes interlocked with hers before he took off into the thicket.

"You don't need to fear him." She spun around and saw Kyros standing before her with a dead pheasant in his hand. "His name is Nemos. He's harmless. He just wants to see who you are."

"How do you know this? How do you know he won't come back with his friends and try to kill us again?"

Kyros stacked up some branches and started a fire. He sat down next to it and pulled out his dagger.

"He's not one of the group that attacked us. He's one of the Centaurs that helped distract our attackers so we could get away."

"How do you know so much about Centaurs?"

Instead of using the dagger to scare off anyone lurking in the bushes as she'd hoped he would, he used it to prepare the fowl for their meal.

"You ask too many questions," he answered without looking up. "Just trust me. Nemos and his friends won't bother you."

"You seem so sure of yourself." She sat down across from him at the fire. "You can't trust a Centaur. They're deceitful and thrive on killing humans just for the fun of it."

His knife stopped in mid-motion and his gaze met hers. A muscle in his jaw twitched. His eyes narrowed.

"Well, now who seems so sure of themselves?"

"I know a lot about those creatures," she reassured him.

"Oh, do you?"

"I've seen them join my father's army and do many wicked things. They're blood-thirsty animals and nothing more."

He jabbed the pheasant onto a stick and placed it above the fire to cook.

"And what makes you think it is the Centaur race that's so blood thirsty? It seems to me the gods are the ones who cause all the trouble."

He was trying to protect the Centaur race. This was clear, yet she didn't know why.

"I wouldn't talk bad of the gods if I were you."

"Why not?" He got to his feet and wiped his hands in his clothes. "Are you going to strike me down for saying something bad about your father? And by the way ... you're so fast to accuse me of not fighting our attackers today, yet you didn't even think about using your own powers to save your hide."

She stood also and met his gaze across the fire. The orange glow lit his face, the heat from the flames making a barrier between them. The fires of Hades come to consume her. Her own nauseous stomach made her break the gaze and she turned away and walked toward the creek.

"I'm not a goddess anymore."

"What is that supposed to mean? Of course you are."

She hugged her arms around the child within her and looked out across the creek to the open sky. The low sun melded into a swirl of blues and golds.

"It means my father and the other gods stripped me of my powers before ... before." A lump lodged in her throat and she couldn't continue.

She felt his presence directly behind her though she didn't even hear his soft footsteps.

"I'm sorry. I didn't know. It must be hard for you."

He was so close she could feel the heat of his breath on her neck as he spoke.

"Don't be sorry." She turned to face him. Her cheek almost brushed his chest. She wanted more than anything for him to put his arms around her the way he did when they sat atop his horse. His hand came up and rested on her shoulder. Warmth traveled through her body and she reveled in the security of it all.

"I'm here for you and the baby, Thera. I won't desert you. You can count on me."

If only he knew how much those words really meant to her right now. She needed someone there with her. She was scared and felt so alone. But Kyros would be there for her and their child now. He told her so and she believed him. She had nothing to worry about and would sleep well tonight. Even if he wouldn't fight the Centaurs, she knew he would keep her and her unborn child safe from the wretched creatures.

She boldly laid her cheek on his chest and he gave her a quick half-hug. Slowly, she met his eyes, their gazes magically making time stand still. She wanted to kiss him. He wanted it too. She could feel the intent in his stare. She closed her eyes and his face came closer, but the kiss she expected never came. Instead, he stiffened and released a small groan. Her eyes flew open to find him no longer standing there. He was already far from her, tying his horse to the tree.

Embarrassed by her own behavior, she turned away, falsely warming her hands at the fire.

"Make sure Hester gets to graze."

"Hester?"

"My horse." He walked over to the fire. "The food looks like it's ready to eat. Have your fill and burn the rest so it doesn't attract any animals."

He sounded as if he were leaving. "Aren't you going to eat?" she asked.

He pulled two blankets from his saddle bag and threw them down next to her.

"I'm not hungry." She could have sworn she felt his stomach convulse when he said it. "Use the blankets to keep warm tonight. And keep the fire going."

"You're leaving, aren't you?"

"Just for awhile." He hurriedly headed toward the woods.

"Wait!" Thera jumped to her feet and started after him. "What if Centaurs attack while you're gone?"

He stopped and turned toward her. "You don't have to worry about any Centaurs you may see tonight, Thera."

"By the gods, I hope not to see any of those wretched creatures while you're gone."

His eyes grew darker and his jaw twitched. She felt his anguish and couldn't help but notice his fists clenched at his sides.

"Maybe you should try and get to know one, Goddess. Maybe then you'd change your mind."

"Wait!" she called after him but he was already gone. She felt a small pain stab her in the stomach and decided not to go after him. Her baby was hungry and she had to eat. She'd just have some food, and she'd talk to Kyros when he calmed down a bit. He had to return soon, wherever he was going. She couldn't imagine he'd leave her alone all night when there were Centaurs roaming the woods.

She ate her fill and still Kyros hadn't returned. She let Hester graze a bit and then tied her closer to the fire for the night.

"So, Hester. Where did Kyros go?" She petted the horse on its nose and reveled in the animal's calmness. Her own insides were jumpy. The night had closed in all around her and still Kyros hadn't returned. She went back to the fire and wrapped up in the blankets and laid her head against the trunk of a tree. He should be back soon. She'd apologize for upsetting him when he returned.

Her body ached and every bone within her felt tired. She tried hard to keep her eyes open but just couldn't. She needed rest after her long day. She needed to sleep to rejuvenate herself. She'd just close her eyes for a few minutes until Kyros returned.

EIGHT

Kyros ran through the woods, trying to get as far away from Thera as possible. The sun had disappeared through the trees and he could feel the chill of nightfall setting in. His legs cramped and his stomach convulsed, causing him to fall to his knees in the dirt. It was happening again. Damn, this curse. When would he ever get used to the wretched transformation?

He clutched his side and fell over on the forest floor. A sweat encompassed him from the heat, so strong that he felt he'd incinerate before the change was finished. He tugged at his sandal laces, ripping his shoes from his body in order to save them from being torn apart. He then threw his sword and scabbard to the side and grabbed for his tunic, trying to pull it over his head.

It was too late. His muscles bulged, his bones stretched and his clothing ripped down the middle. He'd stayed too long at Thera's side and now must suffer the consequences. His body writhed on the ground and though the hum in his ears was deafening he could have sworn he heard Thera calling his name.

His stomach convulsed. His body groaned. His teeth chattered as his hooves and tail emerged, and a chill, colder than an Arctic winter, wracked his body, not to mention his brain. But the pain in his head was nothing compared to the aching in his newfound joints. His ragged breathing slowed as he lay on his side. Beads of sweat clung to his chest and back.

Damn the god of war for putting him through this! And damn Ares' daughter for making him want to kiss her, distracting him in the first place. Usually he could prepare his mind for the change. But lately his mind was preoccupied and the transformations only seemed to get worse.

As Kyros lay with his head on the damp earth, he could hear light hoofbeats coming nearer and nearer. He jumped to his feet—all four of them—in the process grabbing his sword from the ground.

"Kyros, it's me. Nemos."

Kyros squeezed his eyes closed for a second and took a deep breath at the sound of the young Centaur's voice.

"Nemos. Where are you?" Kyros looked around, but his vision was still blurred. Then he saw the boy's shadowy form stepping toward him through the trees.

"Are you all right?" As Kyros' vision cleared he could see Nemos looking at him cautiously, coming nearer but aware of keeping a safe distance from him.

Kyros panted and tried to smile at the boy in between breaths to let him know he was safe.

"I'm fine, Nemos. Come closer." He lowered his sword and ran a hand through his long tangled hair. As a man, his hair was past his shoulders. As a Centaur, his hair reached down to his waist. In his Centaur form, his chest was nearly twice his normal size. Not to mention the muscles that graced his body as well. Everything was exaggerated.

"You ... you looked so ..."

"Vicious? Angry? Pathetic?" Kyros filled in the blanks for him.

"Scared." The boy said the word slow and soft almost as if he wasn't certain how Kyros was going to take it.

Kyros sauntered over to a tree and laid his head against the rough bark, looking into the night as he spoke.

"I'm the most vulnerable when I'm in the middle of a transformation." He spoke to himself as well as the boy, reminding himself just how foolish he'd been not to take cover before the damned curse took hold. He didn't look at Nemos but could hear his light hoofbeats trotting over to join him.

"I was waiting for you at the hovel, but you never came. So I decided to find you. I tried to remind you—I came to your camp."

Kyros turned his head slightly and looked at Nemos in the darkening sky. He knew what a risk it was for Nemos to come to him. And now that the sky was turning dark, he knew he'd have to walk the boy back to the hovel. A Centaur's sight was strong in the sunlight of the day; but when the night fell, every one of them were at a disadvantage of not seeing danger until it was upon them.

"Thank you, Nemos. Your loyalty is true. I know what you risked coming to me. And your devotion has earned your place at my side. If I were king, you'd serve in my court."

The boy grinned and sheepishly ducked his head as Kyros reached out to ruffle his hair.

"I'm a Centaur," he reminded Kyros. "Centaurs don't serve the king, let alone go anywhere near the people of Trozen."

"Not now they don't," said Kyros. "But someday that's all going to change."

Kyros' vision cleared and he first noticed the huge bow and quiver of arrows the boy carried on his back.

"Phylo's bow?" he asked.

The boy grabbed it from his back with a newfound eagerness. He proudly handed it to Kyros.

"It has the strength of ten Centaur bows, twice the speed and an alarming accuracy. Artemis had Hephaestus make it for Phylo. It was to protect the Centaurs from Ares. It's said to have powers against the gods. If a god besides Artemis touches it, it's said to even be able to kill them."

Kyros grabbed the bow in one hand and tested it's weight.

"What do you mean ... said to have? Doesn't anyone know for sure?"

"No one's dared to use it since Phylo was killed. Ares has tried to find the bow but we've hidden it well. Though the bow has a magical air about it, it's also said no one but a king can use it."

"So, Phylo was the king of the Centaurs?"

Nemos' eyes grew wide and he nodded his head. "He was the king until he was killed by Ares. Though the bow is dangerous for a god to touch, the arrows can't kill one. If so, Phylo would have killed Ares first. No Centaur thereafter has claimed the bow and the title. It's said to be cursed since it couldn't save our king's life. The Centaur race believes the next Centaur to use it will surely die."

Kyros leaned his sword against the tree and took the quiver of arrows Nemos handed to him.

"No sense in letting it go to waste. I'm already cursed. And dying doesn't really seem like such a bad thing anymore."

Kyros fastened the quiver on his back and cocked an arrow in place. He pulled back the string and raised it toward the sky. He released it and listened as the arrow whizzed through the canopy above.

"Not bad," he commented, running his hand along the curved wood. Something fell from the sky and landed at his feet with a thump, making them both jump.

Their gaze followed what the arrow had brought down. A warrior with a dagger still gripped in his hand lay at their feet, his eyes round with surprise, his mouth gaping open in protest.

"He must have been in the trees!" Nemos' eyes shot upward, looking for more. "He looks like he wanted to kill us."

Kyros scanned the trees but could see no other warrior. This one must have been a straggler. He poked the dead man's stomach with his bow, surveying the situation.

"Or wanted to kill *me*, anyway. This is one of Pittheus' men. My brother must have sent him."

"Your own brother would have you killed?" Nemos walked around the body, curiously eyeing the dead warrior.

"The feast of Dionysus is coming closer. Pittheus is desperate for the sword so he can claim my father's true title and have the support of the people. Without the sword, the fate isn't sealed and Pittheus will never have true control."

Kyros flung the bow over his shoulder and picked up his father's sword that lay against the tree. He carefully placed it in the scabbard and held it out to Nemos.

"It's in your care now."

Nemos backed away slightly. "Maybe you should guard it."

"Impossible. I need to go back to Thera. If she sees the sword, she'll know my secret."

"But what if I—"

"I trust you, son. You've shown your loyalty and I know the sword of the future king of Trozen is safe in your care. Now let's get this body buried before someone finds it and starts a war. Then I'll see you back to the hovel. I'm certain Chiron will wonder what's become of you by now."

Nemos helped bury the body and the two of them made their way back to Chiron's hovel.

"So you've returned." Chiron stood at the entranceway like a worried mother. A fire flickered at the mouth of the cave. He held out the purple mask to Kyros. Kyros exchanged it with his sandals and torn tunic.

"Time to visit the weaver again, I see." Chiron shook his head.

"This time, get me something that covers my legs," grumbled Kyros.

Nemos excitedly stepped forward, with Kyros' sword in his hand. "Kyros used Phylo's bow and it struck a warrior dead."

Chiron looked over to Kyros, his face clouded. "One of Pittheus' men?"

Kyros nodded. "My brother must know where I am. I need to stay away from the hovel as much as possible or I'm going to lead them right to the sword."

Chiron motioned to the boy and Nemos disappeared inside the cave. "Kyros, you're not safe anymore."

"None of us are." Kyros busied himself tying the purple strip of material over his eyes and adjusting the eye holes so he could see.

"I'm concerned for your safety."

Kyros ran a hand through his hair. "Just take care of yourself and the boy. And watch that sword like a hawk. I'll be fine. They wouldn't dare touch me as long as I'm with Thera."

"What makes you so certain?"

"She's a goddess. They fear her as well as her father."

"So she can protect you then."

"Not so. She's lost her powers. But still, my brother and his men don't need to know that."

"You don't need to do this," said Chiron. "You don't need to put yourself and your father's sword in jeopardy by going to Ares' daughter."

Kyros remained quiet for a moment, but knew he could never even consider Chiron's suggestion. "She's carrying my child, Chiron. I do need to be there. Though Thera means nothing to me, the child she'll bear me is now more important than my father's sword."

NINE

Thera lay still on the blanket, woken from a deep sleep by nothing more than the feeling that something—or someone—was watching her. Even in her sleep her awareness was sharp. She didn't move, yet felt a presence in the trees directly behind her.

Her heart raced and the babe inside her womb stirred. Almost with excitement, the child moved within her. She felt the babe's happiness—calm pleasure—yet her own body was rigid with fear; and that feeling ... that eerie feeling of being watched.

"Kyros?"

Thera called his name but didn't move. Her eyes scanned the grounds in front of her. She saw Hester munching on grass. The firelight flickered over the horse's shiny flesh. There was no reason to be alarmed, she told herself. She felt the horse's easiness and knew the animal would be fidgety if there was danger.

She could hear breathing now from somewhere behind her. And she was sure she smelled the gamy aroma of Centaur. Faintly, but still it was there. She was helpless without her bow and arrows. She was stupid for leaving them behind in the first place. The overwhelming need to protect herself and her unborn child bubbled in her veins. She didn't want to kill again, but would if she had to. She'd do anything—give her own life if needed—just to protect her and Kyros' baby.

She heard a snap of a twig behind her and in a flash she reached for a branch in the fire. She sprang to her feet, swinging the burning log toward whatever wretched Centaur that may have come to claim her.

A strong hand gripped her wrist and stopped her from her action. She found herself looking up into the masked face of the wild-looking Centaur she'd seen in the woods her first night. It was him. There was no mistaking. His long oaken hair hung wildly almost down to his waist. His chest was bare and she almost wished it weren't. She couldn't help herself from letting her eyes wander over his smooth skin and well developed muscles.

From the waist up he was the most pleasing man she'd ever laid eyes on. Though he hid behind his mask, she was sure his face was just as beautiful as the rest of him. He was an Adonis wrapped up in the package of strength, mystery and fatal attraction.

"Didn't anyone ever tell you not to play with fire?" He spoke almost in a half-whisper, his voice low and sultry.

His eyes glistened from behind the purple mask. The firelight from her weapon illuminated his upper body in a soft encompassing glow. She felt her pulse quicken and she noticed her breathing deepen. Then she heard the swish of a tail and she came back to her senses. She dropped the burning stick and it would have landed on her bare foot hadn't the Centaur pulled her out of the way.

She was so close to him now she could feel the heat from his body and hear the rapid beating of his own heart. His musky scent brought to life in her a stirring which she'd only experienced once—when she was mated with Kyros. A feeling she'd rather not be experiencing with a wretched Centaur so close.

She jumped away and headed closer to the fire. She picked up the blanket and wrapped it protectively around herself.

"Who are you?" she demanded.

The Centaur half-smiled, picked up the burning stick and tossed it into the fire. Still, he didn't answer.

"What's your name?" she asked. "And why do you follow me? What do you want?"

He shuffled over the hard ground, making a survey of the surroundings before returning to her side. It was then she noticed the huge golden bow thrown over his shoulder and the quiver of shiny arrows mounted on his back. For some reason she was expecting to see a sword fastened to him. Hadn't she seen a sword the first night she'd met him? Or was it only in her dreams he carried such a weapon? When had it become difficult to tell reality from illusions?

"My name's not important." He talked soft and low, his voice resonating within her. She felt her baby stir. "You needn't fear me," he continued. "I've been sent to protect you during the nights."

"You've been sent to protect me?" Suspicions raised within her. Was this another of her father's allies? Should she trust him or fear him? Her head said to fear him, her heart told her otherwise. "I don't need you to protect me. I already have someone to do that."

The Centaur raised his brow in amusement and his eyes scanned the grounds once again, landing on the horse. "I see."

Her eyes followed his to Hester. "Not the horse," she snapped. "I've got a true warrior. He has a sword big enough to cut through even your tough hide."

He chuckled lowly and his amusement at her expense made her uneasy.

"And where is this warrior of yours?" he asked.

"He's watching you at this very minute. You make one wrong move and he'll slice your throat from ear to ear."

He took his bow from his back and reached behind him for an arrow. He cocked his head to one side and motioned for her to be quiet.

"Who are you to tell me to be quiet?" she snapped. "And who sent you anyway? What's this all about?"

He positioned the arrow and pulled back the bowstring. "Don't move," he whispered and brought his aim closer to her. She wanted to scream out for Kyros to save her. She wanted to grab the bow from his hands and break it in half. But she found herself unable to move. Her lips were dry and she couldn't swallow. She could only watch the tip of the arrow being aimed closer and closer to her right ear.

He released the arrow and it whizzed so close to her ear she could feel the hairs on her skin split. He galloped by her and came back with something thrown over his shoulder. Something besides that big golden bow of his.

She stood frozen to the spot and only turned her eyes to see what he held up in front of her like an offering to a god. An offering she'd never gotten as a goddess and most certainly didn't want now. A huge snake jolted in his grip. His large golden arrow pierced through it.

"It would have bitten you. It was hanging from the branch above your head."

"Oh." Suddenly, Thera felt very foolish for thinking he meant to kill her. "So you *are* here to protect me."

"Like I said."

"Who sent you?"

"Kyros, of course. He can't be with you after nightfall. He asked me to look after you until dawn."

"He didn't mention it."

The Centaur just smiled. She watched in awe at how fast he skinned the snake and spiked up over the fire. The revolting aroma filled the air and turned her stomach.

"What're you doing?" she asked.

"I haven't eaten yet. I'm famished. Just cooking up a little dinner."

Thera wrapped her blanket around her tighter, her body temperature rising and her stomach topsy-turvy. "You plan on ... on eating that?"

His eyes were amused through the deep purple mask. He pawed the ground with one hoof and grinned. "How rude of me. Would you care to join me?"

Her stomach revolted at the mere thought of eating snake. Her hand flew to cover her mouth and she took off in a hurry toward the trees.

All the while she heard the Centaur's deep laugh.

Kyros knew it was going to be a long night. Even if Thera's retching didn't keep him awake, he knew her presence would. How he longed to tell her who he really was. How he longed to reach out and push a lock of hair behind her ear, or have her lay her head against his chest the way she'd done earlier that day.

He saw her emerging from the bushes, bent over slightly and clutching that damned blanket around her so tight there was no way in Tartarus he could even glimpse those beautiful breasts he'd seen so well when he'd caught her bathing in the pond.

He shook the thought from his head when he noticed the disgusted look upon her face as she surveyed him. He had to remember he was a Centaur now, not a man. Why should she treat him any different than she did the rest of the Centaurs she loathed?

He picked up the stick that held the snake meat and waved it in the air to cool.

"Sure you don't want some?"

"Don't start with that again." She hunkered down by the fire but wouldn't meet his eyes.

"Just trying to be friendly." He took a bite of the meat and watched her cringe even though she was looking into the flames instead of at what he was doing.

"Why?" she asked.

"Why what?" He continued with his dinner, thoroughly enjoying it though he would have preferred venison to fill his aching hunger.

"Why are you trying to be friendly and why would Kyros send you to protect me instead of being here himself?"

"Can't a Centaur be friendly to a human without having ulterior motives?"

"Not that I know of. They never have before."

"Maybe you should get to know one before you judge so harshly."

Her eyes shot up at that comment and her face took on a surprised look.

"You sound like Kyros when you say that."

His stomach lurched at the mistake he'd made. He threw the remaining snake meat into the fire, no longer having an appetite. One mistake like this and his whole secret could be exposed. He couldn't let her find out. Not yet. Not when she hated Centaurs so much. He wanted to change her mind about them first, not to mention he wanted her trust. Not only as Kyros the man, but as Kyros the Centaur as well.

"Well, I told you Kyros sent me. Maybe that should prove it."

"So you're close to Kyros then? A friend?"

"Closer than you think," he mumbled under his breath and walked over to Hester. His back was toward her, but still he knew she followed behind him. He petted Hester's nose and the horse nuzzled him back.

"She seems to like you."

"What's wrong with that?"

He turned to see her watching him wide-eyed. The fire behind her cast a glow around her body. Even wrapped in his old blanket she held the air of a goddess. A beautiful goddess, he found hard to resist.

She shrugged her shoulders and headed back to the fire. "So what does Kyros call you?" She held out her hands to warm them from the flames, never turning to look at him when she talked. For a woman who hated Centaurs so much she oddly trusted him enough to turn her back on him and let down her guard.

"I'm not some kind of pet if that's what you mean. He doesn't have a certain name to call me by when he wants me to fetch." She irritated him. She looked down her nose at him since he was a Centaur, and he didn't like it.

"Well, what can I call you then? Shall I just call you 'Centaur' when I need to get your attention?"

That got his attention all right. "My name isn't Centaur. My name is K—" She jerked her head around in anticipation and he knew he'd almost said his real name. "Kaj. You can call me Kaj."

She nodded slowly and let her eyes scan his body from his head to his hooves. He felt so naked in this form. And her perusal excited him in a strange way. That's all he needed now was a huge arousal to add to this wonderful night.

"Get some sleep by the fire. I'll be staying in the woods to watch for prowlers."

He headed into the woods but stopped when he heard her sweet voice calling his false name.

"Kaj?"

"Yes?" He didn't turn to look at her. Didn't want to see her at the moment.

"Thank you."

It was a mere two words but it was a start. She'd thanked a Centaur. Something he was sure she'd never done before in her life.

TEN

Thera woke to the sound of her growling stomach and the delightful smell of breakfast cooking over the fire. Without opening her eyes, she knew it was wild pheasant eggs and some sort of meat. She remembered the snake meat from last night and groaned. Still, the thought of it gave her an urge to see the masked Centaur again. Kaj, he'd called himself. Some strange sort of attraction had pulled her to him. His vibrations were alluring, tantalizing—like Kyros. But yet, they were different. There was a darkness and denseness about Kaj that made her leery, yet she didn't quite know what it was.

She stirred on the blanket, the empty feeling in her stomach gnawing at her. Her baby was going to be a big one with that appetite. She slowly let her eyes drift open, reluctant to leave her cozy dreams of the Centaur with the purple mask. Of Kaj. She was almost surprised, and a bit disappointed when she saw Kyros standing by the fire instead. His hair was neat and tied back, his manners so polite. He didn't have that same raw energy about him that attracted her to Kaj. Yet, Kyros had his own attractiveness, one she knew she could learn to love. He was her protector—her child's protector. He was mysterious, like Kaj, but more predictable and compelling in a noble sort of way. He stirred the eggs in the pan and talked to her without looking up.

"I knew the smell of food would wake you from your slumber."

Suddenly, she questioned his manners. She took his words as an insult. Maybe he was more like that rugged Centaur then she thought.

"Not the right thing to say to a pregnant woman so early in the morning." She threw back the blanket and grabbed her boots and pulled them on, irritated already. She stood and readjusted her skirt which had become a bit snug in the last few days.

"It's not."

"It's not?" she repeated and pulled her fingers through her tangled hair. "What's that supposed to mean?"

"It's not morning, Goddess."

"Quit calling me that." She stretched her aching body. She wasn't used to sleeping on the hard ground. Though she'd lived in the forest on Mount Olympus her entire life, she had a house to live in. Or actually, it had once been a temple for Artemis, but it was old and broken down and Artemis kindly gave it to her as a cast-off. "And what do you mean it's not morning?"

Kyros flipped the food onto two wooden plates and handed her one. "You must have had a busy night to sleep so long. It's well into the day. I would have woke you but I wanted to catch some shut-eye myself."

She gladly took the food he handed her and also the seat he offered next to him on the log. "It was a rather ... different night." The aroma called to her and she took a bite of the eggs. Done perfectly. She savored the creamy texture in her mouth and slowly chewed, reveling in the flavor before she swallowed. Still having her power of sensations worked in her favor when it came to eating. The babe within her stirred slightly.

"And by different ..." He handed her a mug of ale. "You mean ..."

"I had a visitor last night." She picked up some of the meat and looked at it. "Snake meat?"

He flashed her a smile, something she'd never seen him do yet. The brief second illuminated his face and made him seem even more handsome. For the first time, she noticed he was wearing different clothes. Some sort of tunic and breeches, instead of the short tunic-wrap she'd seen him in yesterday.

"Would you have preferred snake meat to ground squirrel?" he asked.

She ignored him and took a bite. Not bad. Of course, with her ravenous hunger, she probably would have eaten the snake meat and not complained. "Where'd you get the new clothes?"

He stopped in mid-motion and she felt alarm overtake him for a second before he took a deep breath and answered her.

"In my saddle bag. I didn't like the other tunic, so I chose to wear the breeches and this tunic instead. I guess I'm shy about women looking at my legs."

She finished off her breakfast and he scooped more onto her plate without her asking. She was still famished and didn't object. His assumption that she'd want more to eat without asking her, made her a bit perturbed. She looked down to her own legs which were very visible with the short leather skirt and suddenly became self-conscious.

"Well, if it'll make you feel better I didn't even notice your legs," she answered and shoveled the rest of the food into her mouth, not bothering to savor the flavor. "But if you don't want that old tunic, I'll take it off your hands. My skirt is becoming a bit snug and I don't fancy you looking at my legs either."

He took her empty dish from her, in the process letting his eyes fall on her bare legs. She placed her hands on her lap in an attempt to block his view.

"I didn't notice your legs either until you mentioned them." He walked to the lake and bent down to wash the dishes. She jumped up and followed him, about to call him a liar when he broke in with, "Of course, I can't say the same about the rest of your body. After all, you had no qualms showing it to me at the pond yesterday."

If anyone could ruffle her feathers beside her father, it had to be Kyros. He had such a sour disposition, and the way he spoke to her, she almost swore he wanted her not to like him. Whatever game it was he played with her, she wasn't going to let him know it bothered her. She wouldn't give him the satisfaction.

"Well, you just may see my naked body again if you don't give me that tunic. My waist is stretching and I'm no longer comfortable in my skirt."

His shoulders stiffened and the scrubbing of the dishes slowed. He answered without looking at her.

"I can't give it to you, or I would. I ...I got rid of it last night."

"Well, where'd you put it? We'll just go get it."

"It's gone."

She let out an exasperated breath and headed over for Hester.

"Well, if I hadn't dropped my saddle bag when the Centaurs attacked, I'd have extra clothes. Of course, I'm sure the Centaurs have stolen it by now so no use even trying to retrieve it. Surely you must have something in here I can wear?"

Kyros turned his head to see Thera by Hester, rummaging through his saddle bag. He sprang to his feet and ran to her. He'd hidden his mask in the bag and she was about to find it. "Wait!" he called and grabbed her hand away just as she was about to discover his secret. He held onto her wrist and she looked up to him with those Olympian blue eyes.

"What's the matter?" She shook her hand loose and was about to dig back into the bag when Kyros spun her around toward him. He had to distract her. He had to make her stop her exploration of his bag or he'd be explaining more than he wanted to right now.

So instead, he pulled her into his arms and kissed her. His lips brushed against hers ever so lightly and when he pulled away, he realized he wanted to do it again. She was beautiful, as beautiful as her mother, the goddess of love, in his eyes. He couldn't help himself from reaching out and tucking a strand of her loose hair behind her ear.

She seemed surprised—actually shocked that he'd done that. But not half as surprised as he was by his own actions. He couldn't help himself. She was staring at his lips and he put his hands on her shoulders and drew her to him. He lowered his mouth to hers and this time, gave her a lingering kiss. One that turned into a deep kiss on both their parts. She tasted like a cross between honey and ambrosia—like the nectar of the gods, or so he guessed. Her lips were soft and moist. Her body pressed up close to his, felt warm and delightfully curvy.

What started out as a distraction turned into an obsession and he had to have more. One kiss led to another and he found his hands wandering down her back, massaging, caressing and feeling her wonderful body so close to his. It was a long time since he'd had a woman. No woman wanted him once she knew his secret. Everyone was repelled by the likes of him. No one wanted anything to do with someone who was half-man and half-beast.

His tongue darted out and traced the line of her lips. Her own hands circled around his waist, pulling him closer. She opened for him and he entered her mouth with his tongue. Their tongues danced a slow rhythm in circles, and as they melded together he felt they were almost one. He'd wanted her so badly last night while in his Centaur form. Something about being part animal brought out his rutting instincts. But he'd known he couldn't touch her then. But today he was human. Today he could touch her, and he would.

His hands traveled to the front of her tight bodice and he couldn't help but let his fingers roam over her rounded breasts. He'd seen them at the pond and knew exactly what they looked like. He'd been longing since to feel them, and now his wish was coming true. He ran his fingers over the bare skin that was exposed and heard her whimper in pleasure.

She grabbed one of his hands and guided it beneath the fabric. His skin against hers was the best feeling he'd ever experienced—besides the actual interchange that'd gotten her pregnant in the first place.

He felt his breath deepen and his loins tighten. So ironic that the woman he wanted to couple with was already pregnant with his child, though he'd never touched her before now. He flicked a finger across her soft nipple and felt it tighten beneath his touch. She moaned and arched back, inviting him to do more. He wanted her more than he'd ever wanted any woman. He wanted to lower his head and suckle her, then pull her skirt up and slam himself into her, delighting in the pleasure he knew he'd feel. He removed his hand from her bodice and let it slip down toward her waist.

She grabbed him and pushed her mouth to his, eager, hungry and definitely willing. It was then his hand passed over the small swell of her stomach. He felt the baby within her stir, and at the same time, Hester neighed in the background. He jumped back and released her. The baby was his. The baby he wasn't even sure was human. It could be a Centaur. And if it was, how would that affect Thera? How would that affect the Trozens and the rest of the Centaur race?

He buried his face in his hands and fought for control. He had no business touching Thera or even wanting her for that matter. She was the daughter of the god of war. A god he hated for ruining his life. A god who was about to destroy the chance of peace between the Trozens and the Centaurs and probably take most of the race in the process.

"What is it?" Thera fixed her bodice and stared at him with those bedchamber eyes. "Why did you stop?" Her lower lip trembled and he was afraid she'd cry. What in Tartarus was he doing to her? What was he doing to himself?

"You don't find me attractive." It was an accusation on her part. One she may have believed, but one he knew was not so.

"No. It's not that. You're very attractive. It's just … I can't, that's all. I just had to stop."

Well, his distraction had worked. She forgot all about the saddle bag. But now she had other things on her mind. She slapped him, totally catching him off guard.

"What was that for?" His cheek stung and he was sure her fingerprints were imbedded upon his skin. He was really glad she didn't decide to punch him instead.

"It's just something I had to do," she answered, and Kyros knew somehow he deserved it. He never did understand women and a goddess was out of his league. Not only didn't he deserve her, but he didn't deserve what may happen if he angered her. He was only glad she said her powers had been stripped away.

"Even Kaj has more manners than you."

That took him by surprise. She almost sounded as if she liked his Centaur form.

"So you met Kaj."

"I did." She crossed her arms over her chest as she spoke and he knew she was still angry with him. He bent down to scoop the clean dishes out of the water.

"Then you didn't find him offensive at all?"

She hesitated before she answered. "For a Centaur, he wasn't all that bad. At least not nearly as offensive as you with the way you lead me on and then toss me to the wolves when you've had your fill."

"Had my fill?" He chuckled as he took the dishes and crammed them into the saddle bag atop his mask and some bread and ale he'd brought with. "I'm far from having my fill, sweetheart. It takes more to satisfy a warrior than just a little heavy petting." He rubbed a hand over Hester's nose as he spoke.

"Well, Warrior, maybe you'll have to restrict your petting to Hester from now on. I'm a pregnant woman and off limits."

"Pregnant with my child, I'll remind you." He made his way past her and picked up the blankets and shook the dust from them.

"With your child, but not by your hand," she remarked. "It's by the hands of a god that you've impregnated me. I never gave you permission to impregnate me; nor did I give you permission to touch me just now."

He folded the blankets into neat squares, holding them against his chest. "I didn't know I needed permission. And by the way you were giving of yourself, I thought you wanted it as much as I did. If I was wrong, forgive me for assuming you were enjoying it."

By her silence, he knew he'd struck a true note. She did enjoy it as much as he did and was probably only angry that he stopped. He finished packing the saddle bag, giving her privacy when she disappeared for a moment behind a bush. When she came back out he could have sworn her eyes were a bit wetter than before and her nose was a little redder.

"I hope you don't mind Kaj spending the evenings with you." That sounded strange and he thought he'd correct the statement before she went off on another temper tantrum. "I mean … watching out for you after nightfall."

"I guess I don't mind. He seems harmless. Or at least to me."

"Good. I'm sorry I can't be here, but I've got other places to be at night. But he'll protect you as well as I would."

"Maybe better," she answered to his surprise. "After all, you didn't seem to use that big sword any to defend us when the Centaurs were attacking."

Kyros instinctively grabbed for the hilt of his sword at his hip, just to assure himself it was safe. "You're safe, aren't you?" he retorted.

"Kaj has a huge golden bow and arrows. He's a master archer and can hunt and shoot better than anyone."

This bothered Kyros. He wasn't a master archer. He barely knew how to hold the bow. He was a master swordsman and proud of it. The bow and arrows were blessed by Artemis, the only reason he could even aim the damned thing at all.

"He's not a master archer. The bow is blessed by the gods."

She looked up at him in intrigue and he now cursed himself silently for mentioning it.

"By Artemis?" she asked, and he felt the can of worms beginning to open. He couldn't lie to her. He had to tell her the truth in a round-about sort of way.

"I think that's what Kaj said. Why does it matter?"

"I overheard Ares and Artemis arguing one day. She supposedly made a bow and arrows for the king of the Centaurs. It was to be used only by him—only by a king—to protect the Centaurs from attackers. It supposedly was faster and possessed a truer aim than any human-made bow."

Well, she was right on track so far. Little Miss Loner did know a little about what went on up at Mount Olympus. Next she'd be asking why Kaj is able to use it. He couldn't very well tell her it was because Kaj was him, and he was the future king of Trozen—down the line after his brother, anyway.

"Kaj is the king of the Centaurs! I knew there was something different about him."

Kyros just stood there with his mouth open. Maybe her days of living as a hermit really did keep her from knowing the history of the Centaurs. And maybe this could work to his advantage after all. But then again, he hated lying to Thera. She didn't deserve it and he was already feeling bad enough that he had to hide his secret identity and use a false name.

"I wouldn't exactly call him king of the Centaurs. That bow kind of has a mind of its own. I wouldn't be surprised if he didn't even know how to use the thing."

She smiled and took a step closer. "If I didn't know better, I'd say you were jealous of Kaj."

Jealous? If only she knew how much he hated Kaj. If he was jealous of anyone, it would be of a man who was just a man and nothing more.

"Let's get going." He reached out and helped her atop Hester. "I know of a place in the woods that even the gods don't know about. It's a ways from here, but you'll be safe there." He would have jumped on behind her to pick up time, but he didn't trust himself so near her again.

"Where is it? And how can you be sure Ares won't find us?" She looked down at him as she sat astride his horse. He couldn't help but see right up that damned short skirt of hers. She wore nothing beneath it.

"It's a chance we'll have to take. But first we're going to find that horse you lost. I hope it's not in too bad condition. We could travel much faster if we had it."

"But can't we just share this horse?" Her voice was just a bit too sultry for him, and after knowing what lie beneath her skirt, there was no way he'd be able to ride with her. He had lots of thoughts in his head of what he'd like to do with her, but knew none of them included getting to safety.

He took hold of Hester's reins and started to walk. "Let's go find the blind old weaver. Hopefully she can spin you something to wear that'll cover up those legs of yours I never look at."

ELEVEN

Ares, God of War, paced the floor of his cave—a palace in his eyes though it was probably one of the worst homes on Mount Olympus. Hundreds of candles lit the dark cave, trophies of war lined the walls. Weapons, torture devices, and tokens of past leaders and human kings graced his presence.

He stopped beside one of his favorite trophies; a gold jeweled crown interwoven with the hairs of horse tail—Centaur tail to be exact. The tail and crown of Phylo, the king of the Centaurs. This was one Centaur he truly enjoyed killing, bringing fear upon the Centaur race. A race without a leader. A race now divided. Just the right makings of the kind of confusion that would lead to war. And a war was just what Ares needed right now. His own warriors were having trouble doing what he ordered, so he decided to take matters into his own hands.

"Ares!" came a voice from the door.

Ares turned to see two of his men escorting Rodas into his cave. The Centaur looked angry and Ares knew exactly what bothered him.

"Don't come to complain again, Rodas. It's not my fault Thera's not carrying your child."

"You promised I'd be the father of the Centaur child that caused the war between the Centaurs and the Trozens. You gave me your word I'd have the pleasure and the power of being a part of the destruction. Centaurs were supposed to fear me. I was suppose to be their new king."

Ares felt his own anger pumping turmoil through his veins. He knew his plan was tainted by Kyros and he didn't like the feeling of not being in control. He raised a finger toward Rodas and shot a beam of light toward him.

"Arrrgh!"

Rodas jumped out of the way just in time, landing sideways on the ground. Ares' warriors scurried out the cave door, obviously not wanting to be near him when he was mad.

"How dare you burst into my domain and complain I'm not carrying out my promises! I should kill you for that, just as I killed your own king for nothing more than irritating me."

Rodas jumped to his feet and held his hands out in front of him in a means of protection. "Now wait a minute, Ares. I didn't mean to accuse you of anything. It's just that—"

Ares threw a ball of fire toward him and this time he ducked behind Ares' throne.

"I'm the god here! I'm the only one who'll do accusing or complaining. I'm the one with the power and you'll listen to me and not complain again or I'll slice off your head and hang it on my wall as the first body-part trophy in here."

A waving hand came up from behind the chair and Rodas slowly poked his head out.

"Get away from my throne! I'm the only one who goes near it."

"Yes, Ares. Forgive me, your Highness."

Rodas darted out from behind the chair and Ares plopped down in it and threw his leather-sheathed legs over the side arm.

"Cut the Highness routine. Now shut up and listen for a change. If you still want to be my warrior, I have a chore for you."

Rodas' tail flicked and his hooves pawed the dirt floor in anticipation.

"Of course, I want to be your warrior. That is, if the deal is still good that I'll be the Centaur king."

Ares sprang to his feet. "I don't make deals with mortals. You do it, or die. Simple as that. If you happen to benefit in the process—good for you. Either way I'll get what I want, with or without you. So what do you say?"

Bravery graced Rodas, but even he wasn't so stupid as to deny the god of war. "I'll do it," he answered.

"Good." Ares half-smiled and ran his fingers over his short beard as he paced the room while he spoke. "The way I see it, the ball's already been set in motion. Thera is pregnant—"

"With Kyros' baby," Rodas broke in.

"Don't interrupt me!" Ares raised a finger but lowered it again when he saw Rodas flinch. "And don't ever flinch. No warrior of mine will ever be caught flinching."

"Got it," answered Rodas. "No flinching."

"Now you're catching on. As I was saying, Thera is pregnant with Kyros' baby. This could work to our advantage. Pittheus hates Kyros almost as much as I do."

"As much as we do," Rodas corrected him.

Ares ignored him and kept his pace as he talked. "When Pittheus finds out his bride is pregnant with his brother's baby, he'll be furious. Pittheus needs an heir in order to ensure himself that Kyros will never get the throne. The whole reason he accepted my gift of Thera's hand in the first place is because he figured an heir that was half-god was even more powerful."

"I thought you told him it was a peace offering for the death of his father, since your curse on Kyros triggered his weak heart."

Ares laughed and walked over to the Centaur crown. He pulled it off the wall and toyed with it. "Since when does the god of war want peace? Any fool could see right through that lie."

Rodas reached out and grabbed a fig from the bowl of fruit that sat on a nearby table. Before he could pop it into his mouth, Ares' iron fist grabbed his wrist and stopped him.

"That fruit is an offering. It's not to be eaten, let alone touched by the likes of you."

"Sorry." Rodas nodded toward his wrist and Ares released it. The Centaur then gingerly placed the fruit back into the bowl. "So," he said as he wiped his palm on his chest. "What is it you want me to do?"

"Get Kyros' sword and bring it to Pittheus."

Rodas' eyes opened wide. "That won't be easy. Kyros is an excellent swordsman. It's not likely he's going to just hand it over."

"Then steal it," snapped Ares. "My men have been watching him. He takes it off when he turns into his Centaur form. He gives it to that child Centaur. Find out where they hide it and then take it when Kyros isn't around."

"I fail to see the logic behind this."

"You fool. Once Kyros knows his brother has the sword, he'll go to the castle himself to retrieve it."

"So?"

"So, he'll bring Thera along to protect her and his baby. I won't have to force Thera to go to Pittheus. Kyros will bring her there for me. Once she's there, our problems will be over. Pittheus will insist on his bride and the fun begins."

Ares chuckled and turned a full circle with his arms outstretched.

The walls rumbled with thunder and the floor shook.

"One question," Rodas spoke slowly.

"What?"

"How are you going to convince Pittheus not to hold me there and use me for sport? After all, he does make entertainment out of the Centaurs he catches. He's even said to kill a few for fun, though it can't be proven."

Ares folded his arms over his chest and raised the side of his upper lip as he spoke.

"Well, now. That's not really my problem, is it?"

"Well, no, but—"

"The way I see it, you can go and take the chance of being captured, or you can refuse me and take the chance of dying right now. So what'll it be?"

"I'm on my way," grumbled Rodas, and with a swish of his tail he was out the door.

Ares held up the Centaur crown and examined it in the firelight.

"Well, now that I've got Rodas out of my way, I've got a few things of my own to do." He hung the crown back on the wall and grabbed a battle ax. Twirling it around in his hands, he called for his guards.

"Yes, Ares," one replied. The other stood silent.

"Have my warriors found Ganymede yet?"

"No, Ares. They've searched everywhere but can't find him."

"Then search harder!" he bellowed. "Ganymede was sent to bring my daughter to Pittheus and he failed. He's a deserter and he needs to be found and punished."

"And what about the other two escorts?" asked the guard.

Ares flung the battle ax in the air and it stuck in the cave wall close to where the guards stood.

"Thera's already killed Akil and Loxias."

"So she's a warrior now?" asked the quiet guard.

"No, she's not a warrior yet. Those two weren't even real. But Ganymede is different. I didn't create him. He came to my doorstep wanting to be my warrior, like so many others. With any luck he'll go back to her and she'll hopefully kill him. That would save me the trouble. Thera's killing instincts are no longer dormant. She shot my raven; so she has killed."

"She killed your raven and you let her get away with it?" asked the first guard.

Ares felt his blood boil just at the mention of the death of his favorite pet. Thera was never supposed to kill the bird, she was supposed to kill a deer. For this, he was going to have to make her pay, but he didn't need his guard to remind him.

"I'm not letting her get away with it," he shouted, blasting the man with a jolt just because he was irritating. Thera was his daughter, and though Ares had many bastards running around, he had hopes for this child. Thera was different, stronger. She had a strong sense of her mother's powers within her, but she had his as well. And now that her war-like abilities were awakened, she'd be in constant struggle of every choice she made. Just the perfect makings of a warrior. He wasn't going to give up yet.

"Hades refuses to give back my raven until I start up a huge war. And that's just what I'm going to do. For if Rodas does what he's supposed to, we're going to see the biggest war in Greece since the fall of Troy."

TWELVE

It took most of the afternoon to find Thera's horse, and when they did, it wasn't what they had hoped for. The horse had badly twisted its ankle and couldn't be ridden. The way it limped, Kyros knew it wasn't going to do them any good. And there wasn't any use dragging it along with them as it'd only slow them down.

"I guess we'll have to leave your horse," sighed Kyros. Thera seemed worried. "Someone is bound to find it in the next day or so," he reassured her. "This area is loaded with soldiers from the castle."

"All right," she agreed, patting the horse on the side in a calming gesture. "How far is the weaver's hut?"

"I'm not sure. But if I understand Chiron's directions, I think it's about a half a day's walk north of here."

"Well, we'd better get going then." Thera looked a bit tired and Kyros knew they'd never make it there before sunset. Or at least not on foot. The only way they'd make it there before his transformation is if they both rode on his horse. Something he wasn't looking forward to doing. Being close to Thera was enough challenge on his part. Bouncing his body up against hers as they rode was something that would drive him mad.

"I think we should just wait until tomorrow." He didn't like the idea of hanging around if Pittheus' men were in the woods, but still it'd be safer than getting close to Thera.

"Nonsense." She put her foot in the stirrup and hoisted herself awkwardly onto Hester. "Just jump up here and we'll both ride. Hester can handle it. We should get there in time for dinner."

It was tempting, but he just couldn't. "I'll walk." He took the reins and was starting away when she stopped him.

"Kyros. There's Centaurs in the woods nearby."

Kyros scanned the grounds, sword at the ready but still he saw nothing.

"I don't see them," he answered.

"Neither do I," said Thera. "But I can smell them and the scent is getting stronger."

He replaced his sword in the scabbard and in one motion hoisted himself up onto the horse behind her. He couldn't take the chance of Rodas and his followers coming after Thera. "Let's ride."

They took off at a gallop toward the north to find the blind old weaver.

Thera felt terrible about lying to Kyros. She didn't smell Centaur. As far as she knew there wasn't a Centaur within a half a day's ride from them. Still, she told Kyros there was, as she knew he'd hop on the horse, and that was what she wanted.

She felt his strong arms around her and she reveled in the warmth, strength and comfort. It felt right to be in the embrace of the father of her child. The baby stirred within her and she knew the unborn child was happy as well. They were a family, the three of them, like it or not. Kyros was the father of her baby and she was glad of it.

She smelled his male scent, spicy, alluring, a powerful river that forged its way to the nearest bank. He was that river, she the bank on which she hoped he'd land and find solace.

He was disturbed, his mind confused. She'd felt it when he pulled away from their embrace. She didn't understand it. He seemed like he wanted to be close to her, yet he fought to keep his distance. The man was a mystery. Kyros of nowhere, going everywhere. She still wasn't sure why he stayed with her, or for that matter, where they were going to end up.

All she knew was that she had no intention of going to the castle and marrying the man who was regent king. Pittheus, her father had called him. The name meant nothing to her, and she was sorry now she'd lived so secluded in her days as a goddess and didn't mingle more with the humans. She had no idea what went on anywhere besides Olympus. It never really mattered to her before, but now that she was human it made all the difference in the world.

She'd have to ask Kyros about Pittheus. She'd ask him many things when the moment was right. But for now, her eyelids grew heavy and the rocking steps of the horse lulled her to sleep. She laid her head back against Kyros' chest and felt his warmth engulf her. She was safe with him. She was attracted to him. But still, as she drifted off to sleep she couldn't help but dream about the Centaur with the purple mask. All thoughts of Kyros faded away as Kaj filled her dreams instead.

The sun was getting low on the horizon when they reached the weaver's hut. It was a little shack, barely enough room for one person. Kyros hated to wake Thera who was asleep in his arms. He rather liked the feel of her so close to him. But it only made him think of the bliss he'd felt while being mated with her. And that only made him want to do it once again, but physically this time.

He gently woke her and slipped off the horse, instructing her to wait there. He walked up to the door and called out.

"Weaver! I'm a friend of Chiron's. I'm here to ask you a favor."

The door to the hut creaked open slowly, but no one came to greet him.

"You said she was old, maybe we should go to her." Thera stood directly behind him. He jumped slightly. Damn her for not listening and staying on the horse. Somehow he was sure she was going to cause trouble.

"I don't think we should go in, Thera. I have a bad feeling about this."

It was too late. Thera disappeared into the dark hut. Kyros had no choice but to follow. A little old lady sat hunched over a loom, spinning, weaving, making cloth in the dim light of the dying hearth fire.

"You are hiding something," came her voice, though her eyes were white and glassed-over and she didn't look at them at all. "You are not who you seem to be." The old woman was definitely blind. Kyros' heart jumped at the accusation and he didn't quite know what to say.

"No, I'm not hiding anything," answered Thera, obviously thinking the woman was speaking to her. "My name is Thera and my traveling partner is—"

"Names aren't important," broke in Kyros. "Thera needs a tunic and we were hoping you could make one for her."

The old woman stopped weaving and reached out her hand. "Step closer, child, so I can feel you and know how big to make the garment."

Thera obeyed and the woman reached out her hand. Her fingers touched Thera's skirt and the old woman pulled her hand away as if burned. She then fell to her knees on the floor in front of Thera, her head hidden in her hands.

"Forgive me, Goddess. I didn't realize, or I never would have touched you."

Kyros was in awe how the blind old hag could know so much by just one touch. And if she knew so much, she was sure to tell Thera all his secrets. He had a bad feeling about all this and knew now that it was a mistake to come here in the first place.

Thera laughed and grabbed the weaver and helped her to her feet.

"True, I was once a goddess, but am not anymore. You can treat me like any other human now." She took the old woman's hand and placed it on her stomach to feel the baby. "I'll need something to wear that will stretch."

"You're pregnant with a very special baby."

"Yes," Thera beamed. "I am. You seem to see the future. Maybe you can tell me if it'll be a boy or a girl."

"Stop the idle chatter," interrupted Kyros. "It's bad luck to know too much too soon. Weaver, will you make her a garment to wear?"

"Have you got anything to offer in exchange?"

Kyros didn't have any money, but then remembered it wasn't money the woman wanted. Chiron had told him they'd exchanged food for clothing.

"We have bread and figs to offer," he answered.

"No meat?" she asked.

Before he could answer, Thera broke in. "Kyros could hunt you some meat. He's an excellent hunter, not to mention cook."

Kyros shifted nervously as he noticed the sky outside the open hut door. Nightfall would be here soon and he knew he had no time to hunt when his transformation was so close at hand.

"We have bread and figs to offer," he repeated.

"You're Kyros?" the old woman asked him slowly.

"Oh, you've heard of him?" Thera seemed surprised and happy. Not what she would be feeling if he allowed the old hag to continue spilling his secrets.

"She hasn't," answered Kyros. "And I think we'd better get that bread and figs now. I'll hunt for you tomorrow as I've got somewhere to go for the night."

"You're leaving again?" Thera looked disappointed, and he wanted more than anything to tell her he'd stay.

"Kaj will be with you to watch you. You have nothing to worry about."

"Kaj?" came the crone's hackled voice, half-laughing.

"Kaj is the king of the Centaurs," answered Thera. "He wears a mask and carries a huge bow."

"Oh really?" she asked with doubt in her voice.

"Let's go," broke in Kyros and pulled her toward the door.

"She can stay here." The weaver smiled a broken-toothed grin. A grin he didn't trust in the least.

"She'll be fine with Kaj." Kyros pulled her back toward the door.

"Oh, I'd like to stay," said Thera, but Kyros didn't slow down to listen. He pulled her out to the horse and tossed her atop it. He then grabbed some food from his saddle bag and went back to give it to the weaver.

"Your secret's safe with me," she said as she accepted the bread and figs.

"I don't know what you're talking about," grumbled Kyros and headed for the door.

"I think you do, Kaj," she said softly so Thera couldn't hear her. "But you'd better tell her soon. For once the baby is born, there'll no longer be any secrets."

THIRTEEN

Thera didn't speak a word to Kyros until they stopped to make camp. He slid from the horse and held a hand out to help her. She brushed his hand away and slid off the opposite side by herself.

"I get the feeling you're angry with me."

"And why shouldn't I be? Who are you to tell me where I can or can't stay for the night?"

"I'm the father of your child, and I'll do what I think is right for the baby."

"I liked the old weaver. You rushed me out of there so fast, I didn't even get a chance to ask her name."

She watched Kyros tie up Hester and quickly make a campfire. He worked so fast, she could have sworn he was in a hurry to get away from her.

"Where do you disappear to at night?" She had the feeling it was the wrong time to ask, but still she had to try. After all, if he had a lover awaiting him somewhere then she had the right to know about it. After all, he was the father of her unborn child.

"Kaj will be here shortly. He'll bring you some game to eat. Stay put."

"And if I don't?"

He stopped his work and looked up at her. "I would stay put if I were you. You don't know what dangers lie out there in the woods."

"And I don't know what dangers lie here at camp with that wretched Centaur you send to guard me."

He looked hurt by that statement and stood up and wiped the dust from his hands on his legs. "You really don't like Kaj?"

"Why should I? Why should I like any Centaur for that matter? Kaj scares me. He's unlike any Centaur I've ever known."

"What do you mean by that?" Kyros went over to the horse and pulled the blankets from the saddle bag. She saw him fussing with something else but didn't know or care at the moment what it was. She couldn't tell him why Kaj scared her. She couldn't tell him about her strange attraction to the Centaur when she didn't understand it herself. She hated Centaurs, so why did she like this one? She didn't want Kyros to think she was being disloyal to him. After all, he was the father of her child and there would be no one else but him in her life.

"Hester isn't spooked by Kaj," she said instead. "I've never seen a horse yet that likes a Centaur."

"Hester is a very different horse. She doesn't get spooked by much."

Maybe he had a point there, but Hester did seem spooked when the Centaurs attacked. It was just one Centaur Hester wasn't afraid of.

"And he eats meat," she added. "What Centaur do you know of that eats meat?"

"Just Kaj."

Kyros fell quiet as he placed the blankets around the fire. Then he looked up at the sun setting behind the trees.

"Just give him a chance. That's all I ask."

With that, Kyros disappeared into the woods without even as much as a good-bye. Thera felt the chill creeping in around her and scooted up closer to the fire. She noticed her breathing had quickened and she felt a strange excitement about her as she waited for the masked Centaur. Apprehensive, cautious and yet curious about Kaj, she decided maybe she'd take Kyros' advice and try to get to know him better.

She sat down on the blanket and waited. It was then she heard the sound of a man's painful scream somewhere in the woods. She shuddered, wondering if one of Pittheus' men was torturing or perhaps killing someone. By the gods, she hoped it wasn't Kyros. This terrified her, and she didn't like this human emotion. She closed her eyes, trying to shut out the noises of the outside world. She was helpless, weaponless and very much alone. Her body shivered if not from cold then from fright. The baby kicked inside her and she rubbed a hand over her rounding stomach. She'd be well protected soon. Just as soon as Kaj showed up. For some reason, when he was with her she felt that same sense of calm protection as she felt with Kyros.

Kyros barely made it in time, taking off his newly woven clothes before his body began to transform. He couldn't help but let out a pent-up cry as his bones shifted and his lower half grew in size. He hadn't had time to prepare his mind again. And each time he'd let it slip, the pain grew more and more intense.

Chiron and Nemos found him just as he started transforming and grabbed his sword and sandals to help him along. He lay on the ground now with his eyes closed. His body shivered and convulsed with spasms. When would this curse be over? How much more could he endure before he lost his composure and decided to take his own life to end it all?

"Kyros." Chiron called his name and through his blurred vision he could see the old man holding out a helping hand. Kyros reached for him and let him pull him to his feet. He was tired and weak, from not enough sleep and certainly not enough food. He'd have to make certain to rest and eat tonight or he wasn't sure he'd have enough strength to pull himself onto his horse tomorrow.

"I can't do this anymore," he panted. His vision cleared a bit and he saw Nemos standing proudly beside Kyros with his sword protected in his arms.

"You have no choice," Chiron reminded him. "You're damned for the rest of your life unless you can find some way to break Ares' curse."

"Don't remind me." Kyros picked up his clothing from the ground and handed it to Chiron. "Thank the gods I didn't rip my clothes or I'd have to ask the weaver to make some more for me along with the ones for Thera."

"You went to the weaver?" Chiron seemed a bit disturbed about this.

"I did. Shouldn't I have?"

"You shouldn't have gone to her, Kyros. She's not to be trusted. She's an ally of Ares."

"Now you tell me. Had I known that, I never would have gone."

"She's sure to tell him where you are. Either that or she'll weave some spell into Thera's clothing."

"What do you mean by that?" Kyros pulled his mask from the pile of clothing and tied it on as he spoke.

"I mean she's been known to sometimes weave ideas or curses into the clothes she makes if she doesn't like the person. No telling what she's done until its too late."

"Thera is a goddess. The old woman wouldn't dare do anything to a goddess." Kyros took the bow and arrows from Nemos.

"A fallen goddess," remarked Chiron. "And who knows what kind of deals the weaver's made with Ares."

"Well, that's just the chance we'll have to take." Kyros patted Chiron on the shoulder and then ruffled Nemos' hair. "Take good care of that sword, boy."

"I'll watch it with my life, Kyros."

"Good," answered Kyros. "Because I'd hate to think what would happen if that sword fell into the wrong hands."

By the time Kyros hunted down two rabbits for dinner and made his way back to camp, Thera was already fast asleep by the fire. He didn't wake her as he skinned the rabbits and speared them up to cook. He took the handful of wild flowers he'd picked for her and laid them on the blanket next to her head. Maybe this would make her accept him. He hoped so, or at least to ease the ill feelings she had toward Centaurs— him in particular. Then he made himself comfortable while he roasted the meat.

She looked so young and innocent as she slept. And so beautiful that it made him want to cry. Even if she was the daughter of Ares he couldn't help but be attracted to her. In a way he was jealous that she was to become his brother Pittheus' wife. Pittheus didn't deserve someone like her. But then again, neither did he.

She stirred in her sleep and cooed softly. Her long dark hair fell gently over her face and he wanted nothing more than to smooth it back and place a kiss gently upon her cheek. But he wouldn't. Couldn't. Not while in his Centaur form. He wasn't even sure how he'd get down there to do it and then back up without hurting himself.

He felt awkward being a Centaur and wasn't at all sure he'd ever get used to it. He'd learned to sleep standing up, like most the other Centaurs did. That way they were always on their feet if there was trouble or an attack during the night.

He reached down and grabbed a rabbit and tore off a limb, blowing on it to cool. He'd made another mistake by eating meat in front of Thera while in his Centaur form. But since the damage was done he figured he'd enjoy a good meal. He just couldn't get used to eating vegetables, fruit and grain and nothing else. He was a warrior with a powerful hunger, and it'd take more than greens to satisfy him.

His eyes went back to Thera and he realized he hungered for more than just food. She was his biggest enemy's daughter, and yet, he hungered for her more than for any woman he'd ever known. She had a raw energy about her that called out to him in every form. He was a part of her now; his seed was growing into their child. And though he'd always longed for the day he'd have a child, the thought now terrified him more than anything ever had.

And the biggest fear he had was that his child would be a Centaur. Not that a Centaur child would bother him, just the fact that if his baby was born a Centaur, it would be hated by all. For his child would be the cause of a horrible war.

Thera's eyelids flickered and then slowly opened. With the way she'd turned in her sleep, the flowers now lay directly in front of her face. She focused on them with wide eyes and then sat up abruptly and fearfully looked at him.

"I'm sorry. I didn't mean to frighten you," he said.

"You didn't." She said the words but he knew they were a lie. She was terrified of him and why shouldn't she be? He was a wretched, horrid creature in her eyes. A creature that to her, symbolized hatred, war, destruction—and her father.

"From you?" she asked, glancing down toward the flowers.

He couldn't answer, just nodded and handed her some meat.

"I hope you're hungry." He knew she would be. With the way she'd been eating, he wouldn't be surprised if she put down two rabbits herself.

She reached out slowly and grabbed the meat. Her eyes glanced at the flowers again and then back to him. "Thank you."

He wasn't sure if she was thanking him for the flowers or the meal, but it didn't matter. All that mattered was that this was the second time she'd thanked him while he was in his Centaur form.

The silence was deafening and he could no longer take the feel of her eyes burning a hole through his skin. He had to say something, anything to break the damned silence.

"So I hear you've outgrown your skirt and the weaver has to make you a new one."

By the look on her face, he knew he should have kept quiet. He didn't mean it as an insult, but knew that was the way she took it.

"Who told you that? Kyros?"

He nodded.

"Sounds like something he would say." She went on eating her meat, but he knew she was fuming about the whole situation.

"Don't you like Kyros?"

Her eyes darted up and then she dropped her gaze back to her food quickly. "Kyros seems to be trying hard to convince me to like you," she answered instead.

"Well?"

"Well what?" She seemed so flippant about the whole thing.

"Well, do you?" He felt like a fool for asking, but had to know.

"I despise Centaurs," she answered. "The only reason I tolerate you is because I do it as a favor to Kyros."

He didn't need to hear any more. He didn't want to. Her answer was clear. She didn't like him in his Centaur form and he wasn't really sure she liked him in his human form either. But her kiss told differently. Her kiss said she liked Kyros, the man more than she was willing to let on. But all that would change once she found out about his secret life. Once she knew that, she'd for certain want nothing to do with him.

A huge flying roach flew toward the fire and landed on Thera's leg. She screamed and jumped to her feet, brushing the bug off of her in the process. Alarmed, Kyros ran to her side and without thinking, scooped her up into his arms.

She automatically clasped her hands around his shoulders and hung on. It was then that he knew he'd made a mistake. He never should have touched her. Her face was just inches from his. He focused on her lips and watched them part slightly. He felt the irresistible need to kiss her and almost felt that she wanted it too. His tail flicked in anticipation and his hooves moved back and forth over the rocky ground.

"Put me down," she said in a low voice. Though he heard the words, she didn't sound like she really meant them. He moved his mouth towards hers.

"Put me down!" she commanded more loudly. And this time he knew she meant it. He placed her on the ground on her feet and in his awkwardness his hooves trampled her flowers. He needed to get out of there and he needed to do it now. One more minute near her and he wasn't sure how he'd react.

Without a word he picked up his bow and arrows and took off into the forest to try to find a place to think.

Thera's body shook slightly and she wrapped her arms around herself, holding back the tears that were destined to come. Kaj was gone and she felt an emptiness within her. She looked to the ground and saw the crushed flowers at her feet. Slowly she bent down and picked up a few broken petals. She closed her fist over them and closed her eyes tight.

What was happening to her? Her own feelings scared her and she wasn't sure how to react. Kaj had brought her flowers. He wasn't like any other Centaur. He had a kindness to him. True caring. He had all the ingredients of a man. All, that is, except his Centaur body.

Thera held the petals to her heart and felt her baby's heartbeat within her. She was confused and angry at herself. Confused, because she knew it was Kyros whom she wanted to be with. Angry, because she let herself have feelings for Kaj. She had never in her entire life felt anything for a Centaur except for contempt. Centaurs were lowly creatures whom she'd always avoided if she could. Now her life was filled with them. She'd almost been impregnated by one and Kyros had best friends that were Centaurs, and now she had feelings toward a Centaur she never should be having.

Kaj was a Centaur. She was a fallen goddess. There was no connection between them and she would never allow one to form. But still, as much as she tried to hate Kaj, she couldn't. Something inside herself held the same kind of attraction for Kaj that she had for Kyros.

She used her senses to make certain Kaj was nowhere near. And when she knew for certain he'd left, she sat down on the blanket and stared into the fire. She held her fist out toward the fire and slowly opened her fingers. With a slow tilt of her hand, the petals from the flower fluttered into the flames.

She wouldn't allow herself to have feelings for a Centaur. Centaurs had ruined her life and a Centaur had worked with her father to try to force her into starting a war. She'd have to watch herself closely from now on. It felt a bit too good being in Kaj's arms. And if she hadn't forced herself to tell him to put her down, she was sure she would have let him kiss her.

She buried her hands in her face and cried harder than she'd ever cried in her life. She wanted a family, her baby, and Kyros. She wanted to live a human life without magic, the gods, or Centaurs. So why was she having feelings for Kaj? Her attraction to him challenged and threatened her chances of attaining her dream. Kaj challenged not only her hopes for the future, but her beliefs and attitude towards Centaurs as well.

FOURTEEN

Kyros went early the next morning to the old weaver's hut and exchanged meat for Thera's clothing. He didn't want Thera coming with him, or she'd want to stay and get acquainted with the old woman—something he couldn't allow. He held her tunic dress in one hand and tucked his purple mask into the waist of his breeches with the other. He felt exhausted from the night before. He hadn't been able to sleep a wink after what happened with Thera.

He couldn't go back to camp after he'd almost kissed her while in his Centaur form. She made it quite clear to him how she felt about Centaurs. There was no doubt in his mind that she would never accept him while he was cursed—cursed by her own father, a god he truly wished he had the power to kill.

He approached camp and oddly heard voices. Picking up his pace, he drew his sword and stepped through the clearing. Thera was having breakfast with a man. His back was toward Kyros, but by the way he was dressed, he knew the man was a warrior. Thera laughed delightfully, not at all seeming to fear her visitor. When they didn't seem to notice him, Kyros cleared his throat to gain their attention.

The man spun around with wide eyes and Kyros recognized him as one of Ares' men. One of the escorts that was supposed to bring Thera to his brother. Kyros had the tip of his blade under the man's chin even before he could draw his sword.

"Not much of a warrior," remarked Kyros. "I could have slit your damned throat and you never even saw me coming."

"Kyros!" Thera looked at him sternly. "Put away the sword. This man doesn't mean to harm me."

Kyros looked from the battle-scarred warrior to Thera and then back again. For some reason he believed that statement, but still the man worked for Ares and couldn't be trusted.

"This is Ganymede." Thera introduced them but still Kyros didn't move his sword. "He was originally sent by my father to bring me to the castle, but Ganymede has decided not to work for Ares any longer."

The man didn't move a muscle under the tip of his sword. And though he should have feared for his life, he had a strange sense of calmness, sureness about him.

"How do I know I can trust you?" Kyros asked.

"You don't know," answered Ganymede. Kyros lowered his sword slightly. The man moved his hand toward his waist, and Kyros kicked him to the ground, resting his foot on the man's chest to keep him from moving.

A bright light encompassed Ganymede and the body beneath Kyros shifted into a different form. To his amazement, he found his foot resting on the beautiful body of a woman.

"Harmonia!" Thera cried out and ran over to them. Before Kyros could remove his foot, Harmonia blasted him with her powers and sent Kyros sailing through the air, landing with his back against a tree. His sword fell out of his hand and landed on the ground some distance from him.

"Enough!" cried out Thera's twin sister. "I'll not be treated like this. You'll pay for it." She got to her feet and stretched out her arm. Kyros could almost feel the next jolt coming, but Thera stopped her.

"No, Harmonia. Leave Kyros alone. He didn't know it was you, neither did I. He thought you were one of Ares' men and he was only trying to protect me."

Thera's sister put down her arm and straightened the thin gown she wore. Kyros couldn't help but notice her beauty, and couldn't help from staring.

Harmonia obviously noticed his perusal and she smiled. Thera noticed also, and a dark cloud passed over her face.

"I'm sorry, Goddess. I didn't know it was you." Kyros got to his feet and made his way slowly toward Harmonia. She held out her hand to him and Kyros bowed and kissed it.

Thera fumed when she saw the way her sister had taken control of Kyros. She had him kissing her hand and who knows what she'd be having him do next. With the translucent gown Harmonia wore, Kyros couldn't keep his eyes off of her. She looked down her own body at the bulge of her stomach and suddenly felt homely and unwanted.

"Harmonia," she interrupted. "Why were you pretending to be Ganymede?"

"I am Ganymede, dear sister. I always was. I only did it for Mother. She insisted I stay by you to protect you, but I won't be entrapped in such a filthy, wretched body again."

Thera watched Kyros' attention for Harmonia, feeling once again she was in the shadow of her beautiful sister. Her heart sank when Kyros picked up one of the uncrushed flowers from the ground and gave it to Harmonia. One of her flowers. One of the flowers Kaj had given to her last night.

She felt anger boil up inside her. One too many times Harmonia had stolen the spotlight and Thera was pushed into the shadows. Kyros was hers now, and she wasn't going to let Harmonia steal him away. He was the father of her child and her sister wasn't going to get him if she could help it.

"Be on your way, dear sister." The turmoil pumped through her veins as she boldly spoke to the goddess.

"Back off, Thera. I rather like Kyros. Besides, you owe me a favor after what I did for you."

"I never asked you to pretend you were someone else and watch over me. If I had known it was you, I'd have ... I'd have ..."

"What?" asked Harmonia. "Struck me down and taken back your man? I sincerely doubt it sister."

Thera couldn't argue with that. If Harmonia wanted Kyros, she could take him back to Mount Olympus with her and Thera would have to stand by helplessly and watch her own life be ruined. She was powerless now, a mere human against an immortal and it felt awful. It made her crazy to think she'd lose the only man she'd ever loved because she couldn't fight for him. Love? Where did that thought come from? She knew she held a special fondness for Kyros and now realized that feeling was love disguised.

"Ta-ta, sis. You're on your own now, as I'm taking this one with me." Harmonia raised her hand to wave her and Kyros away.

Thera could hold back no longer. "No!" she cried and dove for Kyros' sword. She held it up and a beam of lightning went from the tip and pushed her sister away from Kyros.

Thera was just as surprised as Harmonia at what had just happened. She dropped the sword and it clattered to the ground.

"Thera," came Kyros' voice. "What's happening?"

She didn't know, but when she looked up she saw her sister hurling a log at her by the mere twitch of a finger. She raised her hand to block her head and the log shifted around and flew back the other way. Harmonia hit it with a beam and the thing shattered to pieces.

"Well, I didn't think you had it in you, sister. You're finally using your powers after all these years."

"My powers?" Thera asked, not yet sure exactly what was happening to her.

"Don't seem so surprised. You've had them all the time, it's about time you used them."

"But Ares said—"

"Ares lied. You should know him by now. Neither he nor any of us have the authority to take away a gift that was given to you by the king of the gods. If you weren't so sheltered your whole life you would have known that, Thera."

Suddenly Thera felt like the biggest fool to walk the earth. Her father had one over on her again. She had her powers all along. She could have used them at any time. She could have done something to stop all this before it started. And she didn't need to fear anyone or anything anymore. After all, she was still a goddess and still immortal.

"Oh well, I think I'm tired of him already anyway. You can have him," Harmonia commented flippantly. "My work's done here. It's up to you now to get yourself out of this mess." With that, Harmonia dissipated into thin air.

Thera watched her sister's body disappear and felt her own body tingle. It was more than tingling, it was vibrating with the feeling of power. It filled her pores and made her feel strong, invincible, ready to take on the world. A wave of heat washed over her and the baby kicked inside her. It brought her back to her senses and she looked over to see Kyros staring at her, picking himself up off the ground. Her knees became weak and gave way and she fell to the ground.

"Are you all right, Goddess?" he asked in a low voice and held out his hand to help her to her feet.

Now the word goddess didn't seem so foreign to her. She finally realized how it felt to be powerful, invincible. She could go where she wanted, do what she would and no one, not even Ares could stop her. She felt the energy pump through her and wanted to explore her abilities. Something she should have done long before now. Now she had a second chance. She hadn't lost her powers and she was, in all ways, still a goddess.

She reached up to grab Kyros' hand but felt his apprehension. Looking up into his eyes she saw, as well as felt, his confusion and his fear.

She took back her hand and got to her feet by herself.

"Nothing's changed," she told him.

She heard the words coming from her mouth but didn't believe them herself. Everything would be different now. Her life couldn't be the same now that she knew she was still, indeed, a powerful goddess.

Kyros looked at his empty palm and she could feel the rejection that ran through him. She could see it in his face as well. He pulled out a garment from behind his back and handed it to her. She took it and opened it up. It was a tunic wrap. One that could be adjusted to any size. A brown, plain, drab tunic wrap. One made for a mortal, not really suited for a goddess.

"I picked it up from the weaver this morning," said Kyros as he bent down slowly and retrieved his sword. "I guess you won't be needing it anymore. Now that you've still got your powers, I guess you'll just want to conjure up a garment of your own."

She could very well do that and she was half tempted to, just to be able to use her powers again. She rather liked the way they felt. But she didn't like the way she was making Kyros feel.

"No. I think I'd like to wear the tunic you brought me. I think that's what I'll do."

Kyros just nodded his head. "I'd offer to go hunt for something to eat, but maybe you'd just like to zap something up instead. Something more suitable for a goddess. More than I could ever offer."

He turned and walked over to Hester and fiddled with the saddle bag. She didn't know what to say to him. She liked the way she felt when she was around him. She liked when he hunted and cooked for her and she rather liked the way it felt to be dependent upon a man. She also liked the idea of someday hopefully becoming a family. But now that would never happen.

"I suppose you won't need me to protect you or the baby anymore either." He didn't turn around to face her when he talked and that bothered her. "Will you be going back to Mount Olympus?"

"Going back?" She'd never held this as an option before. Matter of fact, she hadn't really thought about where she was going. Only where she wasn't going, and that was to the castle to marry Pittheus. "I … I never really thought about it."

"It's where you belong," he said. "Living in the woods with Centaurs and lone warriors is no life for a goddess."

She clutched the tunic and walked up softly behind him. Deep down, she knew she never really wanted to be a goddess. She never admitted it to herself before, but when Ares told her her powers and immortality had been stripped from her, it was a relief. She was different than the other gods and goddesses of Mount Olympus. She didn't really belong there—never felt she did. Her father was right about everything he ever said about her. She didn't deserve to be a goddess and secretly she'd always wished to be mortal.

"I'm not going back." She put a hand on Kyros' shoulder and he turned his head slightly, his cheek brushing against her skin. "I don't belong on Mount Olympus. And I don't want to be anywhere near my father."

He turned to face her. "Then where will you go? Where will you live?"

"I don't know." She dropped her hand to her side. She couldn't look at him when she spoke. She wanted to stay with Kyros but knew it would never work. A goddess living on earth with a mortal had never been done. It wasn't allowed by Zeus. And if a god or goddess was the parent of a child, along with a human, that child was considered a demi-god and usually disowned. The gods wouldn't accept the child, and neither would the mortals. The poor child would live a life in between two worlds. It would live a life of confusion and abandonment.

"I'd like to stay with you," she finally blurted out. "I … I think I love you."

He reached a hand out to caress her but drew it back instead. He let out a deep breath and she knew he was afraid to touch her now that she was a goddess.

"It would never work, Thera. I'm no good for you. Take our baby and raise it wherever you want."

He was casting off her and the baby just like that? "Why?" she asked. "Are you saying this just because I'm a goddess? We can make it work, Kyros. You may be just a man, but … I love you."

He took a step away, her words somehow seeming to upset him. She thought they would have made him happy. Any man hearing that a goddess wanted to stay with him would be elated. Any man that is, except for Kyros.

"C'mon," said Kyros.

"Where are we going?" she asked, hoping he just wanted her near.

"We can go there like a mortal, on horseback—or we can go like an immortal and use your powers to get us there. Either way, Thera, I'm taking you home."

FIFTEEN

Thera was quiet—very quiet on the trip back to Mount Olympus. Of course, Kyros wasn't talking much either. He felt as if it was over now that Thera had her powers back. She didn't need his protection anymore. She should be the one protecting him. And Hades take him if he'd ever let a woman protect him, even if she was a goddess.

He felt so sad inside. He'd really started to like Thera—more than like her. And she even said she loved him. Maybe she loved Kyros the man, but she'd made it quite clear how she felt about Kaj the Centaur. There was no future for them. She deserved so much better than a cursed man. So much more than he could ever give her.

"We'll stop here and make camp for the night," he announced. The traveling was slow as he refused to ride with her on the horse. Now that he knew she was still a goddess he was reluctant even to touch her.

He made a fire and got the blankets ready. All the while Thera remained quiet. She stared into the flames as if in a trance and he really didn't know what to say.

"Did you ... did you want me to hunt for you, Goddess?"

"Don't ever call me that again." She stared at the fire while she talked. "My name is Thera and always has been. I'd appreciate it if you'd call me by my name."

"I see," was all Kyros could say. "So did you want me to—"

"I'm not hungry. Just go disappear into the woods and do whatever it is you do when the sun goes down."

If only she knew what he did when the sun went down. If only he didn't have to do it.

"I guess I'll be leaving then. I'll be back in the morning. It's a long trip to Mount Olympus and we should get an early start."

She didn't say anything and he thought it best just to go. He went over to the saddlebag and pulled the mask out from inside, hiding it from

Thera.

"What are you hiding from me?" he heard her ask from where she sat. She was too far to have seen him and he figured she just sensed that he had a secret.

"I can't talk now, Thera. Maybe in the morning. We'll see."

He took off into the woods, getting as far away from Thera as he could before he started his change.

Thera waited until Kyros couldn't see her anymore and then she got to her feet and started after him. She would have liked to have taken Hester, but he'd have heard her coming for sure. She didn't want him to know she followed him. But she felt she needed to know where he went at night. Tonight might be her last chance. Once he left her at Mount Olympus, she knew she'd never see Kyros again.

The sun dropped quickly in the sky and night set in before she could catch up with him. Actually, after the first couple minutes she somehow lost his trail. She still had her power of the senses, and tried to use them to track Kyros. Strange, but she knew Kyros' scent and somehow it just seemed to up and disappear. Still, she continued searching.

It was well into the night when she first caught sight of him bathing in a small pond. Something was different about him, but she didn't know what. His hair seemed longer, or was it her imagination? She was going to call out to him but decided not to. Instead she stood behind a bush and watched in the moonlight as Kyros dipped his head below the water and brought it back up. He stood in the water waist high and all she could see was from his chest up. What a beautiful chest as it glistened in the moonlight. Much like Kaj's chest. She'd never seen Kyros' chest before, and had no idea it would be so big and strong under his clothing. It was sensational, as was Kaj's.

She wondered what Kaj would do when he got to the camp and found out she was missing. But on the other hand, she wondered if Kyros told him not to bother coming at all now that she didn't need their protection.

She loved Kyros. She put her hand on her stomach and felt that the baby had grown in the last day. She knew it wouldn't be long before it was born. And she was going to miss the feel of it within her when it was all over. She liked having a part of Kyros within her. It made her feel whole, complete. She wanted him to be with her forever. To be there to help her raise their child.

She pushed aside a branch and watched Kyros. She felt the love for him but yet she had the irresistible urge to also be with Kaj. She didn't understand it at all. Kaj was nothing more than a Centaur. But a nice Centaur. A different Centaur. She had strong feelings for him and they scared her. She knew deep down that Kaj, too, would be a good father.

Kyros started for the shore and Thera felt as if she should get back to camp. Whatever Kyros did in the night was his business. It didn't seem to her that he had a lover on the side, or that he was doing anything he wouldn't want her to know about.

She got to her feet and was turning around when something told her to look back at Kyros once more before she left. It was an eerie feeling. A feeling that she wasn't going to like what she saw, but she did it anyway.

The moon shone brightly on Kyros as he emerged from the pond, and she held a hand over her mouth in order not to scream by what she saw. Kyros walked from the water and onto the shore and it was then that she realized he was a Centaur. She couldn't believe her eyes. His body dripped with water and his horseflesh shone in the moonlight.

She wanted to turn around and run as fast as she could, but she couldn't move. All she could do was watch as Kyros tied the purple mask around his eyes and picked up his bow and quiver of arrows. It couldn't be. She couldn't believe it. Kyros was Kaj. Kaj was Kyros. She didn't know how or didn't really understand it at all, but she was horrified and forced herself to turn and run as fast as she could.

When Kyros got to the camp in his Centaur form, he realized Thera was gone. Something was wrong. There was no sign of any struggle so he doubted Pittheus' men had taken her captive. Besides, she was a goddess now and could fight them off if need be. No, she had gone away on her own. But he hadn't any idea as to where. He missed her already. And he truly wondered if he'd ever see her or his child again.

He looked up toward Mount Olympus and heard a wolf howling to the moon. She didn't go there. He felt it in his soul. She was out somewhere in the woods, and he was going to find her. He took off through the trees, intending to find the mother of his unborn child.

Two days passed and still there was no sign of Thera. Kyros was worried and apprehensive not knowing where she'd gone. He had gotten used to having her around and protecting her. He rather liked it and now that she was gone, a part of him was missing with her.

"Kyros." The sun was low in the sky as Chiron walked up to Kyros with Nemos at his side. Kyros sat on a log polishing his father's sword. He felt so empty without Thera. His mind was in such turmoil that he hadn't even been able to think about bringing peace between the Centaurs and the Trozens these last couple days. All he wanted now was peace between himself and Thera.

"Did you find her, Chiron?" Kyros stood and placed his sword in his scabbard.

"We've been all around the Centaur village and even to the outskirts of Trozen," remarked Nemos.

"You haven't found her." Kyros' heart sank and he sat back down.

"You're in love with her, aren't you?" came a crackly old voice from the trees.

Kyros turned quickly, his hand on the hilt of his sword. Even Chiron and Nemos were ready for action.

The blind, little old weaver woman stepped out from behind a tree. Kyros didn't know how she knew where she walked and how she kept from falling without her eyesight.

"Where'd you come from, old woman?"

"Well, you are, aren't you? You know she loves you," said the woman.

"You know where she is, don't you?" asked Kyros.

"She's been with me for the last two days. All she can do is talk about you."

Why hadn't he thought to look at the weaver's hut? Thera had seemed to take a liking to the old crone. It would only make sense she'd go there.

"I'm going to her." Kyros hopped atop Hester and turned a full circle.

"Kyros," called Chiron. "Do you think it's wise to leave so late in the day? The sun is about to go down."

"I have to see her," said Kyros. "I have to—"

"Tell her your secret?" asked the weaver.

"You told her, didn't you?" he accused her.

"I didn't need to, Kyros. She already knew when she came to me."

"Damn!" Kyros didn't know what to do now. If Thera knew his secret, he was sure she'd have nothing to do with him ever again. No wonder she left. What was he supposed to say to her? All he knew was that he had to see her once more before she dismissed him from her life forever.

"She's waiting for you, Kyros. You'd better go before she changes her mind about wanting to see you."

Kyros nodded silently. "I have to do this." But a pain hit him and he hunched over on his horse. "Damn! Not now. Not now."

He fell from the horse and Chiron and Nemos ran over to help him undress. Kyros handed his sword to Nemos. His body trembled and the convulsions took place. He didn't have time for this. He just needed it to be over. He had to see Thera and he had to see her now.

When Kyros turned back to talk to the old woman, she was gone. Another convulsion caused him to close his eyes and wish the transformation was over. It seemed to last longer and longer now-a-days, and he wondered if someday he might just stay in his Centaur form forever.

"It's over, Kyros." Kyros heard Chiron's reassuring voice. He didn't know what he'd have done without him. Nemos held his sword in one hand and handed him the golden bow with the other.

Kyros pushed to his feet and stretched his stiff legs. His vision was still blurry but he had no time to wait. Out of habit, he grabbed the bow and arrows from Nemos and headed off toward the weaver's hut.

SIXTEEN

Thera waited inside the weaver's hut, but the woman never returned. She'd enjoyed talking with her these past few days, as the spinner was a motherly type of person. Still, she didn't know the woman's name as the old lady said that everyone just called her The Weaver.

She heard hoofbeats outside the hut and ran to the door. She knew it was a Centaur even before she opened the door. And she knew exactly which Centaur it was.

Kaj, or Kyros trotted closer to her, his huge bow and arrows flung across his back. He didn't wear the mask this time. A simple way of telling her that he now knew she knew his secret.

"Thera. I need to talk to you." He moved a step closer but she took a step back into the hut.

"There's nothing to talk about."

"Yes, there is. I'm sorry that you have to see me like this."

"Why didn't you tell me?"

She sensed Kyros' nervousness and it made her a bit jumpy. It was strange to see Kyros with a Centaur body. She accepted it so well when she thought he was Kaj, but this just didn't seem right.

"I wanted to tell you," he said, and she believed him. "I wanted to tell you since the day I saw you at the pond."

Just the memory of him seeing her naked brought a flush of heat through her. Her baby stirred within her and she knew it was reacting to the sound of Kyros' voice. The baby knew Kyros was Kaj. So did Hester, his horse. How could she have been so out of touch with her senses? Maybe her senses were dulled from pregnancy. Or maybe they were dulled from being in love.

"You lied to me," she said. "You made me believe you were someone else."

"Would you have accepted me if you thought a Centaur was the father of your baby?"

By the gods, she didn't want to be reminded of that. If he was half Centaur, then her baby had half a chance of being Centaur also. Her stomach convulsed as the baby kicked wildly inside her. She was sure she felt feet and it felt like sharp hooves to her. Nausea overtook her and she had to grab the doorframe for support.

"Thera, I was scared to tell you. You were so happy that you were having a human baby."

He walked a bit closer to her. He raised his hand as if to touch her and then changed his mind and put it back down.

"I was happy that my father's plan would be foiled. Plus I was happy I wasn't going to die birthing a Centaur."

"Well, now that you know you're still a goddess, you can put your mind at ease. It doesn't matter if the baby is human or Centaur. You'll never die, Thera." He reached out and took her chin in his hands. She closed her eyes and trembled. If only he'd known what she'd done these last two days.

"I would gladly die for my child," she whispered. "And I'd give my own life if it could help break your curse. Who was it that did this to you, Kyros? Tell me so I can make them pay."

"It was your father," he answered softly. "Ares cursed me, hence being the cause of my father, King Mezentius' death as well. You see, Pittheus, the regent king of Trozen is my brother."

She grabbed his hand and looked up into his eyes. Tears formed in her eyes and her heart went out to him. Her father had ruined a man's life and been the cause of the death of a king. And then he had put her in a position right in the middle of it all.

"I'm so sorry, Kyros. I'm so, so sorry."

"Shh," he whispered and gazed at her lips. She felt her eyes close as he lifted her chin in his palm.

He kissed her then. Soft, deep and meaningful. With her eyes closed she tried to pretend it was Kyros, the man. She kissed him back and a warm sensation engulfed her. Then she heard the swish of his tail and her eyes popped open.

"This is wrong, Kyros. I can't be in love with a Centaur. This is all wrong."

"I'm a man, Thera. A cursed man. And you can't tell me you didn't want Kaj just as much as me, though you thought he was pure Centaur."

"You're right," she admitted. "I did want Kaj as much as I wanted you and it confused me. Now I understand why."

She threw her arms up around his shoulders, standing on her tiptoes as he was much higher than her in his Centaur form.

He scooped her up in his strong arms and carried her into the moonlight. He nuzzled his head into her hair and pulled her closer to his chest.

"I've never been kissed by a Centaur before."

"I've never kissed anyone while transformed." He looked down at her and then at the tunic wrap she wore.

"You really did wear the weaver's wrap."

She smiled and was glad he noticed. "Kiss me again," she said. "I want to feel you close to me."

Kyros walked up to a low tree branch and sat her on it. He then took her head in his hands and kissed her slow and deeply.

"I want to be the father of your child, Thera. No matter what it is, I want to raise it with you ... together."

"You are the child's father," she said. "And always will be."

He ran his hands through her long hair and she did the same to him. She liked the way it felt. She liked just about everything about him. His sturdy hands moved down to her shoulders caressing them and she moaned with pleasure. He hesitated only to reach around to his back and remove his bow and arrows, laying them gently at his feet.

"Any time you want me to stop touching you, Thera, just say so."

She didn't want him to stop, but rather wanted him to explore. She let the tunic fall down to her waist and expose her full breasts. They were heavy now that she was pregnant.

His fingers floated down her shoulders and caressed her breasts, rubbing, teasing. She felt a bolt of energy run up her spine when he teased her nipples and they hardened to peaks. She spoke with her eyes closed. "I want to feel more, Kyros. I need to feel more."

He lowered his head and took one peak into his mouth, driving her out of her mind. He suckled and released her and she arched back, pulling his head into her chest. Her chest heaved with her deep breaths and she noticed his did the same.

His hands dropped to her stomach and he ran his fingers over her pregnant belly.

"Thera, I don't want to do anything to hurt the baby."

"The baby is strong, Kyros. The baby is yours, it'll be just fine."

He put his lips to her stomach and kissed her. The baby kicked within her and they both laughed. Then he loosened the rest of her tunic and let it fall to the ground. She was totally naked and his eyes took in every inch of her. She loved the way she felt and she loved the way his eyes devoured her. He pressed his lips to her chest and slowly made his way down her body, kissing, tasting every inch of her. She opened for him, melting in his arms, willing him to continue his exploration. This is what she dreamed of ever since the day she felt the same euphoria when she was impregnated with his seed. This was physical, and more than anything she needed to feel Kyros' touch. Now it was his touch that was swelling her senses. This is the way it should be.

"I have to stop, Thera. If I don't, I may not be able to."

She didn't want him to stop, but she knew he was right.

"I want to be near you, Kyros. I don't want to stop our physical contact."

"Then we don't have to, Thera. Get on my back."

He picked her up and put her on his back. On the back of a horse—yet on Kyros' back. She hung on around his waist as he took off at a full gallop through the trees. Never had she felt so free. The wind blew her hair all around her. His hair blew in her face and she breathed in his musky scent. She was with the man she loved, be he cursed or not, and she never wanted to leave him. He slowed and she laid her head against his back as they returned to the hut. Inside, he gently took her from his back and laid her on the old weaver's bed.

"Kyros." She looked up at him, not knowing what to say. "I wish you could lie down with me. Just to be close. You understand, don't you?"

He ran a finger over her cheek and smiled slightly. "There's nothing that I want more right now than to lie with you in my arms, but I can't."

She knew it was true. He couldn't lie down with her while in his Centaur form. And she didn't know what to do next. "Kyros, I—"

"Shhh," he whispered and bent down and kissed her gently on the lips. "I'll be a man again soon. We'll have plenty of time for that later."

She knew he was right, but pitied him in his cursed form. He didn't deserve this and she hated her father for what he'd done to him. Tears made a path down her face and Kyros leaned over and kissed them away.

"Go to sleep now, Thera." He picked up a blanket from the foot of the bed and placed it over her. He then ran a loving hand over her stomach and smiled.

"Go to sleep my little baby."

She felt such a deep sorrow for Kyros, and a deep love as well. And she had every intention of proving her love to him in the morning.

SEVENTEEN

Kyros lay on the ground just after his transformation with Chiron and Nemos looking down at him. He could feel the smile on his face and he barely even noticed the pain this time. He couldn't help but think of Thera and the closeness he'd felt with her last night. He remembered feeling her body, tasting her, and wishing more than anything he'd been in his man-form at the time.

Chiron cleared his throat and Kyros realized Nemos was staring at his waist with wide open eyes. Kyros looked down and saw himself straight as an arrow. He jumped to his feet and grabbed his clothes from Chiron, making sure he donned the breeches first. He tried to pull the tunic down to hide the bulge, but it was hopeless.

"So," said Chiron. "What happened last night with Thera?"

"Not nearly enough," he mumbled and turned away from Nemos' gaze.

"Is everything all right between you then?" Chiron was searching for information.

"It is, Chiron. And it'll be better just as soon as I see her this morning. Much better," he said not able to hide his smile.

Kyros was about to reach for his sword in Nemos' hands when he heard Thera scream from the hut. He turned his head, and in that instant Rodas darted from the woods and grabbed the sword from Nemos.

"No!" cried the boy as he tried to get it back, but it was just too late.

"Rodas!" screamed Chiron. "What are you doing?"

Rodas held the tip of the sword out toward Kyros as he spoke. "This sword is going to its rightful owner. Pittheus will be glad to see it after all this time."

"I'll die before I let you take my father's sword," said Kyros.

"You just may," snarled Rodas as a half dozen Centaurs appeared from the woods, one of them dragging Thera along stark naked.

"Let her go," Kyros demanded. The Centaur holding her threw her onto the dirt. Thera dived for the golden bow and Kyros tried to stop her.

"No, Thera! Don't touch it." He remembered what Nemos had told him about the bow, that if a god touched it, it would kill them. He closed his eyes, not wanting to witness Thera turning into a pile of ashes. He heard an arrow whiz by his ear. Rodas cursed and took off into the forest. Thera released three more arrows, wounding one of the Centaurs before they all ran away.

"Thera!" He ran to her and threw his arms around her. She dropped the bow and fell against his chest. "Did they hurt you? Did they—"

"No," she answered. "No, they didn't."

"Is she all right?" he heard Chiron ask from behind him. Kyros took off his tunic and wrapped it around her naked body.

"She's fine," answered Kyros, pulling her even closer in his embrace.

"Go find her clothes," Chiron ordered Nemos. The boy trotted away toward the weaver's hut.

"Thera, I don't understand. You touched Phylo's bow and you didn't die," said Kyros.

She looked up at him with tears in her eyes, but didn't answer.

"She's no longer a goddess," came the old weaver's voice from behind him. "She didn't tell you?"

Kyros was no longer surprised to hear the old weaver's voice popping up unexpectedly and didn't even turn toward her.

"Thera, is this true?" he asked. "How?" He looked at her innocent wide eyes and knew she had done something drastic.

"It is," she answered. "I had a lot of time to think these past few days, and I came to the conclusion I want to be mortal."

"She went to Zeus two days ago and asked him to take back his gifts," the weaver informed them. "She's now mortal. A human."

"But Thera ... why?" he asked.

"I want to be your wife, Kyros. I want us to raise our baby together. I want to live with you by my side as mortals. I want you to protect me, hunt for me and someday we'll die together in each others' arms."

Kyros couldn't believe what he was hearing. Thera gave up her powers and immortality just for him. She must really love him to sacrifice such a gift.

"But Thera, if you're human, what if our baby is a Centaur?"

"Then she'll die giving birth." The weaver answered for her. "She'll die giving you a son."

Kyros felt his stomach turn sour. She must have known there was half a chance their baby would be a Centaur before she ever got rid of her powers. Yet, she'd done it anyway. She'd done it out of love and for the chance to someday live with him and their baby as mortals.

"I love you, Thera. I love you more than life itself." They embraced and kissed and when he pulled away, Nemos handed her clothes to her.

"I'm sorry, Kyros," said Nemos. "I've let you down."

Kyros pulled Thera to her feet then walked with the boy in order to give her the privacy to dress.

"What are you talking about, Nemos?"

"You entrusted me to guard your sword and I let Rodas steal it."

"It wasn't your fault," piped in Chiron.

"That's right," added Kyros. "We were all standing right here when it happened."

"I'll make it up to you, Kyros, I promise." Nemos had tears in his eyes and Kyros knew he had to calm him.

"I'll get the sword back, Nemos. Don't you worry."

"But how?" asked the boy. "You don't even know where Rodas took it."

"I know exactly where he took it." Kyros looked up toward his father's castle on a hill in the distance. "And I plan to get it back if I have to die doing it."

"I'm coming with you," said Thera as she walked up, fully dressed and handed Kyros his tunic. He put it on and also took the golden bow and arrows from her hands.

"I can't risk anything happening to you or the baby, Thera. You can stay in the hovel with Chiron and Nemos. I'll return for you later."

"I'm coming with," she repeated.

"Thera, please stay. I can't watch my back if I'm worried about you or the baby getting hurt. I promise you I'll return."

"Well, then, can I help?" asked Nemos. "I feel I should after losing your sword."

"No," Kyros shook his head. "I don't want a single Centaur to try and help me."

"Why not?" asked Nemos. "Why don't you want the Centaurs help?"

"Chiron understands," answered Kyros. "Ask him. I don't have time now to explain."

With that, he gave Thera a quick kiss, hopped atop Hester and headed for the castle.

Ares watched from behind a tree as Kyros left for the castle and Thera stayed behind. Rodas stood next to him with Kyros' sword in hand.

"Damn!" Ares hands clenched into fists and his jaw set to a firm line. "Kyros was supposed to take Thera with him. This isn't going at all how I planned."

"Do you want me to capture her and dump her at Pittheus' feet?" asked Rodas.

"No," answered Ares. "I know Thera too well. She's nothing but trouble. She never does anything she's told to do. She'll follow Kyros on her own. Mark my words."

EIGHTEEN

Thera lay silent on her pallet in the hovel, until she heard the snoring of Chiron. She slowly opened her eyes and looked around the cave. A night candle burned in the corner and she could see Chiron standing there but not moving. She heard the loud snores and there was no doubt he was asleep.

The boy stood in an opposite corner and she tried to listen for his breathing, but couldn't hear it over Chiron's snores. She tried to use her other senses to determine if he was asleep but couldn't tell. Her power of the senses was dulled more and more as the baby grew bigger and bigger.

She turned her head and whispered Nemos' name softly. When he didn't answer, she got to her feet and sneaked to the door. She picked up an extra bow and arrows that hung on the wall, as Chiron slept with his own on his back as did Nemos.

She looked back at them one more time before heading out. It was so strange the way Centaurs slept standing up. She'd never seen Kaj ... Kyros—she corrected herself—sleeping. She wondered if he slept that way too. She also wondered if their child would, if he was a Centaur. She felt a bit saddened at the thought. She'd always pictured herself rocking a baby in a cradle, not closing him into a pen. It didn't matter, she told herself. Not even if Kyros could never lie in bed with her at night. Maybe she'd change her sleeping patterns and sleep during the day, just so she could couple with and lie with Kyros.

She tiptoed through the entrance and made her way carefully through the darkened woods. Her senses were still sharp enough to be able to see, and more or less, feel the branches or rocks that would be in her way.

She headed east for the castle, not at all sure where she was going. The full moonlight spilled through the branches and fell on her skin as she came to a clearing. It reminded her of how Kyros looked while he bathed in the pond: The bluish moonlight lighting up his long, dark hair; his strong chest dripping with water as he bathed himself in the pond.

She missed him deeply. She wanted to kiss him and have him hold her protectively in his arms. Now that he'd awoken her womanly senses, she could think of nothing but being with him. When he touched her, it was just as satisfying as when she'd first been implanted with his seed. But she'd done everything now except for the actual act of coupling. Ironic, she was pregnant with his child and still a virgin. She wanted to know how it felt to physically make love with a man. She wanted to feel him within her. And more than anything, she wanted to please him the way he'd pleased her.

She loved Kyros and had to be by his side no matter what he was going through. She loved him for more than just the physical pleasure. She loved him for who he was, be it man or Centaur. She loved his body, his mind, his soul. She would be by his side, where she was meant to be. And once she got to the castle, then she would decide how she was going to help him.

A twig snapped in the woods and pulled her from her thoughts. It was then she smelled Centaur and jumped to her feet. How could she be so careless as to not be watching out for danger? She picked up her bow and arrows, cocking an arrow in place for protection. She heard another snap somewhere behind her and then a thud and spun around.

"Thera, it's me, Nemos. Don't shoot," came the voice.

She put down her weapon and ran to help him. She could see him lying on the ground with his own weapon next to him.

"What are you doing, Nemos?" she asked.

"Coming to help you save Kyros," he answered, getting to his feet.

Just what she needed: A child Centaur who couldn't see in the dark to tag along and give away her element of surprise.

"You knew I was going?"

"I pretended to sleep," he told her. "Just like you did. Then I followed you here."

"It's amazing you didn't break your neck, Nemos. I took the most rockiest, tangled trail in order to throw off anyone who may follow."

"I know," he mumbled and picked up his weapon.

"You can't come with me." She crossed her arms over her chest as she spoke.

"I have to," he answered. "It's my fault Kyros lost his sword. I was supposed to be guarding it. I have to help him get it back."

"He doesn't need your help, Nemos."

"Why?" he asked. "Because I'm a child?"

That—not to mention a Centaur—she thought, but didn't say it.

"I'm going to help him, Nemos. You just go back to the hovel and wait with Chiron."

Nemos' face saddened and Thera could feel the struggle within him. He wanted to prove himself a brave warrior. He wanted to show Kyros he could be trusted and depended upon. Totally different than her reasons for going. Or were they?

"So he needs the help of a pregnant woman and not that of a Centaur child?" he asked.

"Yes," she answered and realized how absurd it sounded. Kyros didn't need her nor Nemos slowing him down. Maybe her own reasons for wanting to be with him were self-centered. By going to him she was sure to get into trouble, not to mention endanger Kyros' own life. After all, he had said he couldn't watch his back if he had to look after her and the baby.

Suddenly she felt foolish for thinking she was going to be of help to him. The baby kicked and she felt a sharp pain. She couldn't even move stealthily if she wanted to. She was heavy with child and she already felt it taking its toll from the short distance she'd traveled. She was out of breath and tired. She knew it was because of carrying the heavy baby up hill. She was exhausted, not to mention hungry. As much as she wanted to continue, she also wanted nothing more than a nice, warm, safe pallet for the night.

"You're right," she said. "I don't have any business going after Kyros either. We'll just endanger him if he has to worry about us. He'll be all right." She tried to convince herself of this but felt it in her bones that he was going to have problems.

"So we should go back and just wait for him?" asked the boy.

"Exactly," answered Thera and patted him on the shoulder. "Let's go back before Chiron awakes and knows what we planned to do."

They started through the dark woods, but Thera realized she'd left the bow and arrows behind. She had to get them and return them or Chiron would know something was amiss.

"I forgot the bow and arrows," she told Nemos. "You wait here and I'll go get them."

"All right," agreed Nemos, rubbing his shoulder. She knew he'd gotten scratched a bit from his fall and wasn't eager to tramp blindly through the woods any more than he had to.

Thera made it back to the small clearing and spotted the bow and arrows on the ground where she'd left them. Thoughts of Kyros flooded her head or she would have been more aware of her senses and would have known she wasn't alone. She reached down for the weapon but a hand closed over her wrist. She screamed and looked up into the eyes of a warrior; one she was certain was from Pittheus' castle. Two other soldiers joined him.

"Well, look what we have here," sneered the guard. "It looks to me like Pittheus is going to be pleased with what we found."

"I'm not going anywhere near Pittheus," she said.

"Pittheus has been waiting for you," sneered the guard.

"For me?" she asked, trying to call their bluff. "I think you're mistaken. I don't even know the man."

"We know who you are."

"Then you know I'm a goddess and can use my powers to stop you."

They didn't seem at all alarmed and she knew she was doomed.

"A fallen goddess," said one of the men. "We know more than you think. Now come on."

Thera wondered who had told them. Had they captured Kyros and made him talk? Or was it the old weaver, or perhaps Ares?

Thera realized Nemos was still waiting for her and would have heard her scream. He would come to help her and he'd be captured as well. She couldn't allow that. She had to get out of there before they captured the boy too.

"Let's go," she said.

"In a hurry to meet your future husband?" the guard asked and Thera wanted to protest him but couldn't waste time and endanger Nemos.

"I don't want to cause trouble," she said, though she knew it was too late. "I'll go with you and not put up a fight."

"Good girl," chuckled the guard. "Pittheus likes a woman to be willing."

As they dragged her away she glanced back towards the place she'd left Nemos. Hopefully his poor nightsight would slow him down so they could be out of there before he showed his face.

The guard hoisted her up onto his horse and they all rode across the open field. She knew Nemos would hear them even though he was too far away to follow. And she knew Chiron would be furious when Nemos went back to the hovel to report that she'd been captured.

NINETEEN

Kyros approached the castle cautiously in his man-form, with the golden bow and arrows thrown over his back, taking the place of his stolen sword. He'd hidden away all day the day before, waiting, watching, hoping to find a way to enter the castle unnoticed. And then nightfall had set in and his transformation took place. He waited through the night without sleeping, keeping watch, but yet knowing he'd have a harder time sneaking in as a Centaur and would have to wait until sunrise.

He sat atop Hester now as he rode slowly up to the drawbridge. He cursed his rotten luck that he'd been in Centaur form when darkness cloaked the earth. If he had been in human form, he could have found a way to sneak in. But he was only in human form in broad daylight. There was no way he was going to enter the castle now without being seen. The only way was to face Pittheus head on and ride right in. It was the only time he'd be able to confront his brother man to man.

A few of the guards looked his way as he entered through the gates of his late father's castle, but none stopped him. It was easy. All too easy, and Kyros was sure he was being set up. But there was no other way to retrieve his father's sword than to just confront his brother face to face.

"Kyros, we knew you'd come." His brother Pittheus stood just inside the drawbridge waiting for him. His father's sword was in Pittheus' hand, and Rodas was by his side.

"Thanks for the invitation," mocked Kyros as he rode on Hester a bit closer. "I didn't realize I'd be such a guest of honor."

"Father's sword is mine now," smiled Pittheus. "It's right where it belongs. And in three days time the feast day of Dionysus will be here. I'll sit on the throne with my sword raised to Artemis and the fate of Trozen will be sealed. I'll rule as king of Trozen and the people will accept me as their king."

Kyros looked at Rodas who seemed a bit uneasy. Several more Centaurs stood inside the castle walls and Kyros couldn't help but notice how many of Pittheus' men surrounded them.

"Accepting gifts from Centaurs now, brother? I'm glad to see you've changed your attitude about them."

"Who said anything about me changing my attitude?" Pittheus waved a hand toward his guards, giving them the signal. Rodas, seeing what was happening, gave his men the order to attack also.

An all-out battle started between the Centaurs and the Trozen warriors. Kyros felt his gut wrench, knowing this was just the beginning of the wars to come if Pittheus should indeed become king. He couldn't just sit there and watch it, but then again he couldn't really take any side either. Instead, he went after Pittheus, hoping to get his sword and escape before it was too late.

Pittheus saw Kyros coming and ordered his men to attack. They were no match for Phylo's bow which Kyros found himself having to use for defense. He shot one arrow and took down two of Pittheus' warriors. He then aimed for his brother, but couldn't shoot to kill. Instead, he shot him in the leg, jumped off the horse and grabbed his father's sword.

"You'll never be king, Pittheus, as long as I'm alive." He hoisted himself back up onto Hester and heard his brother's reply.

"Well, we'll have to take care of that then, won't we?"

Pittheus gave the command to his men to hoist up the drawbridge. Kyros sank his heels into Hester and charged for the opening. He could have made it. Would have just gotten through before it closed if it wasn't for what he saw just inside the gate. One of Pittheus' men held Thera in front of him, a dagger pressed to her throat. Damn, he hadn't seen this coming. They must have sneaked her into a back entrance during the night.

He pulled on the reins and brought his horse to a stop. He saw the drawbridge closing and knew with it went his only chance for escape. But he couldn't leave Thera. Not even to protect his father's sword and the fate of the Centaur race. It was over now and there was nothing he could do. He looked back to the battle and realized Pittheus' men had captured the Centaurs and were putting them in chains. Defeat was all around him.

"Drop the sword," commanded his brother as he limped over toward Kyros with the golden arrow still sticking out from his leg. "Or I kill the girl. I hear you've taken a liking to her."

Kyros looked toward Rodas and wondered just how much the Centaur had told his brother. "You're not going to get away with this, Pittheus."

"And who's going to stop me?" he chuckled. "Seems to me I'm the one holding all the cards now. If you were smart you'd start begging me to spare your life."

Kyros found himself surrounded by warriors with swords aimed at his heart. He reluctantly dropped his father's sword and Pittheus wasted no time in picking it up.

"The bow and arrows too," he commanded.

"It's the bow of Artemis," Kyros told him. "It'll do you no good. It was made only for the king of the Centaurs."

"Drop it, or lose your life," came his command and Kyros had no choice but to obey. He may have been able to use it to take down a few more warriors, but Thera's life was at stake and he couldn't risk it. He wasn't going to lose her or his baby over a bow.

"My life's no longer important, brother. With the curse that's been placed on me, I think I would rather die than to see you create a war between the Centaurs and the Trozens."

"If that's what you want," answered Pittheus, "so be it."

He waved his hand and commanded his guard to kill Kyros.

"No!" screamed Thera, fighting to get out of the grip of the guard. "Leave him alone."

Kyros reared his horse and set the guard off balance. He rode over to Thera, kicking the guard in the face who held her. He grabbed her and pulled her up in front of him atop Hester.

It was then he felt the burning fire piercing him through his shoulder. He looked down and saw the tip of a golden arrow sticking out from his flesh, his blood pouring out of the wound.

His head went dizzy and Hester reared up nervously. He lost hold of the reins and fell to the ground. Thera was crying. She jumped off the horse and kneeled at his side.

"You're forgetting something," snarled Pittheus as he stood above Kyros. "I'm a king also. I, too, can use this bow."

"And you're forgetting something also," said Kyros. "That the bow is said to be cursed. Whoever uses it is sure to die."

"Then I guess we'll both die, won't we, brother?" The courtyard was silent—the Centaurs now captured. Pittheus nodded to one of his men.

"Finish him off."

The soldier raised his sword but Thera laid her body across Kyros, trying to save him.

"Please," she begged Pittheus. "Please let him live and I'll do anything you ask."

"I don't like my future bride to be seen begging." Pittheus grabbed her arm and pulled her up to stand next to him. He then grabbed the back of her head and smashed his lips into hers.

Kyros wanted to kill his brother. He didn't want Pittheus anywhere near Thera, and he wouldn't let him get away with the way he was treating her. He pushed himself up to a sitting position, but the guards pushed him back down on the ground.

"I've waited a long time for this, my dear. Your father promised you to me and now I hear you've given away your powers."

"You don't want her," Kyros tried to convince him. "She isn't a goddess anymore so she's not going to meet your needs."

"And how would you know what needs I have, Kyros? You, who are nothing more than a Centaur lover—a turncoat. Trying to bring down this kingdom to the lowliness of those wretched creatures. You deserve the curse Ares put upon you. Maybe I'll let you live just so you can suffer with your horrible curse. That's much worse than dying, Kyros. Don't you agree?"

Kyros saw the fear in Thera's eyes as his brother held onto her arm so tight it turned a shade of blue. He knew he had to help her and his unborn baby. He no longer cared about his own life, but he had to live just so he could help Thera escape.

"You're too much of a coward to kill me yourself," Kyros taunted him. He knew by baiting him this way, his brother would get his attention off Thera. Not to mention, if Pittheus thought Kyros wanted to die, he'd do just the opposite in order to spite him.

Instead of responding, Pittheus turned to Thera and raked her over with his eyes. "Let's see what my little bride looks like, shall we?"

The men-at-arms whistled, as they knew what Pittheus was about to do. He took a hold of Thera's clothing and tugged, ripping it from her body. She stood in front of the whole army of men naked and did nothing to try to cover herself.

"No!" Kyros fought against six men as he tried to get to Thera. The arrow in his shoulder was pushed in a bit further and blood squirted from the horrible wound.

"What?" screamed Pittheus when he eyed her rounded stomach. "You're already with child." He grabbed her in front of him and turned her so the entire courtyard could see.

"Ares tricked me!" he screamed. "You were supposed to bear my heir. Who is the man responsible for this? Let me know so I can kill him for what he's done."

Kyros was about to admit it was his child when Rodas, struggling against five men called out. "It's my child, Pittheus. I was the one who got your bride pregnant, so kill me now and be done with it."

Kyros couldn't believe what Rodas was doing. He was covering for him and by doing this he was sacrificing his own life as well.

"A Centaur?" Pittheus was in a rage. "No filthy Centaur will soil my bride and live to speak of it." He threw Thera to the side and raising his father's sword, he limped over to Rodas. "I'll kill you myself for what you've done."

"It's my child," came the voice of another Centaur and Pittheus turned around in confusion.

"No, it's mine," said still another Centaur and Pittheus grew even madder.

"Then I'll kill you all," he screamed. "I'll kill every last one of you for trying to protect the louse who got my bride pregnant."

"No," said Kyros and pushed to his feet. The guards were still holding on to his arms. "It's my child, brother. I'm the one they're trying to protect. Let the Centaurs go. They had nothing to do with any of this. It's me that's to blame."

"Your child?" asked Pittheus. "You ... half-man, half-beast convinced a goddess to couple with you? Don't ask me to believe this absurdity."

"It's true." Thera stood up, having donned her ripped tunic wrap. "Kyros is the father of my child, but it's not his fault. It's Ares you should be angry with. It's by his doing that this all came about."

Pittheus rubbed his leg. The arrow that pierced it was obviously causing him much pain. The ball was in his court now. Kyros' life as well as the others' lie in his hands. Kyros wished Thera hadn't given up her powers right now. If she'd still had them, none of this would be happening.

Pittheus called to his steward and leaned on him as he talked.

"At the moment, I'm in need of some sewing up. So I think we'll talk about this more over dinner. You will join me and my bride for dinner, won't you Kyros? After all, I do think you'll enjoy the entertainment I've got planned."

Kyros didn't understand that statement at all. His brother was inviting him to dinner as if nothing had happened? Not but a moment ago he was giving the order for his men to kill him.

Pittheus grabbed Thera and dragged her along with him. His low, evil laughter echoed in Kyros' ears as he made his way to the castle.

Thera was handed over to the ladies-in-waiting and bathed, perfumed and dressed in the fanciest of clothes. They washed her hair and braided it into a circle around the top of her head. Flowers adorned her hair and she actually felt pretty for the first time in her life. Or actually the second time—Kyros had always made her feel pretty, just by the way he caressed her or made love to her with his eyes.

"Why am I being dressed up?" she asked one of the ladies-in-waiting. The woman didn't answer. "Why is Pittheus going through all this trouble just over dinner?"

She decided not to even try to get an answer from these women. Their lips were sealed and she was sure Pittheus must have told them not to say a word. Thera was led through corridor after corridor until they finally made their way to the great hall. Most of the people were already seated at the long tables inside, but Pittheus waited for her at the door. He held out his arm and smiled at her. The gesture made her cringe. She could feel his false pretense. She could feel the lust he held for her, and also his hate for Kyros.

"You look lovely, my darling. Now hold my arm and join me as we make our way to the table. We have a guest of honor tonight. Someone I think you'll be especially interested in seeing."

Thera had no idea who he was talking about. Not until they rounded the corner and entered the great hall. There, sitting at the dais with his feet on the table and lounging back on the chair was Ares. He held a huge tankard up in his hand as they entered.

"A toast," he spoke and everyone in the hall was silent. "To my daughter Thera and the new king of Trozen, Pittheus."

The crowd was silent, and it wasn't until Ares stood and looked around the room that they cheered half-heartedly.

"Father!" She let go of Pittheus' arm and ran to him. She stopped in front of the table and met his eyes. "What are you doing here and what is going on?"

"Why, Thera, I thought you would have figured that out by now. I'm here for the celebration."

"What celebration? What are you talking about?"

"Thera, I'm here for your wedding."

TWENTY

Wedding. The word stabbed a pain through Thera. She sickened when she realized her father really meant to go through with this after all. Somehow she was hoping things would be different now that Pittheus already knew she was pregnant. She figured he would just refuse to marry her and it would all be over. But obviously Ares had other plans. Plans that would not only ruin her life but end up causing a war after all.

"You've got it wrong, Father. I'm not getting married. I'm here as a prisoner."

Ares stroked his short beard and looked up to the ceiling. "A prisoner of love as your mother would say."

"Love has nothing to do with this. I'll not marry Pittheus and there's nothing you can do to make me."

The room fell silent except for the shuffle of feet and hooves behind her. She didn't dare turn around and look. She didn't want to turn her back on her father.

"Well, that's brave talk for a goddess who has given away her powers. Maybe I can't do anything to convince you, Thera, but I do believe Pittheus can make you change your mind."

She sensed Kyros somewhere in the room now. She felt the hatred burning in his veins for Ares, and also the love he held for her. She turned abruptly and saw him being dragged in by guards. His hands were chained together and his shoulder was wrapped up sloppily. The wound still leaked. Behind him, the guards brought Rodas and the other Centaur prisoners. They, too, were in chains.

"Ares," growled Rodas. "This is your fault. Now get us out of this mess."

Ares laughed. "No one tells me what to do."

"I shouldn't have trusted you," sneered Rodas. "I never should have done your dirty work. I never should have turned against my own kind."

"Such a touching confession, but I don't care to hear it. I no longer have need of you." He raised a finger and Thera knew he meant to kill the Centaur.

"No!" shouted Kyros. "Leave him alone."

"Interesting," Ares said in surprise. "The way you stick up for each other though you hate one another."

"Gag the Centaur," Pittheus ordered his men. "Gag them all but my brother."

Thera's heart went out to Kyros and she wanted to throw herself into his arms. They were going to use him against her. They were going to hurt him. She just knew it.

"You'll either marry me," said Pittheus, "or you can watch Kyros die right now." They threw him to the ground and one man held him with his foot; another of Pittheus' warriors held a sword to his neck.

She felt the dormant force of war within her stir. Her war-like abilities were being prodded and she'd never felt more like picking up a weapon and killing someone as she did right now. If she'd had her bow, she'd kill Pittheus and then anyone who dared to hurt Kyros. He didn't deserve this. He didn't deserve to suffer and be humiliated. And most of all, he didn't deserve to die because of her.

"Don't do it, Thera," cried Kyros. "I'd rather die than see you married to Pittheus."

"Shut up," commanded the guard and kicked him in the stomach.

Thera's baby kicked at that exact moment and she felt Kyros' pain as well. She put her hand on her stomach and tried to soothe the baby. It knew what was going on, and that its father was in danger.

"Kyros," she cried. "They'll kill you if I refuse to marry him."

"He'll only start the war between the Trozens and the Centaurs, Thera."

"I'll start it anyway, brother," snarled Pittheus. "I don't need a Centaur baby to spur me on. As a matter of fact, I don't even want your baby at all."

Ares slammed down his tankard and walked over to Pittheus. He had a look of disgust upon his face. "You mean to tell me, I went through all this trouble for nothing? You would have started the war on your own?"

"I'd planned on it long ago," answered Pittheus. "But I was waiting to find my father's sword and claim my right as king before I did it. Now, thanks to your daughter, Kyros has gotten careless and the sword is all mine."

"Then on with the war!" hailed Ares, raising his warrior fist to the sky.

"Not yet," said Pittheus. "First I'll claim my title. The feast of Dionysus is in three days time and it will be then the people of Trozen accept me and agree to fight this battle."

"Good enough," agreed Ares, nodding his head. "That'll give me enough time to talk to Hades and convince him to give back my raven when I start sending him hundreds of soldiers."

"Is that what it's all about?" asked Thera, shocked to hear such a thing. "Father, you want your raven back and you're willing to start a war and kill hundreds of Trozens and Centaurs in order to get it?"

"Tsk, tsk, Daughter. It's not just that. You know I need war in order to survive. I am the god of war. When you killed my raven ... let's just say that was the frosting on the cake. I had plans for you, Thera. Plans for you to become a great warrior and fight at my side. A warrior princess. After all, I couldn't very well get Harmonia to help me. Her mother's got her so spoiled she'd probably complain she didn't want to break a nail."

Thera walked up to her father and reached her arms out to him. "Accept me as I am. I was never meant to be a warrior and you know it. But I am meant to be a mother. And you're going to be a grandfather soon."

Ares stared at her and his cheek quivered; yet, he did nothing to embrace his daughter who was asking for his love.

"Don't call me a grandfather. I don't ever want to be referred to as old. And I don't ever want to be related to a child that was sowed by his seed!"

He pointed a finger at Kyros and a beam of light went out from him. Thera jumped in front of it, being knocked half-way across the room by the force. "Now you act like a warrior," Ares said to Thera. "Only you do it for the wrong reasons. How can you want to protect that beast?"

"He's a man," Thera corrected him as she got to her feet, feeling every muscle in her body hurt from Ares' bolt. "And when he turns into a Centaur it's only because you made him that way. Take the curse off of him, Ares. Take it off him right now."

"No, I won't, Thera. When I make up my mind, I don't change it. I'll never remove his curse."

"Then at least save him from being killed," pleaded Thera. "Do something to help him."

"You want to save his life," laughed Ares, "then marry Pittheus." His laugh grew deeper.

"But if I marry Pittheus," choked out Thera. "I can't be with Kyros. I love Kyros and want to marry him."

"You figure it out." Ares waved her away from him. "I've got more important things to do. I've got to see Hades about my raven."

With a flash of light he disappeared. Pittheus broke the silence.

"Well, I'm hungry. Thera, I'll give you until after the meal to give me your answer. Meanwhile, let's eat and start the entertainment."

He gave the order to chain Kyros to a chair in the middle of the room. The guests were cleared to the side tables and the Centaurs were brought down front. It was only when she'd taken her place at the dais next to Pittheus and seen the look on Kyros' face that she knew exactly what was about to happen. Kyros flinched a bit and coughed and Thera realized the sun was about to set. His change would come soon. Thera was horrified. She knew now that Pittheus meant to humiliate his brother. For there was no doubt in her mind that Pittheus meant for Kyros to be the evening's entertainment.

TWENTY-ONE

Kyros' body wracked with pain as he sat chained to the chair in the middle of the room. He felt so helpless, so wounded and so angry that his own brother would treat him this way. But then again, Pittheus had always been jealous of Kyros. After their mother had died, Pittheus turned against him, not having the attention he wanted from his father.

Kyros knew his father had always wished his younger son could inherit his castle and become king once he passed on to the afterlife. King Mezentius never expected to die so soon or he would have made some sort of arrangements giving Kyros his thrown. Kyros felt certain of it. Pittheus knew this and was always causing trouble for Kyros.

Even in childhood, their games of war were real to his brother. Pittheus would fight with sharp weapons instead of blunted ones when they were in training. And more than once Kyros had taken the blow and felt the pain of the wound he'd inflicted.

But he'd always recovered, as he was a warrior and used to pain. But the pain his brother inflicted upon him now was more than he could bear. The pain of the heart. The pain caused by his love for Thera. Loving her so much hurt. He watched as Pittheus put his arm around Thera at the table and took it upon himself to feed her by his hand from his own plate. He picked up a piece of venison and popped it into her mouth. He then made a big show of licking the juices off his fingers and licking them off her lips as well.

He saw Thera cringe and back away. But every time she started to object to one of his actions, Pittheus would take her chin in his hands and turn her eyes towards Kyros sitting helplessly chained and wounded in the middle of the great hall.

He couldn't help but remember their intimate night together. Her beautiful nakedness and the sweet taste of her soft skin. He eyed her breasts trussed up and all but popping out of the bodice of the garment

Pittheus had her dressed in. He saw his brother's eyes drop down her cleavage and he felt his stomach tighten. He didn't want to think of Pittheus fondling her the way he'd done. It tore at his insides to even think of him kissing her sweet lips.

He'd get out of these chains somehow and stop his brother from looking at Thera like he was going to devour her. He'd stop him from touching her and most of all from making her his bride.

"Bring on the entertainment," called Pittheus, and his men pushed the Centaurs into the middle of the room where Kyros sat. Rodas and his men were bound hand and foot by chains. They had huge iron balls connected to their legs so they couldn't run. Their legs were chained together so they could only take small steps, and they were all chained to one another. They had gags in their mouths and couldn't even defend themselves with words.

"Bring on the archers," called Pittheus, and half a dozen archers drew themselves up to the front of the dais.

"What are you doing?" asked Thera.

"Just having a bit of sport," answered Pittheus. He then gave his men the order to shoot.

Kyros jolted as food just missed hitting his face. He watched in disbelievement as the archers hurled rotten fruit and stale bread toward Rodas and the others. The Centaurs tried to get out of the way, but every time one of them moved, they pulled to the ground the others that were chained with them.

"This is absurd!" shouted Kyros from his place on the chair. "Pittheus, stop this at once. These Centaurs did nothing to deserve this kind of humiliation."

Pittheus laughed and threw a piece of food himself. It hit Kyros in the chest and dripped down the front of him.

"This is all in good fun, brother. Just relax and enjoy it."

Kyros' anger raged within him. He knew his brother was trying to anger the Centaurs enough so when he'd release them, they'd go back to the Centaur camp and round up the others and declare war on the people of Trozen. Pittheus had tried this before. But when the Centaurs he'd captured and tormented were released and came back to camp, it was Chiron who talked the group out of declaring war.

But now the Centaurs being humiliated were Rodas and his men. Pittheus knew Rodas was a rebel. If he wasn't, he never would have stolen the sword. And Kyros knew once Rodas and his men were released, they'd come back to fight. He had no doubt in his mind this would be what would start the war.

When the archers got tired of throwing food at the Centaurs, Pittheus told them to pick up their bows. Kyros watched as they picked up arrows and started shooting them all around Rodas and his men. Rodas fought against his chains as did the others. The fire blazing in his eyes told everything. Kyros had to do something to stop this before it was too late, but he was as helpless at the moment as the Centaurs. And wounded also.

"Pittheus, stop this absurdity now!" Kyros exclaimed. "This won't solve anything. War isn't the answer to anything. It's power you seek. War will only kill off the soldiers who are in your command. Without an army you're nothing."

Pittheus laughed and took a deep swig of ale. He banged the tankard back down on the table, the contents spilling over the edge of the cup.

"I'll have a strong army, Kyros. Don't you worry about that. My men won't be the ones to die. But the Centaurs will cease to exist when I'm through with them. And don't ask me to stop my entertainment again. For my bride is the only one who can stop it. All she has to do is agree to marry me without a fight."

"Then you'll stop all this?" asked Thera.

"Of course." He gave her a peck on the cheek.

"Don't believe it, Thera," called Kyros. "Don't say you'll marry him. Don't do it!"

Thera felt more confused than she'd ever been. Pittheus was telling her she had the power to stop the Centaurs from their torture and humiliation. All she had to do was agree to marry him without a struggle. Then the Centaurs and Kyros would be free to go.

But Kyros was telling her not to believe him. Not to trust his brother's word and not to agree to marry the man. By the powers of Zeus, marrying Pittheus was the last thing she wanted. But watching the Centaurs and Kyros suffer hurt her more.

She wasn't sure where this feeling was coming from. She'd always abhorred Centaurs and shouldn't care what happened to them. But since she'd met Kaj, her opinions of the creatures changed. She saw them in a different light. She saw that Centaurs weren't really any different than humans.

She looked at Pittheus who blew his drunken breath in her face. Then she looked over to Kyros who sat pitifully helpless chained to the chair in the center of the room. The torment of the Centaurs continued and the people crowded around as they drank and laughed. The sounds echoed in her head and she felt a knot in her stomach. The baby lay still and she worried if it was all right. She hadn't felt it stir since she'd been hit by her father's beam. She put her hand on her stomach and rubbed it.

It was then the crowd became silent and the archers stopped their shooting. She looked through the crowd and saw just what it was that captured their undivided attention.

Kyros' face was twisted and his body convulsed. He twitched in the chair in a contorted way. Then she noticed his clothing splitting. His muscles bulged beneath the material and his legs seemed to grow in size.

"Stand back," cried a guard and the crowd moved further from Kyros. The Centaurs themselves stopped fighting as they got to their feet and focused their attention on Kyros.

"What's happening?" shouted a child from across the room.

Thera knew exactly what was happening. The sun was setting and Kyros was going through his change. She'd never seen it happen before and felt scared, confused and pity all at once. It was torture for her to watch him as his hooves emerged and the convulsions wracked his body. The sweat beaded his brow and glistened off his huge, bare chest. His hair grew in length, tangling around his arms.

Thera's own stomach convulsed as she felt Kyros' pain. It was as if he was connected to her somehow. As if they were one and she was experiencing his transformation with him.

The women in the crowd screamed and the men laughed nervously. Kyros' body from the waist down grew, breaking the chains that held him. A guard stepped forward, meaning to restrain him, but Pittheus stopped his action.

"No!" he said. "Leave Kyros be. I want everyone to witness what my brother really is. The man who wants be king of Trozen and take my place. The man who is not really a man at all."

Thera's head grew dizzy and her vision blurred as she watched Kyros fall to the floor helplessly. He shook and convulsed; his teeth chattered. She felt horror at having to witness his transformation, yet at the same time she felt love for Kyros. He never should have to be so humiliated. He should have the people of Trozen look at him with respect, not laugh at him and call him names as if he were nothing but a freak.

Thera jumped to her feet, knowing she had to go to him. She wanted to comfort him and hold him and tell him she was there for him. She stepped away from the table, but Pittheus grabbed her by the arm and stopped her.

"Just say the word," he told her. "Just say you'll marry me willingly and do your part in being my rightful wife and I'll stop all this."

Thera took a deep breath, trying to calm her nerves. She didn't want to marry Pittheus. She wanted to marry Kyros. But if she didn't agree, Pittheus would continue to put Kyros through this sort of humiliation. That, or kill him. She couldn't allow either. Maybe by marrying Pittheus, she'd help Kyros after all. She'd give him up if it meant saving his life.

"So if I marry you, you'll let the Centaurs go and Kyros live?"

"Just to show you I mean what I say ..." He called a guard over to him.

"Yes, Pittheus?" asked the guard.

"Have the men take the Centaurs to the edge of the forest and release them."

"But—"

"Do it!" he commanded.

"Yes, sir." The guard motioned for help and they took Rodas and the others from the great hall.

"You see, my dear. I've already kept my word."

"Half your word," she ground out. "Now are you going to keep the rest?"

"Yes, I'll let Kyros live. You won't have to worry about your ex-lover dying at my hand."

Just then, Kyros let out a tortured cry and Thera looked up to see his transformation was over. His body convulsed in spasms on the floor and his teeth chattered as he shivered. The people gathered around to get a closer look and the soldiers held them back.

Thera bit her lip to keep from crying. She wanted to run and comfort him but couldn't. Pittheus was to blame for the humiliation. Ares was to blame for the cursed transformation. But no one but herself was to blame for not stopping all of this.

She put her hand on her stomach and felt relief as the baby stirred. She knew she'd always have a part of Kyros with her in their baby. She couldn't imagine a life without Kyros, but then again, she couldn't imagine a world without him either if Pittheus decided to kill him.

"I love you, Kyros," she whispered to herself and then turned to face

Pittheus. "I'll do it," she said. "I'll marry you to save Kyros' life."

"I knew you'd come around," he smiled. He then hailed the crowd and they gave him their undivided attention. "I want to make the announcement that Thera has decided to become my wife."

The crowd spoke in hushed tones to each other when they heard the announcement. Kyros raised his head and looked straight at her. It was then she knew that she'd made the wrong decision. The pain she felt within Kyros was worse than any pain she'd ever felt in her life. His look was one of sadness, defeat, and abandonment. One that said all that he'd worked so hard for in his life had been shattered by her decision to marry his brother.

She had to go to him. She wanted to tell him she'd done it for him because she loved him and thought more of him than she did of herself. And that she would gladly give up her own life if it meant saving his.

She tried to go to him but Pittheus held her back.

"Where are you going my dear?" Pittheus asked. "I reserve a dance with my bride-to-be. Minstrels, start up the music."

Some cheery music started playing but it did nothing to lift Thera's mood. All she could do was stare at Kyros and feel the disappointment that dwelled within him. She also felt the rage he held for his brother and his disappointment of the people who laughed and scorned him. But try as she did, she could no longer feel the love he once held for her in his heart.

Tears welled in her eyes and she tried to mouth the words to Kyros that she was sorry. But she knew he couldn't see her. By the way he shook his head she could tell his vision was still blurred from the transformation. She closed her eyes willing this all to be nothing more than a bad dream.

"What shall we do with the beast?" came the voice of one of Pittheus' men.

"Take my brother to the dungeon," answered Pittheus.

Thera's eyes snapped open and she pulled loose from Pittheus' grasp. "You promised to set him free!"

"I did no such thing," he chuckled. "Our deal was that I let the Centaurs go and let Kyros live if you were to marry me. I've kept my word and now you'll keep yours. We'll be married tomorrow at mid-day. Now come, as I want that dance."

Thera didn't want to dance. She realized now she'd been careless in wording their agreement and Pittheus had been a snake enough to trap her into marrying him. She had said she wanted the Centaurs set free and Kyros' life to be spared. But she meant she wanted Kyros set free as well. Pittheus knew that, but trapped her into making a deal that he alone would benefit from. What good was saving Kyros' life if he was to live with his curse in the dungeons and be brought out for the entertainment each night when his transformation took place? She was sure Kyros would rather die than live like this, and she couldn't blame him. She had only herself to blame for the torture and humiliation Kyros would now have to live with for the rest of his life.

TWENTY-TWO

Rodas and his men freed themselves from their chains and gags, but it took Chiron and Nemos coming to their aid to do it. Chiron reached up and pulled the gag from Rodas' mouth and almost wanted to replace it when he started shouting.

"We'll kill them for what they've done to us. We'll get our weapons and kill every stinking one of the Trozens for the humiliation they put us through."

"Calm down," said Chiron. "Now tell me everything that happened."

"Pittheus betrayed us. He betrayed us and he'll pay for it with his life."

"And you didn't betray Kyros?" asked Chiron in a steady voice.

Rodas was silent and so were his men.

"You stole his father's sword and handed it over to the enemy," said Chiron.

"The sword I was suppose to be guarding," added Nemos.

"Why, Rodas? Why did you do it?"

Rodas looked at Chiron and shook his head. "I don't know. I guess I was just so angry with Kyros for jumping in front of Ares' beam and fathering Thera's child."

"Mad enough to put his life in jeopardy and ruin his dreams of peace?" asked Chiron. "He only dove in front of that beam to save you from what he thought was a curse."

"I wanted to lead a war," said Rodas, "but now I can see I was wrong. Peace truly is stronger. Kyros proved it when he spoke up against Ares at the castle to save me. And though I still want Pittheus and his men to die, I don't want innocent Centaurs to die in the process. I guess I was blinded by greed, wanting the power Phylo, my brother had. I wanted to take over as king of the Centaurs and thought war was the way."

126

"You were Phylo's brother?" Nemos looked on with wide eyes.

"He was," Chiron answered for him. "But Phylo and Rodas were more like enemies than they were like kin."

"But either way, Rodas should be our king," said Nemos. "He should be our leader since Phylo's gone."

Rodas walked up and put a hand on Nemos' shoulder. He raised the boy's chin and gave him a half-hug. It was something Chiron had never seen Rodas do in all the years he'd known him.

"I think it's time he knew the truth," said Rodas. "I'm willing to accept it now, and willing to bring this secret out in the open."

"What secret?" asked Nemos. "What are you talking about?"

"You're our next Centaur king," smiled Chiron. "You were the offspring of Phylo."

"What?" asked Nemos. "You're saying Phylo was my father?"

"He was." Rodas smiled, and Chiron could see that something happened at the castle to bring about this major change in him. "Phylo was your father and I'm you're uncle. Didn't you ever wonder who your parents were?"

"Chiron told me I was an orphan," answered Nemos.

"You were," said Rodas. "When Phylo died, Chiron took you into his care to train you. He hid the golden bow from me because he knew I had bad motives and contempt in my heart. We've lived for too long without a Centaur king. I know you have peace and love in your heart and will lead us better than I ever could."

Chiron looked at Nemos and he nodded. "That's right, Nemos. You are our king. I was waiting until you were old enough to tell you. But I think you're ready for it now, after the way you've grown up just since you met Kyros."

"But I let the sword be stolen," remarked Nemos. "What kind of king am I going to be if I can't even watch a sword?"

"A good one," answered Chiron. "One that needs a bit more training, but with my and Rodas' help, I think you'll be even better than your father."

Rodas looked at Chiron with a questioning brow. "Do you mean it? You want me to help train our king?"

"I do, Rodas. I'd like for you to move into our hovel and take your place as the boy's uncle. You and Phylo were my best students. I could really use your help in training our new king."

"I'd be honored," answered Rodas. He then extended his arm and he and Chiron interlocked in a grasp. "And as trainer to the future Centaur king, I suggest we find a way to free Kyros."

Kyros shivered in the darkness of the cold cell. It was over. Thera had agreed to marry Pittheus and there was nothing he could do to stop her. She'd made her decision despite his warning. And the worst part was, he felt as if he was the one to blame.

He shouldn't have fallen in love with her and he shouldn't have wooed her. She obviously was in love with him and it was clouding her better judgment. If she hadn't loved him, she never would have agreed to marry Pittheus. He knew that was the case. It was her desire to save his life that would cost the lives of so many of the Trozens and probably the entire Centaur race.

The main door to the dungeon squeaked open and he could hear light footsteps coming his way. The torches on the wall flickered, causing a shadow to fall over the ground. He knew it was her even before he saw her face. She walked up to the barred door with a plate of food in her hands.

"I thought you might be hungry." She had her head down, not able to bring her eyes to meet with his.

"That's not why you came. Admit it."

Her head came up and he could see the tears staining her cheeks. Her eyes were glassy and her mouth turned down in a little pout. A pout Kyros would have liked to kiss away had circumstances been different.

"You're right," she said in a shaky voice. "I came … I came to say I'm sorry."

Kyros couldn't stand it any longer. Even if she'd made the wrong decision, crushed his plans and basically sent the Centaur race into extinction, he still loved her. He reached through the bars and cupped her cheek in his hand. She leaned into him with her eyes closed and he lost himself in the warmth of her skin.

"I love you, Thera. You know that. And even though I don't agree with your decision, I'm still the father of your child. I'll always love you and I'll always love our child no matter what happens."

Her Olympian blue eyes opened and he could see the love that shone within them. He couldn't help but think of their times together. Nor could he help but think of her lying down in a bed at night with Pittheus. Something he'd never be able to do as long as he was cursed.

"I love you too, Kyros," she said. "And that's why I made my decision. I was trying to keep him from killing you. You didn't deserve the humiliation he put you through."

"Shhh. I know all that, Thera. You don't have to explain that to me."

"Maybe I'm just trying to explain it to myself," she answered. "You warned me not to trust Pittheus. You told me not to agree to marry him, but I—" Her tears choked her and Kyros knew he had to do something to calm her down.

"We'll figure something out, Thera. Somehow we'll find a way to make it all right."

"I know how to make it right. I'm supposed to marry Pittheus tomorrow at mid-day, but I'm not going to."

"Thera. You gave him your word."

"His word means nothing, so why should mine?"

"He kept his word. He agreed to let the Centaurs go and let me live and he did just that."

"But he tricked me, Kyros. And by refusing to marry him I'm going to get my revenge."

He saw her flinch and move the plate to one hand so she could put her other hand on her stomach. He reached through the two horizontal bars made for meal deliveries, and took the plate from her. He placed it on the floor and then put both his hands through the bars, putting them on her stomach.

"I can feel our baby kicking," he said with a smile.

She smiled through her tears and he felt his heart drop in his chest. How was he going to live without her and their child? How would he be able to watch her marry his brother while he stood by helplessly and did nothing to stop it?

"He's a strong one. He's going to be just like you, Kyros."

"No. Not just like me. He'll either be a Centaur or a human. I'm neither and yet both at the same time."

"Either way, I'll love him just as I love you. It doesn't matter to me if he's human or Centaur."

"Well it does to me, Thera. By the power of the gods, I can only pray our child is not a Centaur."

He saw the confused and shocked look in her eyes. He knew she didn't understand his words, as she'd always been the one to despise Centaurs, not him. She was accepting the fact her child may be a Centaur, but he couldn't. Not when it meant her life was in jeopardy.

"I don't want you to die birthing a Centaur baby."

She smiled and rubbed her hands over the tops of his. "Oh. Is that all?"

"Is that all?" he repeated and they both laughed.

Kyros raised his hands and put them around the back of her head. He pulled her closer and through the bars he brought his lips to meet hers. When he pulled away, her eyes were closed, her head tilted up to his.

"I want to couple with you, Kyros." She opened her eyes. "I want to lay with the man who fathered my baby."

The sound of a slamming door made them both jump away from each other. And also the sound of Pittheus' voice.

"I won't ever let that happen." Pittheus walked up to the cell looking so sure of himself. "The only coupling my wife will be doing is with me."

He put his arm around Thera and pulled her into him. Kyros' gut wrenched and he wanted to reach right through the bars and strangle his brother.

"Get your hands off of her," Kyros warned.

"And what are you going to do?" mocked Pittheus. "Kick me with those horse legs of yours right through the bars?"

"Such an idea," answered Kyros. "What did you come here for anyway? Just to taunt me again? Didn't I already have enough of that tonight?"

"Brother, brother. You make me out to be so evil, when I was the one who allowed Thera to bring you your dinner in the first place. I thought you two might like to say your good-byes before she becomes my wife. Actually, I came down here myself to invite you to join us at the wedding tomorrow."

"Never!" exclaimed Kyros.

"Your choice," chuckled Pittheus. "But you're going to miss the best wedding of all times."

"No, he won't," interrupted Thera. "Because there's not going to be a wedding, Pittheus. I'm not going to marry you after all."

"Oh, but you have to Thera. We made an agreement."

"One that you tricked me into. Set Kyros free."

"I can't do that, sweetheart." Pittheus kissed her atop the head and Kyros clenched his fists as he looked on. "I'm not king yet and won't be until the feast of Dionysus. If I let Kyros out before then, he's sure to find some way to spoil my plans."

Pittheus' words brought a new hope to Kyros. He'd almost forgotten that his brother wasn't king yet, even though he had their father's sword. Pittheus would have to sit on the throne with the sword raised to Artemis on the feast of Dionysus. That wasn't for a few more days. He still had time to think of something. Some way to get the sword back and stop Pittheus from becoming king.

"I accept your invitation to the wedding after all," said Kyros. If he could at least get out of this cell, he may have a chance. Maybe with the confusion of the wedding, he could manage some sort of rescue.

"I knew you'd come around," smiled Pittheus.

Thera's face clouded over and Kyros hoped she'd understand. He hoped she'd figure out that he needed her to go through with the wedding. It was probably their last chance of retrieving the sword, keeping Pittheus from becoming king, and maybe even stopping the war between the Centaurs and the Trozens, which now looked to be inevitable.

"Kyros," said Thera. "I told you, I'm not marrying Pittheus."

"Do it, Thera. You gave your word and you have to see it through. No future queen will be respected by her people if they can't trust her. Trust me, Thera. You need to keep your word and marry Pittheus."

She still looked at him with those big, blue, innocent eyes. But she had a clouded, confused look upon her face. He hated putting her through this, but there was nothing else he could do. It stabbed at his insides to have to tell her to marry his brother when he wanted her so bad for his own wife. But if she didn't obey, Pittheus might take to beating her or harming their baby. He couldn't risk it. If she obeyed, it would be easier on her and the baby. And then Kyros could stop worrying about her and concentrate on how to get them out of this mess.

"Until tomorrow," Pittheus called as he took a struggling Thera under his arm and left the dungeon.

"Until tomorrow," whispered Kyros with a sadness in his heart.

TWENTY-THREE

Thera cried herself to sleep that night, not understanding why Kyros insisted she go ahead and marry Pittheus after he had been so upset in the first place that she'd agreed to do it. But he asked her to trust him. That message got through very clear. All she could think of, is that Kyros had a plan. A plan to help her. A plan to steal the sword and for both of them to escape.

But if she figured this out, then Pittheus was sure to figure it out also. And if he knew Kyros was up to something, he'd have him guarded heavily, not to mention be watching him himself.

Kyros would never escape that way. And if he couldn't escape, there was nothing he could do to stop the wedding. She had to think of a way to help him with his plan. She had to find a way to get back down into the dungeon and ask him just what that plan may be. But Pittheus had forbid her to see Kyros again. And he had instructed his guards not to let her enter. She was doomed. So was Kyros. She cried hysterically and the baby kicked within her. She rubbed her hand over her stomach, trying to soothe it. But how could she comfort her baby if there was no one to help comfort herself?

A knock on the door caused her to sit up in bed and momentarily stop her crying. She stayed silent wondering who it was. She didn't know anyone in the castle and the ladies-in-waiting were already dismissed for the night. That left only one person that could be behind the closed door and she didn't want to open it. Pittheus must be there, wanting to see her. Possibly wanting to touch her or worse yet, wanting her to warm his bed before they were even married.

The knock came again and Thera remained quiet, pretending she was asleep. If he thought she was sleeping, maybe he'd go away and leave her alone. Thera heard the door open and squeezed her eyes shut, burying herself deep under the covers. She didn't want to see Pittheus;

didn't want anything to do with him, and it turned her stomach sour just to think she was going to have to marry him in the morning.

"I know you're not sleeping, Thera. I heard you crying from the hall."

Either Thera's ears played tricks on her or the gods were smiling at her. It wasn't the deep voice of Pittheus she heard, but the high crackling old voice of a woman. And if her memory served her right, that voice belonged to someone she knew.

She whipped the covers back and sat up straight in bed. There, standing before her was the little old weaver woman who had made her tunic; the woman who brought her and Kyros together and let them borrow her hut for a night of privacy. Relief washed over Thera as she released a deep breath and smiled.

"Thank the gods it's you and not Pittheus."

"Yes," agreed the old woman. "It would have been Pittheus had I not run into him in the hall and convinced him it was bad luck to see the bride the night before the wedding."

"Oh, thank you," cried Thera and got to her knees, hugging the woman from the side of the bed.

"You may not be thanking me when you find out why I've come, Thera."

Thera dropped her arms from around the woman. She didn't like the way that sounded. She tried to pick up the old woman's emotions, but couldn't. Ever since Thera met the old weaver she didn't know what to make of her. She couldn't read her the way she could read others. The old weaver was mysterious, secretive, and didn't even have anyone call her by a rightful name. Still, Thera was glad to see her and was happy for the company.

"I guess you didn't come to set me free?" asked Thera.

"I can't do that," the woman replied. "After all, I am blind, and it's hard enough to get around by myself, without trying to help a pregnant woman hide or escape."

"You seem to do a good job anyway," commented Thera.

"So, the reason I'm here." She changed the subject.

Thera saw the solemn look on her face and a thought hit her head on. What if something happened to Kyros? What if the woman was here to give her the news that he was dead?

"By the gods, don't tell me something happened to Kyros?"

The old woman placed her hand on Thera's and patted it gently.

"Nothing you don't already know about. And as far as I know, Pittheus hasn't killed him yet."

"Yet?" Thera was mortified. "So you think he really will kill him after all?"

"Nobody but the Fates know for sure when someone is going to die, child. The reason I'm here is to measure you for your wedding gown."

"No!" Thera pushed away from the woman and snuggled back down into the covers. "I've decided I'm not marrying Pittheus. I can't. I'm in love with Kyros and he's the one I'm going to marry."

"You won't be marrying Kyros if he's dead. And if you refuse Pittheus, you realize that will seal Kyros' fate."

Thera grabbed a pillow and hugged it to her body. "I don't know what to do, Weaver. I just don't know what to do."

"Trust your heart, child. Let your heart tell you what's right."

Trust. Just the word triggered off her conversation with Kyros. He'd told her to trust him and go ahead with the wedding. She didn't understand why, but her heart told her to listen to him.

"Kyros told me to trust him. He said I had to marry Pittheus."

"Then that's what you're to do." The old weaver pulled Thera out of bed and onto the floor. She took a piece of string and started to measure her for her gown.

"How were you chosen to make my wedding gown?"

"Everyone calls on me when a special cloth is to be woven. Pittheus sent for me this evening. I am to finish the gown by morning."

"But how?" asked Thera. "How can you possibly weave an elaborate wedding gown overnight?"

"I have experience," she explained, moving the string around Thera's waist. "I will have it done, don't worry. My," she commented as she felt Thera's thickened waist. "The baby sure has grown. It seems to me you'll be birthing it soon."

"Do you think so?" asked Thera. "How can you tell?"

"It doesn't matter. We've no time for that now. I have a dress to weave and you should get rest so you're not tired on your wedding day."

"When do you think my baby will be born?" asked Thera excitedly. "I can't wait to hold it in my arms."

"It'll be born before the feast day of Dionysus is here. But I wouldn't be so anxious if I were you."

"Why?" Thera backed away from the woman. Her body tensed in apprehension. "Do you know something about my baby that I don't? Is my child going to be born a Centaur? Will I die giving birth?"

"I can't foresee the future. I only have feelings. And the feelings I'm having are that both you and Kyros are going to be in grave danger."

"Then you have to help us somehow. You have to help us escape."

"I don't believe escape is possible. Pittheus has this castle severely guarded."

"Then go to Kyros and ask him if he has a plan. Tell him to tell it to you so you can let me know."

"That I can do," she remarked as she wound up her twine and pushed it into her sleeve. "I'm to bring Kyros some clothes as well. Clothes he'll wear at the wedding, since he's ripped his others and will be in human form at mid-day tomorrow. Pittheus didn't want you too distracted having Kyros attend naked."

"Thank you," said Thera. "Thank you for helping and thank you for being a friend."

"Get some rest, child." The weaver fluffed Thera's pillow and tucked the blankets around her. "We don't want anything happening to that baby."

Thera watched the old woman waddle across the floor and close the door behind her. The weaver's words had upset her. She'd never thought of anything happening to her child. But now she wondered if it would be safe. If it was born human, she doubted if Pittheus would let her keep it and raise it. She prayed he didn't slay it just because it was his brother's. And if it was born a Centaur, she would die in the process. If Kyros was still locked away, who would raise their child?

Thera felt pains again in her stomach and this time she knew she wasn't picking up the pain of Kyros. This pain was different. This was the pain of a fetus grown to completion, struggling, kicking to be released from its mother's womb. She rubbed her stomach and turned her head on the pillow. She was so tired she could barely keep her eyes open. She had to rest, as the weaver told her. She had to regain her strength for the escape plan tomorrow.

Kyros heard the door to the dungeon opening for the third time that night. First it had been Thera, then it was Pittheus come to get her. Now he wondered who would be coming to see him at this late hour. He had dozed off once or twice but found it impossible to really sleep. And he needed sleep more than anything as he hadn't slept much at all in the last couple of nights.

He heard the shuffling footsteps lightly on the stone floor and waited for the person to appear before his cell. He knew it was either a woman or a boy by the lightness of the steps and wondered if Thera had come back down to see him. But as much as he wanted to see her again, he prayed it wasn't her. He knew she'd be punished if caught, and he knew just how capable his brother was of inflicting pain when he wanted to.

"Kyros?" came a crackly voice as the old weaver stepped in front of the bars. "Are you in there?"

"I'm here," he answered, surprised and curious as to why and how she got there. Then he noticed a bundle in her hands, just as he heard the guard call from the door.

"Just give him the clothes and get back already. This is no place for a little old lady."

Kyros stuck his hands through the bars and grabbed the bundle of clothes. "Thank you," he exclaimed and pulled them inside. He noticed the clothes were a bit heavier than they should be. He started to open the package to inspect it, but the old weaver's hand shot out through the bars and stilled him.

"You won't want to open these now. They're for after your transformation. You'll need them then, not before."

"I see," answered Kyros, wondering what the old woman was up to and how she knew he was about to inspect the package.

"Thera sent me to find out your plan," whispered the weaver.

"Plan?" Kyros whispered back. "What plan?"

The old woman's face scrunched up impatiently. Or was it disgust?

"The plan you have for freeing her. To stop her from marrying that ogre."

"I have no plan to free her," he whispered back. "The only plan I have is to steal back my father's sword during the wedding ceremony. I need her to marry Pittheus to distract him. When he takes his attention off of me, I'll go to work."

"No plan to stop the wedding?" she snarled. "What kind of a man are you to let the woman you love marry your evil brother?"

Kyros lost his patience. Couldn't the old woman see that he'd been wracking his brain for hours trying to find a way to stop the wedding and at the same time steal back the sword? He didn't know how to do one, let alone the other.

"Well, perhaps you'd like to suggest a plan old lady?" Kyros whispered but had a hard time from shouting. "This place is so well guarded, even if I do manage to retrieve my father's sword I'll probably never get out of these walls alive."

"Your Centaur friends are planning on doing something to help you escape. I believe they're preparing their weapons right now for an attack on the castle come morning."

"No!" Kyros almost shouted. "If you're in contact with them, tell them not to do anything to try to help me. It'll only start a war. It's just what Pittheus wants. Tell them to stay back at the village and wait for word from me. I'll only call them in if things get so bad that Thera's life is in danger."

"So then the wedding will continue as scheduled?" asked the woman.

Kyros' heart sank to think he had no other choice for now. He hated the idea. He wanted to stop Pittheus from marrying Thera. He wanted to kill him. And wanting to kill one's own brother was not good. He'd just have to let the wedding go as planned, or at least until he found a way to stop it and save the sword too. Maybe after Pittheus was married he'd let down his guard. Then Kyros would still have a day to retrieve the sword before the feast day of Dionysus. If Pittheus wasn't crowned king, he'd have no need for Thera and would hopefully cast her off. Then Kyros could step in and take her for his own wife somehow.

"The wedding will go as planned," Kyros said as he shook his head slowly. "Tell Thera I'm sorry, but there's nothing I can do. Tell her ... tell her I love her. And that's why I have to let her marry my brother."

TWENTY-FOUR

Kyros lay on the floor of the dungeon cell, writhing in pain from his morning's transformation. He was so cold he felt frozen and only wished to be in the warmth of Thera's loving arms so she could warm him. He felt his bones moving, and his tail and horseflesh disappear. He could barely feel his human limbs as they took formation, but knew they'd be there once his vision cleared.

He lay naked on the cold stone, not wanting to go through this transformation again. He'd been cursed for nearly a year, but it seemed to him like eternity. He pitied himself and he had the right to do it. His brother—his human brother—was going to marry the woman he loved; the woman who was carrying his own child.

He wrapped his arms around his bare chest and curled into an embryonic ball. He wondered how his baby would feel about this someday when he got older. He was sure to hate his father for doing nothing to stop Thera from marrying an ogre of a man. But then again, his child would be sure to hate him anyway, once he found out his true father was half-man, half-beast.

Maybe Thera would be better off with Pittheus than with him. She could learn to love him in time. Maybe Pittheus would change. There was a possibility once he was king and married he'd see things differently. Thera would be coupling with Pittheus tonight, and that thought drove a stake so far into Kyros' heart that he thought he'd die. He wanted to die. And after Pittheus would make love to Thera, they'd lie together in his bed and sleep throughout the night side by side. Something Kyros would never be able to do.

His vision cleared and he got to his feet. He thought of the look on Thera's face when she'd left the dungeon last night and it pained him.

"Get dressed," snapped a guard from outside the cell door. "You don't want to be late for the wedding." He left laughing, his voice echoing off the stone walls and off Kyros' heart as well. There must be something he could do to stop this, but he didn't know what.

He grabbed for the bundle of clothes the weaver had brought him the night before. He pulled out the tunic and something went clattering to the floor. It was a dagger, bless her little heart. She'd brought him a weapon to use. Something he was very happy to see. He hurriedly pulled on his clothing and boots she'd sent. He wasn't used to wearing boots and thought it odd she'd sent them instead of sandals. Then he realized it was a great place to hide the dagger. Maybe all hope wasn't lost after all. He pushed the weapon out of sight in his boot when the guard came to unlock the door. Maybe he'd be able to do something about stopping the wedding after all.

Thera held her arms out as the old weaver slipped her wedding gown around her. It was of a white, dull material with many pleats in the lower half. It criss-crossed over her full breasts, clinging to them and making her look bustier than she'd ever been. Her breasts were so trussed up that she could barely see her huge stomach that lie hidden beneath the folds.

"This is beautiful!," exclaimed Thera. "You did a wonderful job. I've never looked so good."

The old weaver smiled a broken-toothed grin and held out a rose-colored flimsy shawl that Thera was supposed to wear over her shoulders. It was made of thick threads that looked almost like string. It was woven in an intricate design, and one thread hung down loose from the end.

"If you don't mind me saying, I'm not fond of the shawl. I don't think I'll wear it to the wedding. It'll cover up the beautiful gown."

"And it'll cover up that cleavage as well," agreed the weaver. "Unless you want Pittheus looking at you throughout the ceremony."

"You're right, give me the shawl," she said and slipped her hands through the arm loops to hold it on. "Why didn't you make the dress less revealing in the first place?"

"Pittheus ordered me to make it that way. Although, the shawl was my idea."

"Thank you," said Thera, grabbing the old woman's hand.

The weaver took Thera's hand and placed it on the loose string. Thera started to pull and the shawl began to unravel. "Don't pull that string unless you want the shawl to unravel," she commented.

"Why would I want it to? I don't understand," said Thera.

"You may need to use it unraveled … or maybe you won't. But if you do, you'll know how to do it."

Thera was thoroughly confused. She had no idea what the crazy old woman was talking about. Why would she need to unravel the shawl, and what good would it do her if it was nothing but a pile of string? She sat in a chair as the old weaver fixed her hair. The woman was a wonder as her fingers flew through the braids and she wound them into a pattern.

Thera had grown to like the old woman. She felt she had a friend in her, something she'd never really had before except for Persephone. But Persephone was taken from her when Hades came to claim her as his bride of the underworld. She wondered if Persephone felt as she did at this very minute. Pittheus came to claim her, and living with him would probably be no different than living in Tartarus. She'd never met her uncle Hades, but the things she'd heard about him weren't so good. Still, Persephone was fond of him, and talked well of him on the few occasions when the topic of Hades was mentioned.

"There," said the weaver. "You are ready now for the wedding."

Thera's body froze as she heard the music starting up below stairs. The weaver still hadn't told her what Kyros' plan was to save her. Surely he didn't mean for her to actually marry Pittheus? Wasn't he going to come bursting through the door at any second and save her from this awful fate?

"So what's Kyros' plan?" she asked the weaver. "Is he going to come rescue me here in the room or do I have to pretend to be marrying Pittheus before he'll stop this nonsense?"

"He doesn't have a plan," the old woman finally admitted.

"No plan? You are jesting!"

"I jest with you not, Thera. When I went to visit him in the dungeon last night, he told me he had no idea what he was going to do. But I did slip him a dagger, so I'm sure he'll see to use it and somehow save you from marrying Pittheus."

Thera was no longer certain this was true. She couldn't pick up the old woman's emotions for some reason, but her intuition told her she was destined to marry Pittheus.

"I think I was meant to marry Pittheus." Thera looked at the floor when she talked.

"Why do you say that, child?"

"Because I was able to use the golden bow of Artemis. No one can use it unless they're a king. Or in this case, I believe the wife of a king. Pittheus now has the sword and I don't see any way Kyros is going to retrieve it before the feast of Dionysus. Pittheus keeps him chained up and well guarded. I'm to marry Pittheus today and Kyros has no plan to stop it. It's obvious to me; I was destined to marry Pittheus and become queen of Trozen, although I'm in love with his brother Kyros."

"Don't fret, child." The weaver pulled Thera to her bosom and hugged her. It felt good to Thera. It felt so motherly. The motherly affection she'd never known from Aphrodite. The love she'd never known from Ares. But she had felt love from Kyros, and now from the old weaver. It was too bad she was marrying a man with only lust in his heart. She enjoyed being human and would like to experience this thing called love more. If only she was marrying Kyros.

"I've been in contact with the Centaurs," said the weaver.

Thera's spirits lifted. "Then they'll come to save Kyros and he can then save me."

"I'm afraid not. Kyros told them not to interfere unless your life was in danger. He's afraid it'll bring about a war."

Thera rose from the chair. "I no longer care what happens to me. As long as Kyros' life has been spared by my actions."

A pain shot through her abdomen and she bent over and clutched herself. The old weaver held on to her shoulders and told her to take deep breaths. In a minute the contraction had eased and Thera was able once more to stand upright.

"It's the baby," said Thera. "The time is coming closer, isn't it?"

"I believe so," smiled the old woman and Thera could have sworn she saw a twinkle in her glazed, blind eyes. "Too bad the baby wasn't a little faster, though. Too bad it couldn't stop the wedding."

TWENTY-FIVE

The guard pushed Kyros in front of him as they made their way to the great hall where the wedding was about to take place. He still didn't have a plan, and this worried him. His hands were tied in front of him in rope instead of chain, and this he felt was the best thing to happen to him yet. The dagger stashed away in his boot rubbed against his leg as he walked and it pinched him in the ankle. He thanked the old weaver silently for bringing this to him as he knew it would cut right through his ropes.

He stopped at the door to the great hall and took in the beauty of it all. An altar was set up on the dais, huge flowers and greenery stood all around. The crowd was gathered in their finest garments. Pittheus stood high on the dais next to the altar, wearing a fine-looking tunic wrap and an olive branch wreath around his head. Soon to be a crown, Kyros thought and wondered if Pittheus had done it on purpose to get his people used to seeing his head crowned. But it was so ironic; he wore the symbol of peace when all he really wanted was war.

Then Kyros' eyes fell at his father's sword strapped around his brother's waist. It looked so foreign there. Kyros cringed at the sight, wanting it back on his own waist where it truly belonged. Damn, he thought. If Pittheus was already wearing the sword, it was his subtle way of saying he'd won. And if the sword was strapped around his brother's waist during the ceremony, he would have no chance at all of stealing it back. Things were going from bad to worse.

"Get moving!" The guard pushed him from behind, his hand slapping against Kyros' freshly-mended wound. The pain sliced through him and he knew with one more blow like that he'd be bleeding again in no time. He moved forward into the room and Pittheus limped up to greet him.

"So good you decided to join this happy occasion," he bellowed out for the entire hall to hear. Everyone hushed their conversations and all eyes followed him.

"Happy for who, Pittheus? Certainly not me, and I don't believe for Thera, either. And why should your people be happy?" He addressed the room when he spoke. "After all, you're not only stealing my bride who's carrying my child, but you've already announced you'll be starting a war with the Centaurs as soon as you become king."

"My people are happy the Centaurs will no longer be bothering them," said Pittheus, a bit nervous if Kyros wasn't mistaken.

"Don't let him be your king," he said to the people. "For if you do, he'll bring war to the land and many of you will die. The Centaurs have never done anything against any of you. They only fought to protect themselves. My father knew that and wanted peace as much as I do between the races."

"Enough!" shouted Pittheus.

Kyros ignored him and continued addressing the crowd. "If I were your king, I'd carry on in the footsteps of the good King Mezentius. Have you all forgotten how happy you were when he was your king and still alive? Things were different then; things were better. They could be again if I—"

"I said enough!" shouted Pittheus and threw a punch at Kyros' face. Kyros stumbled backwards, but the guard caught him and set him straight on his feet. The crowd mumbled their protests and Kyros could only hope he'd gotten through to them. If he had the people on his side then maybe there'd still be hope after all.

"Put him in a chair far from me," snarled Pittheus. "And make sure he's tied."

"I will," answered the guard.

"You're responsible," Pittheus warned the man. "If anything happens here to upset my wedding, I'll have your head."

The guard swallowed deeply and nodded to Pittheus. He then dragged Kyros over to a chair on the far side of the room, near the door to the corridor. He pulled some strong rope from a bag at his waist and tied Kyros' chest, then feet to the chair.

The music switched to something a little slower and the crowd parted as Thera walked in with a bouquet of flowers resting on her belly. She looked more beautiful than Kyros had ever seen her. Little flowers encircled her braids which were woven in a design high on her head. She had delicate sandals gracing her feet. She wore a long, white pleated gown that flowed to the ground and wrapped around her legs as she slowly walked to the altar. Then he noticed the rose-colored ugly shawl that hid the top half of her body, contrasting with the rest of her beautiful outfit.

The blind old weaver stepped out in front of her, sprinkling rose petals where Thera's sandaled feet would step. He was amazed at the old woman's agility and the fact she didn't stumble although she couldn't see. They stopped in front of the dais and the music stopped also. Pittheus reached his hand down and grabbed Thera's. He made a big show of kissing her hand before helping her up the few steps to where the priest waited with book in hand.

Pittheus then motioned for the crowd's attention as he turned Thera for them to see. "I don't like this ugly shawl," he growled at the weaver standing nearby and tore it from Thera's shoulders. It hung behind her from the straps that secured it to her arms.

"That's better," smiled Pittheus. "Now the whole room can see your beauty and what will soon be mine."

Kyros had a good view of Thera now, and couldn't help but notice her exposed cleavage. Then he noticed the way Pittheus' eyes were fastened to it as well. Kyros could have sworn his brother was about to drool as he picked up his hand and reached out for her.

"No!" Kyros screamed, not wanting his brother to touch her.

Thera wasn't even aware of Kyros' presence in the room until she heard his voice. She jerked her head toward the back of the room where she'd heard him, searching with her eyes for a strong warrior standing in the doorway with weapon in hand, coming to save her.

Her heart fell when she saw him sitting tied to a chair, a guard standing over him. This wasn't her warrior come to save her from marrying Pittheus. This was a prisoner who could do nothing but watch as she gave her life away to a man she didn't love.

"Keep him quiet," snarled Pittheus. He reached out and grabbed Thera's chin, turning her attention away from Kyros. "There's nothing he can do to stop this, Thera. And if you refuse to go through with the wedding, I'll kill him. You know I will. I'll even make you watch."

"No!" Thera shook her head in his hand and tears welled in her eyes. "No, you can't do that. I'll marry you if it'll save his life. I'll do whatever you want, just don't hurt him." A tear dripped down her cheek and landed on her chest. Pittheus followed its path with his eyes as the tear disappeared down her cleavage.

"I would have licked that tear from you right now, you realize. But I don't want any more disruptions from Kyros. But tonight I'll have you, Thera, mark my words. I'll taste every part of you and bury myself to the hilt between—"

"Let's get on with it," she bravely answered, not wanting to hear any more of Pittheus' wretched ideas on how he planned to take her.

"That's the spirit," he replied and turned her toward the priest. Thera looked over her shoulder once more at Kyros. His face stone-like, he wiggled in the chair. He didn't even seem to be paying much attention to the ceremony, as his gaze was focused on his feet. She looked over to the old weaver, and though the woman couldn't see her, still, she gave Thera a reassuring smile. Thera shook her head and turned back to the priest as she was forced by Pittheus to say her vows. She barely remembered anything. Didn't even hear herself saying the words 'I do', but knew she must have said them, as Pittheus was smiling at her. A smile that gave her a pain in her stomach. She bent over, feeling the baby kicking within her. He objected to the wedding, she was sure, and didn't blame the child for wanting out.

"What's the matter with you?" Pittheus grabbed her shoulders and turned her to face the crowd. "My bride," he announced. "And your queen."

The crowd cheered, and Thera felt her mind spin. The pain came again and she could do nothing to stop it. She felt the hands of the old weaver helping her to sit on the steps of the dais.

"She's having contractions," the weaver told Pittheus. "The baby is trying to come out. She must sit down and rest now."

"Not now!" snapped Pittheus. "Not in the middle of my wedding."

"She can't help it," said the weaver as the pain subsided.

"Damn my brother for ruining my wedding night. His child will not ruin my plans."

Thera was afraid for Kyros and also afraid for the baby. The pain had passed and she had the weaver help her to her feet so Pittheus would not be angered more.

"I'm all right," she said. "I think I'll feel better once I have some food in my stomach."

"Bring on the food," ordered Pittheus and grabbed his wife and headed for the trestle table.

Wine and ale flowed abundantly at the meal, and Kyros was glad it did. He sat tied to the chair, trying to loosen his bonds but with little luck. He needed the dagger to cut through the ropes and he couldn't very well reach for it while his hands were tied. But the guard watching over him was now sitting down with some of his friends and eating as well. He was too close to risk trying to get the dagger, and Kyros was beginning to think he'd never get free.

His body ached from his wound; his stomach ached from hunger. His heart had the worse ache of all as he watched Thera sitting next to Pittheus eating the meal—now his brother's wife. He felt like a failure knowing he had been unable to stop the wedding. If he could have, he would have done anything in his power to keep it from happening. But he never had a choice. It was him against Pittheus and the rest of the castle. If only he'd had some help.

He wondered if he should have told the Centaurs to come after all. Maybe peace between the races wasn't as important as he and his father thought. Maybe his goals were all wrong and he should re-evaluate them. After all, where had peace gotten him so far? Beaten, humiliated and tied to the chair as a prisoner, while his bride and baby were given away to his evil brother.

"I brought him a bite to eat," came the weaver's voice. Kyros saw the guard nod his head and lose himself in a tankard of ale as the old woman came forth.

"I'm not hungry," Kyros told her as she broke off a piece of bread and held it up for him to eat.

"You're hungry for Thera, aren't you? Now eat this and be quiet so we can get that dagger out of your boot already."

Kyros understood now that the old woman was there to help him. He took the bite of bread into his mouth as the woman laid the plate on his lap. Next she bent over to pick up a goblet of wine, using it as cover as she slipped her nimble fingers into his boot and drew out the dagger. She slipped it under the trencher on his lap.

"She's married to someone else now," whispered the weaver.

"Don't remind me," said Kyros as he opened his mouth and she raised the goblet to his lips. His throat was parched and the wine felt good going down. He'd like to drink a barrel of it and drown himself in his sorrows.

"Not too much," she said and pulled it away. Some dribbled down his chin and onto his tunic. She picked up another piece of bread and dabbed his chin with it before putting it into his mouth. He marveled at how she knew exactly what to do when she couldn't even see. "You have to be sober so you can at least stop him from coupling with her tonight."

"I'll die before I let him touch her," he whispered back.

"Forget the heroics and do something about it," she crooned. "Cut yourself free when the guards are too drunk to notice."

"I will," said Kyros with a newfound strength. "Thank you, Weaver for your help."

"You could have had the Centaurs help you, but they're waiting for your signal. That boy king was the one to decide to wait, though the rest of them wanted to storm the castle."

"Nemos is king?"

"Phylo's son. You'll find out more later. Shall I tell them to come help you now?"

Kyros looked at Thera doubled over at the table and then at his brother drinking and laughing away as if nothing was wrong. The sword lay across the dais table and Kyros knew he had to somehow get it. If the Centaurs came in now, it would ruin everything. He still may have a chance to retrieve it on his own.

"No. Tell them not to come unless something happens to me. Then, you instruct them to storm the castle and do what it takes to rescue Thera and the baby. I have a feeling our baby is going to be a Centaur. It should be raised by Chiron."

"And what about Thera?" asked the woman. "Where would she go?"

Kyros looked down to his lap and shook his head. "If our baby is a Centaur … they won't have to worry about that. But by the grace of the gods, I hope she goes to the Elysian fields and not to Tartarus."

TWENTY-SIX

Minstrels struck up the music as the meal ended. People chose partners and took to the floor to dance. Thera, downright miserable and a bit nervous, felt Pittheus' lust for her body every time he looked at her over the brim of his raised tankard. She also couldn't help but notice the bulge under his tunic as he stood up to ask her to dance.

"I don't care to dance," she said and looked over to Kyros still bound to the chair. He looked upset, but she also felt something different in his gaze now. She felt a certain strength that hadn't been there earlier. She couldn't identify it, but it gave her a false hope of comfort. The contractions in her belly stopped for the time being. And although she welcomed the break from the pain, she'd almost wished they would start up again just so she didn't have to dance with Pittheus.

"Get up, Thera," he ordered her and she just sat there, looking at Kyros. "You're my wife now and will do as I command. Get to your feet and dance with me now."

Thera obeyed, just so he wouldn't think to hit her and harm the baby. He held out his arm and she laid her own hand atop it as he led her onto the floor. The crowd parted and one of the soldiers yelled, "Hail to the new king and queen of Trozen."

"Not yet," Thera reminded him and saw Pittheus reach for his waist. He weaved back to the dais, obviously having too much ale. He then picked up the sword and scabbard and fastened them around himself.

"Careless of me to leave the sword at the table. Thank you for reminding me with your words."

If she had known it was going to remind him of the sword, she wouldn't have said anything. Now with it fastened around his waist, Kyros would have no way of laying his hands on it. It was almost nightfall and his transformation would take place soon. If he was going to do something, why didn't he do it already?

Pittheus twirled Thera around and she thought she was going to be sick to her stomach. Her eyes focused once more on Kyros and she saw him jerking his head toward the corridor. What was he trying to tell her? She didn't understand any of this.

"Remove this damned shawl so I can see those big, beautiful breasts." Pittheus lowered the shawl from her shoulders and it hung again from the straps on her arms. He ran his cold hands over her bare shoulders and let them wander lower and lower to her cleavage. She jerked away but he only pulled her closer. The sword at his side was nothing compared to the one she felt pressed against her from under his tunic.

"I think it's time we go to our bedchamber, wife. I need to instruct you in your wifely duties."

"No!" Thera was terrified of being alone with him. Horrified of what he'd do to her in the bedchamber and how helpless she was to stop it.

"Yes!" cackled the crone's old voice beside her. "It is time to retire for the evening to the bedchamber. I'll take your bride and prepare her for you, my lord."

Pittheus gave a nod of approval and grabbed a tankard from the table and downed the contents. "Good, old woman. But make it fast as I'll be right behind you. I can wait no longer to sample what my wife has to offer."

Thera didn't understand. The old weaver was her friend and yet she was the one bringing her to the bedchamber so Pittheus could have his way with her. She passed Kyros sitting on the chair and paused. He looked at her but didn't say a word. No, *I love you, Thera.* No, *I'm sorry, Thera,* or *I'll rescue you somehow.* Instead he'd only given her a little smile. A smile she wanted more than anything to slap off his face.

"Come along, child," said the old weaver and led her up the stairs into the bedchamber that would seal the act of her becoming Pittheus' wife.

Kyros waited until Pittheus had followed Thera upstairs before he attempted his escape. The guard was too well into his cups to notice what Kyros was doing and with any luck wouldn't notice him missing for a while. Hopefully, long enough to give him time to steal the sword and stop Pittheus from coupling with Thera. Then, somehow they'd have to find a way to escape and make their way back to the Centaurs' village.

He held the dagger edge up between his knees and rubbed the ropes of his hands against it. It cut the rope in two and he quickly looked over at the guard to make sure he hadn't noticed. The guard had a whore on his lap and thankfully would be distracted for some time. Everyone was in the midst of merrymaking, and with the flow of the wine and ale, this was going to make his escape even easier.

He reached down and cut away the ropes at his feet and then the ones that held him to the chair. Hiding the dagger in his boot, he backed toward the corridor and ran up the stairs to Pittheus' bedchamber.

Thera broke down into hysterics when the old weaver closed the door to the bed chamber.

"How could you suggest he bring me here?" she asked. "And how could Kyros just sit there and do nothing to help me?"

"Hush, child and jump into bed. Pittheus is anxious and right behind us. We don't have much time to talk." She pushed Thera over to the bed and took the flowers from her hair and started to undo the braids.

"But Kyros—"

"Is doing all he can to help you," she assured her. "Now just do your part and keep Pittheus' attention off the door. Hopefully Kyros will use that dagger I gave him to cut himself free and get up here without the guards noticing."

"So he is coming for me?" she asked, feeling a new hope within her.

"If he can," she said as her nimble fingers undid the last braid and she picked up a brush from the bedside table. "Now just play your part and help him out."

Thera didn't really know what her part was, but didn't have time to ask, as the door banged open and Pittheus walked in with two of his men right behind him.

"Part your legs wife, as I'm bigger than a bull and hotter than the fires of Tartarus."

"She's not ready yet," said the weaver as she ran the brush slowly through Thera's hair. "And what about those other two?" she asked, somehow knowing two men entered with him.

"It's the custom to watch the lord on his wedding night," blurted out one while the other one snickered.

Thera was horrified to think she'd have an audience when Pittheus claimed his husbandly rights. She looked at the old weaver who was taking her time brushing her hair. She wished the woman could see her so she'd see the fear in her eyes and do something to help her.

"It may be awkward mounting her as you must remember she's heavy with child," reminded the weaver. "Not that your lordship would have any problems being pleased, but I just thought you'd want your privacy since this is a new experience to you as well as to Thera."

"Oh." Pittheus rubbed his chin and looked over to his guards. Thera hoped his pride would get the best of him, not wanting to let his men see him fumbling with such a pregnant woman. "You two can stand outside the door. Watch and make certain no one interrupts me."

Thera could see they were obviously upset by not getting to witness the coupling act.

"But Lord Pittheus—"

"Go!" he bellowed. "You'll be able to hear our mating sounds from the doorway. I'll be sure to leave it open a crack. That should satisfy you and you can still be a witness to the act that we're truly man and wife."

The guards seemed to be satisfied with that and took their places outside the door.

"Out of my way, old woman. Make yourself scarce as I have an aching need to itch."

The weaver laid the hairbrush down on the bedside table and slowly made her way to the door. "Be gentle with her," she warned him. "Any sharp movements can bring about more contractions and the birth of that baby."

"I don't care about the baby," he grumbled. "I'll have my way with my wife, baby or not."

Thera lay fully clothed on the bed as Pittheus pushed the old weaver out into the corridor and left the door ajar. Thera could see the guards peeking in and felt a wave of heat and nausea hit her. Pittheus stood at the foot of the bed and unfastened the scabbard, letting the sword clank to the floor. Thera knew Kyros would never treat the weapon with such disrespect, and knew Pittheus had no business being king of Trozen.

He slipped out of his sandals and let his tunic wrap fall to the ground. The guards stood in the doorway, not guarding at all, but waiting for the show to begin. Thera gasped as she viewed Pittheus' naked body and his fully stretched manhood that was already making her insides ache. She pushed herself up on the bed and tried to back away as he came closer.

"I guess you like what you see," he sneered, "as you can't seem to keep your eyes above my waist."

She heard a small thud from the doorway and noticed the guards no longer peered in. She could only hope it was Kyros come to rescue her, and now she had to play her part as the weaver suggested. Pittheus lowered himself atop her on the bed and reached to her bodice.

"Wait!" cried Thera, wondering herself what she was going to say.

"What is it?" asked Pittheus. "I don't like to have to wait for what is mine."

"I … I just thought it would be more private if we drew the drapes around the bed." She wiggled out from under him and pulled the heavy velvet drapes around them, blocking Pittheus' view of the door. Hopefully that would give Kyros an advantage. The sword still lay on the floor at the foot of the bed and he'd be able to get it without Pittheus seeing him now.

"I like that," said Pittheus and snuggled with ale breath close to her ear. "I like a wife who wants to be alone—all alone with her husband."

Thera knew that was true, but not with him. She'd love being alone with her husband if her husband was Kyros. It disgusted her to be so close to this wretched man. But she only did it for Kyros and their baby. She tried to put her own fear aside as she did nothing to stop him from kissing her mouth.

"I'm going to have you now," he announced and pushed her to the bed and mounted himself atop her. Thera's mind screamed out but still she said nothing. He pushed up her tunic wrap and was about to enter her when she stopped him.

"Wait!" she called once again, and he looked up at her with angry eyes.

"What now, wife!" He was running out of patience and Thera was running out of excuses to stall him.

"I … I just thought you'd want to take pleasures in the rest of me before you thrust yourself within me." She lowered the top of her tunic wrap and Pittheus forgot about what dangled between his legs for a moment as he reached out to touch her.

Thera closed her eyes and bit her tongue from crying out. Where was Kyros? Why wasn't he stepping in to stop this? Had she made a mistake thinking he lurked out in the hallway? By the gods, she hoped not, for she didn't know how much longer she could take Pittheus fondling her like this.

Kyros had no trouble knocking out the two guards at the door to the bedchamber with an iron candleholder he'd grabbed along the way. After all, they had been so engrossed in what was going on inside the room, not to mention their busy hands under their own tunics that they'd never even seen him coming. He stepped over their prone bodies and entered the room silently.

The bed curtains were closed and he could hear Thera's voice offering her body to Pittheus. Had he heard wrong? Was she really offering herself to him of her own will instead of fighting him off like he'd expected?

He noticed his father's sword lying on the floor at the foot of the bed. His eyes swept the room before he rushed over to pick it up. He was glad the bed curtains were closed so Pittheus had no idea of what he was doing. He strapped on the scabbard as he heard Thera's delighted little moan of pleasure.

His heart sank in his chest at the thought that someone besides himself could pleasure her like he could. He wanted to rip open the curtains and kill his brother, but then again he felt he had no business doing that if Thera indeed enjoyed and wanted her now rightful husband.

He heard his brother make a comment about her breasts and then he heard her heavy breathing. He couldn't help himself. As much as he respected Thera, he wouldn't let his brother have her, even if it was what she wanted.

He raised the sword to his shoulder and ripped open the curtain. Thera had her hands on her belly as she lay there naked and Kyros realized he'd mistaken her heavy breathing and moan of pleasure for labor pains.

Her eyes met his and she cried out.

"Kyros!"

Pittheus removed his hands from her breasts and swung around. He was naked and weaponless and it would be so easy to kill him at that moment. Kyros had his father's sword and knew one swipe would end his brother's life. He reached out with the tip and pressed it under Pittheus' chin.

"Brother!" Pittheus exclaimed. "What a surprise."

"I bet it is, Pittheus. But then again, you were the one to invite me. Or did you mean to invite me only to the wedding? I should kill you right now for what you've done to Thera."

"I haven't even entered her yet, to my regret," answered Pittheus.

Thera was married to him but the marriage was not yet consummated. He'd gotten there in time after all.

"Kyros!" Thera called again as she had another contraction. The split second Kyros let his eyes leave Pittheus, his brother pushed aside the sword and leapt from the bed.

"Guards!" called Pittheus, but no one came.

"They won't be able to join us for awhile," Kyros told him. "I've taken care of them, and you're next on my list, brother."

"You wouldn't do that. You couldn't take my life and you know it." Pittheus made his way around the other side of the bed as he spoke.

Kyros knew he was right. As much as he hated his brother and everything he'd done to him and Thera, everything he stood for, he still couldn't kill him. He'd been raised differently by his father, King Mezentius. He couldn't kill Pittheus—his father's flesh and blood with his own sword. Pittheus was part of him, and of his father as well. Just as the baby inside Thera was a part of both of them. And he prayed that his own child would someday feel the same way about him.

Kyros followed his brother around the bed, his sword outstretched in a threat. He couldn't stand the thought of not comforting Thera who lay naked upon the bed and in pain from the baby, but he just couldn't go to her yet.

"Thera," he spoke but kept his eyes on Pittheus. "Get dressed. Hurry. We've got to get out of here."

Thera was still moaning and clutched over in pain. "I don't think I can, Kyros."

"You can do it, sweetheart. Do it for me. Do it for us. This may be our only chance to escape—and with the sword."

Pittheus chuckled a little as he backed toward the window. "You don't really think you're going to escape and get away with this, do you little brother? After all, you're taking my wife, remember. My men won't just let you walk out of here with her."

Kyros knew this was true. He hadn't yet figured how to make it past the soldiers in the great hall, not to mention the ones that guarded the gate. But still he had to try. He had to take his father's sword and Thera and get out of there fast.

"I'm ready," came Thera's voice from behind him. Kyros could see her from the corner of his eye. She was dressed in her wedding outfit and had the ugly shawl wrapped around her tight as if it were a means of protection. She was standing upright and Kyros realized the labor pains must have subsided for now.

Kyros' eyes scanned the room but he couldn't find anything to use to tie up Pittheus. Then he noticed the string hanging from Thera's shawl. "Give me your shawl, Thera."

She looked at him wide-eyed and clutched it even closer. "Why?"

"I need it to tie up Pittheus. I have nothing else to use."

"Why don't you just kill him?" came her venomous words. "Or if you won't do it, give me the damned sword and I'll do it for you. I'll cut off his head and stick it on a spike and put it on display in front of his own castle."

Kyros couldn't believe his ears. Thera was starting to sound more and more like her father, Ares, every day. He thought he knew her, but this was a war-like side of her he didn't know. He wasn't sure if he liked it.

"No need to bother with that, dear wife." Pittheus smiled and hoisted himself onto the window ledge. He then leaned backwards and fell from sight.

"Pittheus!" Kyros ran to the window, not believing that his brother took his own life. He leaned out and looked to the ground below expecting to see him splattered on the stones of the walkway. Instead, he saw Pittheus' naked back end as he climbed out of a wagon of hay.

"Damn." Kyros ran his hand through his hair. Thera rushed up behind him and saw what was happening.

"Maybe we can escape this way also." She had one foot on the ledge when Kyros grabbed her arm and stopped her.

"What are you thinking? I may survive the jump, but if you jump our baby will be harmed or killed for sure, not to mention yourself. We can't do it, Thera. We'll just have to find another way."

"Then you go," she said. "Save yourself, Kyros. Forget about me." Another labor pain hit her and she gripped Kyros' arm for support.

Kyros looked back out the window and saw Pittheus running stark naked to the drawbridge. Obviously to tell his men to seal it off so there'd be no chance for Kyros and Thera to escape. He felt a pain of his own this time and realized the sky was darkening as nightfall set in.

"Damn," he said aloud and Thera breathed away her own pain and noticed the sky out the window.

"Kyros, what are we going to do?"

"Well, we're not going to stand here any longer. Come on." He grabbed her hand and headed for the door. They stepped over the guards that still lay unconscious in the corridor.

"You?" Thera looked at the guards and then at Kyros.

"Me," he answered.

"Why couldn't you kill Pittheus?" she wondered. "Especially after what he's done to you?"

"He's my brother, Thera. I can't take the life of my own kin no matter how evil he is."

Thera nodded, although she truly didn't understand Kyros' thinking. Pittheus deserved to die. He'd humiliated the Centaurs, tortured and shamed Kyros in front of everyone and took her as his bride. He'd even threatened to kill Kyros, his own brother, yet Kyros wouldn't take Pittheus' life. She felt the rage and also the sadness within him. She felt a bit of honor, respect or love for his family name. He must want peace between him and his brother as much as he wanted peace between the Trozen and Centaur races.

Here was a man who stood for what he believed. He had ideals and beliefs she'd never seen on Mount Olympus. Her own mother and father didn't want anything to do with her. Her own sister, Harmonia, couldn't care less if she lived or died. If only the strength and honor of Kyros could be imbedded in the gods; then, what gods they would truly be.

Thera gripped Kyros' hand tightly as she picked up her gown and ran quickly down the steep steps with him. She felt his anguish and his body tremble and knew his transformation was coming and there was nothing they could do to stop it. They were half way down the steps when Kyros let go of her hand and doubled over in pain. It set him off balance and he tumbled head over heels down the remaining steps to the ground below. His sword fell from his hand and clattered on the stairs loudly in the process.

Thera rushed to Kyros' side, his body trembling and curled in a ball at the bottom of the steps. He was still breathing and it didn't look as if any of his bones were broken, and she sighed in relief. She watched his eyes swell out and his face contort while a sweat broke out on his brow. He managed to unfasten the scabbard from his waist and pushed it into her hand.

"Thera, take this and the sword and get out of here before Pittheus comes back with his men."

She looked at him and shook her head. She felt so helpless. He had no care for his own life. Pittheus was sure to kill him now, no matter of any deal he'd made with her. If she left him now, it may just be the last time she ever saw him alive. He risked his life to save her, and she'd burn in Tartarus before she left him alone at such a vulnerable time like this.

"I can't, Kyros. I won't leave you like this."

His teeth chattered, and she could tell he was losing his patience by the way his lips curled back when he spoke.

"Do it, damn it! Get the sword to Chiron. Tell him to hide it and never let it get into the hands of my brother."

"But what about you, Kyros? What's going to happen to you? To us?"

He was silent for a moment and Thera could feel the grief that swept through him. He did still love her and their baby. He wanted to be with them more than anything, but he didn't want to endanger her by telling her to wait for him.

"I'll catch up with you as soon as I transform. I can travel faster as a Centaur. I'll find you and give you a ride. Together we'll take the sword to Chiron. Now go fast, as I hear someone coming."

Thera heard the footsteps as well, and the shouting voices of the guards as they came closer. She grabbed the sword and placed it into the scabbard. She then turn and ran down an opposite hall. She stopped when she was around a corner safely, and looked back to see Kyros shifting into his Centaur form. The guard who was assigned to watch him ran up. Pittheus was right behind him, fastening a robe around himself.

"I can't leave him," she spoke softly to herself. The baby kicked and she felt another pain coming on. She gripped her stomach and almost dropped the sword. The noise of it falling would have given away her hiding place.

"Give me the sword, Thera." It was the blind old weaver suddenly standing next to her with her hand outstretched. "I'll get it to Chiron for you. You're in no condition to try to escape. Plus you want to stay with him, so go to him where you belong."

"But ... but how will you get the sword out of here?" Thera thought it highly impossible for a blind woman to try to smuggle the sword past Pittheus if she couldn't even do it.

"I'll manage," smiled the woman and somehow Thera believed her. She handed the old weaver the sword and scabbard and thanked her for helping, hoping she could trust that the sword would end up with Chiron and not back in Pittheus' hands.

"Don't thank me," said the weaver. "I'm only doing what I should. Now get over to Kyros and comfort him. You'll have the chance to save him later."

"I will?" she asked. "How do you know this if you're not a seer?"

"Just keep the shawl with you, as you'll need it. And when the time is right, you'll find Artemis' golden bow and arrows hidden on the wall behind the tapestry in Pittheus' bedchamber."

Thera winced and closed her eyes with the next contraction. And when she opened them, the old woman was gone.

"There she is," shouted one of Pittheus' men. Pittheus himself came to get her.

"How dare you turn against me, wife. I'll have you punished for this."

He reached out and slapped her across the face, the blow sending her into the wall.

"Don't touch her!" Kyros got to all four feet, wobbling, and made his way over to Pittheus. "She's not your wife. She's mine. Now leave her alone." He reached out and grabbed Pittheus around the neck. In a choking voice, Pittheus called for his soldiers.

"Grab him, you idiots. He's twice as strong when he's a Centaur. Get him off of me."

Thera's pain passed and she stood upright, watching Kyros be seized. She loved him so much it hurt. He'd called her his wife, though they all knew it wasn't so. But she wished in her heart she was his wife instead of Pittheus'.

Kyros used his back legs to horse-kick several of the guards. They went sailing across the corridor and with Pittheus' bellow, even more soldiers came to his aid. They had a rope lassoed over Kyros' body as if he were some kind of wild animal. Her heart just about broke when she saw them beating him. Then she noticed his wound had re-opened and blood trickled down his chest.

"Leave him alone already," she cried. "Stop hurting him."

"Where's the sword?" Pittheus growled at Kyros. "What did you do with the sword?"

When Kyros didn't answer, Pittheus himself gave a blow to Kyros' head. Kyros obviously hadn't his clear vision yet, for he did nothing to dodge it.

"He doesn't have it." Thera stepped in between Kyros and Pittheus. "I have it, but you'll never get it, as it's safely out of the castle now."

"Thera!" warned Kyros. "Don't tell him anything."

"What did you do with it?" Pittheus grabbed her arm tightly and she cried out in pain.

"I have an ally who helped me," she admitted. "By now the sword is safe in the hands of Chiron."

When she'd said the Centaur's name she knew she'd made a grave mistake. Kyros' face clouded over and he shook his head defeatedly. She never should have told him where to find it; yet, she was only trying to get him to stop hitting Kyros.

"Why thank you, wife, for telling me who to kill next to get it. And now, maybe you'll tell me who your ally is so I can have him hanged for betraying me."

"She doesn't have any friends," said the guard who'd been assigned to watch Kyros in the hall.

"Shut up, Ercole," Pittheus snapped at the guard. "This is all your fault that Kyros escaped in the first place. You were supposed to guard him at the wedding party. You will now pay as well as him for ruining my wedding."

"But sir—"

"Take Kyros and Ercole to the labyrinth," Pittheus ordered his men.

"Lord Pittheus," spoke Ercole. "You don't mean to leave me in the labyrinth as food for Demogorgan? This is not just punishment for what I did."

"I'll decide what's just and what's not. Demogorgan hasn't eaten yet today. You take Kyros blindfolded into the heart of the labyrinth and leave him there. The beast will find him. If you find your own way out, then I'll let you live."

"But sir, no one knows the way out of the labyrinth but you. No one has been able to find their way out yet."

Pittheus laughed and waved his hand for his men to take them away. "Then if you make it, you'll be the first, I guess. Won't you?"

Kyros focused on Thera this time and she knew he had his eyesight back. "I love you, Thera," he said for all to hear and she wanted to say she loved him back, but couldn't find the strength to speak.

"Get him out of here," yelled Pittheus and took hold of Thera's hand and dragged her after him into the great hall. The hall was almost empty of the merrymakers from the wedding, and only some of Pittheus' soldiers and half a dozen servants cleaning up remained.

"Wench, bring me ale. Lots of it," he bellowed and sat at the fire and pulled Thera onto his lap. Thera knew he'd already drank too much at their wedding and couldn't believe he was still sober enough to down more. "I don't like having my wedding ruined like this." The buxom wench came with a pitcher of ale and also a tankard on a tray. He grabbed the pitcher and bringing it to his mouth, chugged half of it. "Bring me another pitcher," he ordered.

"Yes, my lord," the wench curtseyed and gave a full view of her nearly naked breasts that were trussed up much like Thera's.

"Wait! Come here," he ordered and the wench did so. He grabbed a hold of the bodice of her dress and pulled her into his face. He buried his head in her cleavage and ran his tongue up her chest. The wench giggled. "I'll expect you in my chambers later. Right after I've had enough of my wife."

"Yes, my lord. Anything you say." She then hurried off to get more ale.

Thera's stomach turned in disgust. She was glad it was the wench he was tasting instead of herself, but she knew it was only a matter of time before he brought her back up to bed and had his fill of her. And Kyros wouldn't be there to save her this time. And neither would the weaver, as she would probably spend the rest of the night making her way to the Centaur village—if she ever got there at all.

"So who's this ally who helped you, Thera?"

She jumped a little at his words and hoped she wasn't thinking too loud. She tried to get up off his lap but he pulled her back down.

"Oh, never mind," he said. "It doesn't matter, since you told me where to find the sword. Now I'll have it back by the morrow and just in time to be king."

Thera's gut wrenched at the thought. She knew it would be so, unless she could do something to help Kyros.

"So, where is this labyrinth you spoke of?" she asked.

He raised the pitcher and chugged the rest of the contents. "Slick little thing you are, trying to find out so you can go and help Kyros."

"I'm just trying to make conversation," she tried to convince him.

"Well, then I can tell you that I had Daedalus the inventor make the labyrinth for me. He's sworn to secrecy with his life of the way out of the maze. I, and only I, know the way out. And to make the story even sweeter, I house my new pet there."

"Demogorgan?" she asked, repeating the name she'd heard earlier.

He chuckled and accepted the new pitcher of ale the wench brought him. He then slapped the woman on her rump before bringing his attention back to Thera.

"Yes. Demogorgan is the offspring of Hades' pet Cerberus."

"The three-headed monster-dog that guards the gates of Tartarus?" she asked.

"Oh, so you've heard of it."

"I have. Uncle Hades loves that wretched thing almost as much as Ares loved his raven."

"It is our wedding present from him," he told her, his eyes half closing as he spoke. "He gave it to me as soon as he heard Ares gave me your hand in marriage."

"What a thoughtful gift," she murmured and held the pitcher to his lips for him to drink more. She could see he was highly intoxicated and about ready to pass out. Still, she needed more information before he did.

"So, what does Demogorgan eat?" She'd already figured this out, but had to keep him talking.

"He eats one human a day. But tonight is special. Tonight I've sent him two, since it's my wedding night."

"And does he like his new surroundings?"

"He does. The underground surroundings are nice and dark just like Tartarus, so it's almost like home to him."

Great, she thought. Now, at least she knew where to find the labyrinth. It was somewhere in the bowels of the castle. It had to be somewhere close to the dungeon. She thought of poor Kyros and the fate that would befall him if she didn't do something to help him escape. She jumped off of Pittheus' lap, knowing what she had to do next.

"I'm going to bed," she announced.

The look of surprise on Pittheus' face was amusing. "Let's go," he said and got to his feet. Thera watched the pitcher waver in his hand and then crash to the ground. Pittheus followed it as he collapsed into a drunken slumber. Thera looked around, but no one seemed to pay much attention to her. The serving wench walked up with another pitcher of ale.

"Will he be needing this, my queen?"

"Oh, yes, I do believe so." She grabbed the pitcher and emptied the contents onto his head. He snored and didn't move. "I think that will be all for now." She replaced the pitcher on the tray and wiped her hands in her wedding dress. "I'll be going to our bedchamber now and I don't want anyone bothering me for the rest of the night."

"As you wish, my lady." The serving wench curtseyed and Thera took off at a fast pace for the stairs. She knew exactly what she had to do now, and with a new-found strength she knew she'd have half a chance of carrying it through.

TWENTY-SEVEN

Kyros was led blindfolded into the middle of the labyrinth. Ercole nervously led him there, taking most of the night to find the right way.

"Here we are," he snarled and removed Kyros' blindfold. He took the rope that bound his hands and tied it to a metal post that stood dead center in the room.

Kyros looked around his surroundings. It was dark except for the torch that Ercole held in his hand. Shadows shuddered off the stone walls of the maze and he could hear a low sort of growling getting louder and louder.

"It's Demogorgan." Ercole whispered this time. "I forgot. He can't see or smell worth a damn but he's got ears sharper than my sword. He must have heard us coming. I'm getting out of here."

"Wait!" Kyros whispered back. "Take me with you. I'll help you and we can both escape Pittheus and his plans for us."

The growl got louder and now they could hear the beast's footsteps as it came closer. Ercole took the torch and shone it around the cubicle, his eyes wide with fright and his breathing labored.

The beast came closer and Kyros could even smell it now. He glimpsed its rugged fur as it passed by them in an adjoining corridor.

"No!" screamed the guard. "No!"

"Shh," whispered Kyros. "You're telling him right where we are."

The beast turned its head toward them, saliva dripping out of its mouth, its breath foul and revolting. Its head was huge, but then so were its teeth—all three rows of them. The two bottom rows overlapped and sharp incisors stuck out from the sides of its mouth. It had small, beady eyes that glowed a strange shade of orange-yellow, and tall, pointy ears that were three times too big for its body. Smoke came out of its nose every time it took a breath. Its arms were small, but it had many, and each had talon-like claws that looked sharper then his own sword. It was a disgusting creature, and the stench from its body was wretched as well. Kyros' tail swished nervously and he willed it to stop before the beast heard him with those keen ears.

The guard dropped the torch and backed into the wall, screaming even louder as he did so. Demogorgan approached Ercole, a claw-like paw outstretched and grabbed him, bringing him closer to inspect him. Kyros squinted and turned his head as the beast devoured the screaming guard whole. His stomach lurched and his body shook. He felt so helpless to save the man from the beast. So helpless indeed.

Kyros was alone now with this monster and knew he'd be consumed next. And he could do nothing at all to escape it. Nothing to defend himself from his attacker. The beast turned its head as if to look at Kyros and then cocked it as if listening.

Kyros held his breath and prayed his tail wouldn't swish. The thing obviously didn't see him or smell him but was trying to hear if someone else was there.

Satisfied that the guard must have been alone, Demogorgan lay down on the floor and closed its eyes. Kyros figured it had a full belly and would sleep for now. But when it awoke it would be hungry again, and he was sure to be its next meal.

Kyros had to work fast. He was standing in the same room of a beast that would consume him if he couldn't get away first. He knew morning was going to be there soon and he also knew he'd have to wait until he was in human form before he tried to do anything. If he tried to sneak around now, his hooves would echo off the cobblestone and give his presence away. No, he'd just have to wait until he transformed and then sneak away on bare feet.

Kyros tried to breathe quietly and realized his own fear had him panting. He knew he would have to sleep in order to stay as quiet as possible and to keep his tail from swishing. He'd just close his eyes for awhile until his transformation took place. And by the gods, he hoped he had the strength not to scream with the pain it would cause him.

Thera made her way up to the bedchamber, thankful that the guards were no longer in the corridor as she entered. She remembered the old weaver's words and rushed over to the tapestry hanging on the wall. Sure enough, the golden bow and arrows were hanging on the wall hidden behind it.

She had no idea how the old weaver knew where to find it, but was thankful to be holding a weapon once again in her hands. She liked the way it felt in her hands. Power. Strength. Confidence. She almost understood for a split second how her father must feel when he started up a war.

She shook the thought from her head and strapped the quiver of arrows beneath her shawl on her back. She then held the bow flat against her, with her huge stomach sticking out in between the wood and the bowstring.

"This'll never do. How am I ever going to hide this bow?"

She looked around the room and found a cloak hanging by a nail from the wall. It was an ornate type of cloak, dark blue with intricate designs woven through it in gold. It was majestic, and somehow she knew it wasn't Pittheus'.

She threw the cloak around her and pulled the hood up over her head. This would be a little better in trying to hide the bow and arrows. And hopefully most of the castle's occupants would be sleeping about now as it was well into the night. She had her hand on the door handle when another pain wracked her body. The baby was feeling heavier and heavier; her own body ached and was in need of some sleep. She gritted her teeth and breathed her way through the pain. It was more intense now and she knew the baby would be born at any time.

She wished for someone to go through this with her. She wished for the old weaver by her side, and Kyros there to guide her. Unfortunately she had neither of them. But by morning she would have Pittheus trying to mount her even though she was in the midst of giving birth. This may be her last chance to save Kyros. And if it was the last thing she did before she died, she would see to it.

She pushed the thought from her mind, bit back the nausea that threatened to overtake her, and headed out the door to find the labyrinth. She put her hand on her stomach to calm the baby.

"Don't worry, baby," she whispered. "I'll get you to your father before I die."

It took Thera a bit longer to find the labyrinth than she'd hoped. By the time she'd managed to sneak past all the guards and then by the time she found her way through the dark dungeon, she was sure it must have been almost morning. She wondered if the old weaver made it safely with the sword to Chiron. And she prayed Kyros was in the labyrinth still alive.

She reached the entrance to the labyrinth and thanked the gods that the guard sitting watch at the door was sound asleep. She tip-toed past him, holding the bow awkwardly in front of her and trying not to trip on the long cloak that pooled around her feet.

She opened the wooden door to the labyrinth slowly, hearing the creak louder than it probably really was, and hoping the guard hadn't heard it as well. She held her breath and looked back at him, thankful to see his head still resting against his chest and to hear his loud snoring.

She slipped inside and closed the door behind her. It was dark inside the labyrinth. Very dark. There were no torches lit anywhere and she now wondered if she should have grabbed the one off the wall by the guard. But if he awakened, he'd notice the torch was gone and she'd give herself away. Plus, she couldn't risk opening the creaky door again to go back and get it.

Instead, she took a deep breath and tried to calm herself. Her keen senses smelled some sort of wild beast, mixed with the scant scent of Centaur and the strong scent of fear. Not only her own fear, or Kyros' fear, but the fear of another. The fear that somehow seemed strong, but muffled. Like perhaps the fear of a dead man inside the belly of Demogorgan.

She shivered in the cold room and hoped—prayed—it wasn't Kyros who'd been eaten. She hoped she wasn't too late to save him, and that she could somehow find him before the beast did.

She took a few steps into the labyrinth, feeling her way along the cold, stone walls. Then the thought struck her, that even if she did find Kyros alive and manage to help him escape the beast, they'd probably never find their way back out of the maze.

She needed something that would lead her back to the entrance. She needed to drop bread crumbs or something to leave a trail. It was then that the old weaver's words came to her mind. She'd said Thera would need to use the shawl. She also said, by pulling on the loose string, the whole shawl would unravel.

She felt underneath her cloak for the shawl. Holding the bow under her arm, she grabbed the loose string and pulled. Sure enough, the thing unraveled, leaving her with a long lead. This would work. This would be how she'd find their way back out of the labyrinth. She tied the end to the door latch.

Thera unraveled the shawl as she walked, letting the string fall to the floor to hopefully guide her way back to the entrance. She had no idea where she was going, but used her senses to guide her way. Although she couldn't see much, her eyes eventually became accustomed to the dark. And her eyesight was ten fold of any human's since Zeus let her keep her power of the senses. She could make out the outline of the walls, and also she could hear the sound of the beast snoring.

She followed her ears, not to mention the strong smell that was coming from the right corridor. Unraveling the string as she made her way into the depths of the labyrinth, she couldn't help but wonder what she'd do if Kyros was indeed already dead. She couldn't live with Pittheus the rest of her mortal days. She wouldn't. Kyros had to be alive. This all just had to somehow work out, though she had no idea of how it would.

The baby kicked within her and she stopped in her tracks. Something was different with this pain. The weight of the child had shifted lower and she felt a surge of liquid beneath her robe. She remembered the time she'd gone with Persephone to witness the birth of a human baby. She remembered that the mother felt this way just before she delivered. The pain intensified and Thera did all she could to keep from crying out.

Why did this have to be happening now? She didn't have time for the birth of a baby just yet. She had to get to Kyros first. This would just have to wait. She pressed on, though the pain was becoming more and more severe with each step she took. She had no idea how much longer she'd be able to stay on her feet. And she could only hope she'd find the center of the labyrinth and Kyros before she fell to the ground helpless to birth their child.

"Kyros," she closed her eyes and whispered. "Kyros, please be alive. Please."

Kyros awoke from a deep sleep by a dream of Thera calling for him. She was about to birth their baby and she wanted him by her side. He shook his head and looked around, suddenly remembering exactly where he was and what was about to happen. He was still in Centaur form and still had his hands tied together, and the rope was tied to a pole in the center of the room.

Demogorgan lay sleeping a short distance from him, and he couldn't help but hear in his mind the awful cries of the guard as he was devoured. Kyros knew he could wait no longer to try to escape. He'd just have to risk the beast hearing him. He had to get to Thera. He was sure she needed him.

He moved his hooves as silently as possible toward the pole that kept him prisoner. He carefully used his fingers to untie the rope that held him there. He looked over his shoulder and was thankful the beast still hadn't heard him. He then spotted the torch on the ground, somehow still burning from the night before. Only it was a bit too close to the mouth of the beast. Still, he knew he needed to use it to get the ropes off his wrists. With his hands tied together he'd never even have a chance of fighting off the beast.

He took a step and his tail swished in anticipation. The beast stirred. Kyros stopped in his tracks and held his breath. When the thing rolled over and went back to sleep, he continued. He made it to the torch and held the ropes above the flame. The burning rope made an odor and he was glad the beast didn't have a good sense of smell. He gritted his teeth at the pain that burned at the edges of his wrists.

When the ropes were burned away enough for Kyros to work them, he pulled his wrists from the fire before they were burned further. He was wiggling out of his bondage when he heard a noise from the corridor. Then he saw her. Thera was standing there, doubled over, looking scared and in more pain than he'd ever seen her in before. Her hand was on her belly and she looked as if she were ready to pass out.

"Kyros, help me." She reached out her hand to him. Kyros put his finger to his mouth to silence her, but it was too late. Demogorgan had heard her as well. The beast opened its eyes, seeing Thera and got to its feet.

She first noticed it and screamed a blood curling scream, much like the one the guard had given just before he was eaten.

"Thera, get out of here!" Kyros threw the ropes from his wrists, just as the beast heard him and turned to find the second person in its lair. Kyros picked up the burning torch and held it out as the beast reached for him. Thera screamed when she saw what was happening.

The beast turned back to her, and Kyros realized if he was to save Thera, he'd have to get the beast's attention off of her.

"Thera, be quiet. The beast is attracted to sound."

Demogorgan growled, and when it did, fire sprang from its lips. Kyros side-stepped it barely, and horse kicked the beast as it tried to get him. He galloped over to Thera and ordered her to get on his back.

"I have the bow and arrows," she told him as she pulled the bow from beneath her cape.

"Good girl," he answered and grabbed it from her. He grabbed an arrow and used it on the beast. The beast screamed and retreated to lick its wound.

"That'll slow it down for awhile." Kyros tried to help Thera get onto his back, but it was awkward and he knew she was in much pain. "We've got to try, Thera. We've got to get out of here."

"I can't," she cried. Tears flowed from her eyes as she clutched her belly and fell to the floor. "Go on without me. Save yourself, Kyros."

Kyros noticed Demogorgan coming for them again and grabbed another arrow from the quiver on Thera's back and shot at the beast. It screamed, madder than ever.

Kyros reached down and pulled Thera to her feet. He picked her up in his arms, as he still held on to the bow. He wouldn't be able to fight off the beast this way, but at least he'd get Thera out of the line of danger.

Just as he moved with Thera, the beast shot fire at them once again.

"Follow the string," Thera mumbled. "I've marked the way."

Kyros looked down and saw a string coming from Thera's never ending ugly shawl. He then realized what she'd done.

"You're wonderful, Thera. I love you."

He did the best he could with his poor Centaur eyesight to follow the string through the passageway. He'd had to leave the torch behind when he decided to pick up Thera, but the fire from the beast was lighting up the passageway enough for him to see.

Thera cried out in pain again, and the beast heard them and followed.

"Thera, you've got to try to be quiet," explained Kyros. "I know it's hard, sweetheart, but the beast hunts by sound."

"I'll try," said Thera and buried her face into his shoulder in order to keep quiet.

Kyros got far enough away that he felt he could stop for a moment. He was starting to feel pains of his own and knew his transformation was about to begin. He didn't want to drop Thera or the baby when it happened.

He put her on her feet and adjusted the bow on his shoulder. He grabbed Thera's face in his hands and raised her tear-stained cheeks to look at her. He could barely see her, but still, he knew she was beautiful.

"I love you, Thera. No matter what happens, I want you to know that." He kissed her on the forehead as he spoke.

"And I love you, Kyros. I'm sorry for all the mistakes I've made. I just wish things could be different. I wish we could be together—"

"Shh." Kyros tried to quiet her, as he heard the beast's footsteps again and knew that it had heard them as well. "We'll talk later, Thera," he whispered. She nodded her head and he felt a pain in his heart. A pain that said he wasn't really sure if there would be a later for them.

Thera winced, and Kyros helped her over to the wall to sit down. There was no way he would get her on his back in her condition. Plus, he knew his transformation was coming. He felt his own changes as he doubled over for a second and then stood back up. The bow was still on his shoulder, but Thera had the arrows. He knew the beast was coming nearer, but he also felt a shiver go through him as he felt another presence in the labyrinth. One he somehow knew was even more dangerous than the beast.

"What a lovely sight." Pittheus' voice came from behind him, and Kyros turned around, his Centaur body already writhing in pain.

"Pittheus." Kyros' voice was quiet, but Pittheus made no motion to silence his. He'd obviously had too much to drink and was forgetting his pet hunted by sound.

"I want my wife back," said Pittheus taking a step closer, sword in one hand, torch in the other. Kyros realized the sword he held was not their father's. This meant he hadn't yet found the sword. This was good news indeed.

"She's not your wife, Pittheus. Although the ceremony was completed, the marriage was never consummated."

"Well, I'm going to see about that as soon as I get rid of you, Kyros." He took a drunken step forward.

Kyros' body stiffened as his transformation began. He took the bow from his shoulder knowing it would do him no good now. He slid it on the floor over to Thera. She was curled in a ball and crying softly.

"Well, brother, I guess this is the end," said Pittheus.

Kyros bit his lip and couldn't help but fall to the floor. His body shook and his voice came out shaky. "I'm the most vulnerable when I transform. But then again, I'm sure you know that. I can't do anything to defend myself now. Go ahead and kill me, brother, but just please take good care of Thera."

"Kyros, no!" Thera cried from the floor and reached out her hand to him. He grabbed her hand as he started his transformation. Kyros could see Pittheus with raised sword, standing above him. Why didn't he just bring it down and kill him? What was he waiting for?

"You two really do love each other, don't you?" asked Pittheus.

Kyros couldn't answer him, as his teeth were chattering and his muscles were too cramped to move. Thera didn't answer him either.

Pittheus took a step forward and Kyros closed his eyes, awaiting his death. When it didn't come, his eyes opened and he saw Pittheus lowering the sword before him.

"It's a touching scene, you two," said Pittheus. "Almost touching enough to make me want to spare your life."

Kyros thought for a moment Pittheus had found a bit of goodness inside himself after all, a goodness that maybe stemmed from the love of their father.

"But I can't do that now, can I?" said Pittheus, raising his sword again for the final blow. "Please forgive me, brother, for what I must do."

Kyros was transforming, and totally vulnerable. All he could do was wait for his own death. He knew he had every right to hate his brother for all he'd done, but somehow he couldn't. Pittheus was his brother, he had to forgive him. In his last moment of life he had to show Pittheus that even in death, love would still survive.

"I forgive you," he whispered and realized Pittheus was hesitating once more to carry his act through. He couldn't kill Kyros after all. Maybe after all these years he had broken through his brother's hatred. But then again maybe he was wrong. He wanted to say something to Pittheus, but couldn't talk. His body ached and his bones shifted. Once more his wretched curse had come at the most inappropriate time. His vision blurred and he couldn't see much. But he did hear Thera's scream and then the loud roar of the beast followed by his brother's sword clanking to the floor. Pittheus' cry of defeat echoed in Kyros' ears as his brother was devoured by the beast.

His first thought went out to Thera, and he hoped she would remember the beast hunted by sound, and keep quiet. The creature was standing right before them but didn't seem to notice them in the dark. If they were quiet, it may just leave. Thera was silent too, and he knew it was all she could do to keep quiet through her pain. It was all he could do to keep quiet through his own. Then he heard the beast moving away from them through the labyrinth, obviously full and sated for the time being.

The transformation was complete, and Kyros shivered and waited impatiently for his vision to clear. All was quiet and he could only hope

Thera was still all right.

"Thera?" he whispered. "Are you all right?"

He felt her loving arms dropping the cloak around his naked, cold, shaking body. His vision returned and he could see her face. She was terrified, in pain and in anguish—a way he never wanted her to be. It hurt him immensely to see her this way. She lay on the ground next to him with her hands on her stomach.

"Pittheus is gone," she wept. "The beast just—"

"Shhh. I know, Thera. Don't think of that now. We've got to stay quiet."

He felt a sadness of his own to think his brother was gone. Even after all the evil things Pittheus had done to them, he was still his brother. Pittheus had hesitated to kill him, and Kyros wondered if maybe somewhere deep down his father's love still existed between them. But now Pittheus was gone and he'd never know for sure. There was nothing anyone could do to help him any longer. Now Kyros had something else to concern himself with. He had to get Thera to safety and also, he had to protect their baby.

"Thank you for the cloak." He wrapped it around himself, feeling somewhat comforted. "It was my father's."

She nodded her head and bit her lip to keep from crying out once again.

"We've got to get out of here, Thera, before the beast comes back for us. Can you stand?"

She gripped his hand tightly, her eyes squeezed shut.

"It's time, Kyros."

"It's time?" he repeated.

"I can't move now. Our baby is about to be born."

Kyros shook his head. As if it wasn't bad enough he had to transform at a time like this, now their baby was about to be born in the lair of a beast that would no doubt consume it.

"Thera, can't we try to get out of here first?" He realized how ridiculous it sounded after he'd said it. There was nothing they could do but wait for the baby to be born and hope Demogorgan was satisfied enough not to come back for awhile.

"Kyros, I'm scared." Her cold hand gripped his.

"I know, Thera. But I'm here for you. We'll do this together and get out of here before the beast comes back, don't worry."

"That's not what I mean." She gritted back another pain and Kyros could tell her breathing was very labored. "What if our child is a Centaur?"

"I'll love it no matter if it's Centaur or human." He tried to smile. He knew what Thera was aiming at, but didn't want to think of the consequences himself.

"But if it is, I'll die. Don't you understand?"

"I understand only too well, Thera. Don't think of it right now, just think that we're going to be parents."

"I want nothing more than to be the mother of your child, Kyros. To be able to sit at your side as your wife and raise our child together."

The pain stopped her as she couldn't help but cry out. Kyros raised her gown to expose her bottom half. He'd never assisted with a birth before and didn't even know exactly what to do.

"Thera. This is all new to me."

His own heart beat wildly and his head spun in a thousand different directions.

"Just love our child, Kyros, and promise me you'll take good care of it."

"Stop talking as if you're going to die."

"Kyros." Thera tried to sit in an upright position and Kyros held her head on his lap. "Tell me you'll take care of our child if something happens to me."

"You know I will, Thera. And I'll take care of you as well. Nothing's going to happen to you, now stop talking like that."

"I'm not so sure. I feel like—"

"Shhh," said Kyros and kissed her lightly on the lips. The talking can wait till later. We have a baby to birth right now."

TWENTY-EIGHT

Kyros held Thera tightly as her body wracked with pain and she tried to keep from crying out. He was anxious, excited, and at the same time scared more than he'd ever been in his life. If their baby was a Centaur, he'd lose Thera. That was something he couldn't accept. And if she died, it would be all his fault. If he hadn't been cursed, then she'd have no worry of dying from giving birth.

"Thera, darling. It's my fault you're going through this. If we have a Centaur, it's my fault of what will happen to you."

"No," Thera gasped as she breathed heavily and started to push. "It's because of you I may have the chance of birthing a human after all. Don't you see, Kyros? If you hadn't interfered with Ares' plan I'd be birthing Rodas' baby right now. A Centaur baby. At least now, you've given me hope."

"True. But if you hadn't fallen in love with me, you never would have given away your powers. You know as well as I you'd have no fear of birthing a Centaur if you were still a goddess. I'm so sorry about everything, Thera. I'm sorry I couldn't stop the wedding and you had to live through that humiliation with Pittheus. I'm sorry I—"

"Shhh." This time it was Thera who quieted him. "It's time, Kyros. Put your hands down below and catch our baby."

Kyros nervously did as instructed. As he witnessed the miracle of birth, he held his breath. The head of their child was born, but he still didn't know if it was human or Centaur. Thera was amazingly quiet through all her pain and Kyros knew she, having her power of the senses, must have felt all this twice as much as any other human.

"I can see it's head, Thera. It has dark hair like you."

Thera gave a slight smile and bit her lip and continued breathing.

"Push, Thera, push. It's almost here."

Kyros felt excitement fill his body. This was his child. Thera's child.

A child that would join them together as one for the rest of their lives. He had such plans for their baby. So many things he wanted to teach it. So many things he wanted to do together as a family.

The baby's shoulders were born and he let out his breath as he next saw its legs. Only two. Not the cursed four legs he had almost expected to see.

"It's a boy, Thera! It's a human boy."

Thera laughed and cried at the same time. So did Kyros. She was alive. The baby was human. He picked up the child, still connected to Thera and cradled it in his arms, bringing it closer to her so she could see him as well.

"He's beautiful," she laughed. "We did it, Kyros. We're the proud parents of a new baby."

She hoisted herself up a bit and took what was left of the shawl from around her. She gave it to Kyros and he wrapped the baby in it.

"I guess the old weaver wasn't jesting when she said this shawl would come in handy," said Thera. "Now we just need to find something to cut the baby's cord with. You don't happen to have that dagger with you yet, do you, Kyros?"

"No, said Kyros. I lost it when I transformed. We'll find something worthy to use to bring our baby into this world."

Kyros spotted Pittheus' sword lying on the ground a ways from them. He hesitated in using it, but Thera grabbed his hand.

"It's all right, Kyros. Get the sword. We'll cut the baby free and then we'll get out of here."

The baby looked up at them with wide eyes and Kyros felt a warmth in his heart he'd never felt before. He couldn't wait to take his family far away from this awful place. And now that he was in human form, he could do just that. It saddened him to think what his child may think of him in years to come when he found out he was a Centaur. But no matter what, he knew he'd always love his son.

"I think we should name him Lippio," said Thera. "Lippio means lover of horses."

Kyros looked at Thera and smiled. She must have been reading his mind. He hoped his son would love horses. And he hoped his son would love Centaurs, and him as well.

"I think it's a wonderful idea," he agreed. He encompassed Thera and the baby and hugged them. He then gave her a sensuous kiss on the mouth. She tasted so gloriously wonderful. And he wanted to take her back to the bedchamber and spend the rest of the day lying down with her and Lippio. Lying down in a bed as a man—with his family at his side.

"Let me get that sword," he said and left her side.

The baby wailed just then. Such a loud wail, it echoed off the walls and he was sure the whole castle could hear it.

Then Kyros heard the beast. It was closer than he'd thought it was. It must have been lying just out of the way, digesting its last meal. He grabbed the sword and headed back to Thera. But the beast jumped out of the shadows and swiped her with its claw-like paw. Thera cried out in pain and Kyros could see she was bleeding. He could also see she was trying her best to protect their baby in her arms.

"No!" Kyros screamed, getting Demogorgan's attention. The beast turned its head and let out a breath of fire. Kyros dodged it and lashed out with the sword, severing several of its arms. The beast slowed, and Kyros could see the two golden arrows sticking out from its shoulder.

He battled with the beast, but when he glanced over to check on Thera, Demogorgan swiped the sword from his hand. Kyros dived for the sword, turning around and throwing it at the beast just as it reached out for him. It struck the beast in the eye and the thing bellowed out with fury.

Kyros felt himself being lifted into the air. The sharp talon-like paws of the monster dug into his side. He was thankful for the thick cloak around him, but knew he was weaponless now and helpless as well.

As much as he struggled, he couldn't get free. He knew this was the end, but didn't feel for himself, but rather for Thera and the baby. He could hear Lippio crying, but couldn't hear a word from Thera.

The beast raised Kyros to its mouth and Kyros screamed out, "I love you, Thera!"

These would be his last words and he meant for them to be the only ones that were ever important.

He heard the beast scream and then its claw released him and Kyros fell to the ground below. Demogorgan fell after him and Kyros moved out of the way in order not to be crushed by its huge body. He saw the golden arrow sticking out from the monster's heart and then he saw Thera lying on the ground, curled up to Lippio. The bow was clutched in her hand.

"You did it, Thera! You killed the beast." He ran over to her and the baby, but Thera was still, not answering him. "Thera?" His heart beat a bit faster. Lippio cried in her arms, but she didn't move. "Thera, are you all right?"

He turned her onto her back and noticed her eyes were closed. Then to his horror, he noticed she wasn't breathing. Her face and chest were scratched from the beast and blood dripped from the wounds. She was still ragged from birthing their baby and Kyros' heart went out to her.

"Thera!" He grabbed her by the shoulders and shook her. "Thera, don't die on me. I need you. Don't leave me." He put his arms around the crying baby and Thera, trying to breathe life back into her, but with no luck. He laid his head on her chest. Her heart was no longer beating, and as much as he willed it to start back up, it wouldn't. He cried as he rocked her and the baby in his arms. Just when he thought all this madness had ended, he knew it hadn't. Although he didn't want to accept it, he now realized Thera was dead.

TWENTY-NINE

Kyros cradled Thera and the baby in his arms, rocking them, crying and no longer having the courage or strength to carry on without the woman he loved. They'd come so far together. This was just the beginning of their life as a family. And as much as he loved Lippio, he didn't want to raise him without Thera.

The boy deserved a father. A human father who could watch over him and protect him, and not have to worry about transforming into a beast every time the sun set. The boy also deserved a mother. He needed Thera, and so did Kyros. He would never forgive himself for what happened. He cursed himself for the day he jumped in front of Ares' beam. He never should have gotten involved. He never should have fallen in love with the god of war's daughter.

"Arrrgh!" cried out Kyros. "Damn you, Ares, for starting all this!" The baby wailed louder and Kyros looked to the ceiling. "Your daughter is dead, Ares. Don't you even care? Look what you've done to her! Look what's happened."

Suddenly there was a blast of light and Ares, frown on his face, stood before him with his hands on his leather clad hips.

Startled at his sudden appearance, Kyros had the feeling he shouldn't have cussed at the god of war.

"How dare you talk to me like that, Kyros. I ought to kill you for your disrespect."

"Go ahead, kill me. Kill me just as you did Thera." Kyros clutched the crying baby to his chest and watched Ares raise a finger.

"Ares! Don't you dare touch him." The old blind weaver stood in the corridor, threatening Ares as if she had the right to. Chiron and Nemos arrived in the passageway behind her, watching the drama unfold.

"Old weaver? How'd you come back from the dead?" asked Ares.

"Dead?" Nemos bravely trotted forward. "She's not dead. But she should be for betraying us. She led us into an ambush with Pittheus' men."

"I didn't betray you," said the weaver. "Pittheus had already sent his men. I didn't tell them you were coming."

"It's true," added Kyros. "Thera gave her the sword and she thankfully brought it to you. It was Pittheus who got the information out of Thera as to where she'd taken it."

Nemos nodded his head in acceptance. "In that case, I'm sorry for accusing you." Chiron nodded his head as well.

"You're dead, old woman. I saw you myself when I visited my brother Hades just yesterday. He showed me the Elysian fields and you were there weaving clothes for everyone."

"It can't be," said Kyros. "She's been with us for the past few days."

"Unless she's not who she pretends to be. Let's find out." Ares threw a lightning bolt at the old woman and if Kyros hadn't been holding Lippio, he would have dived in front of it to save her. History repeating itself of his mistakes.

The bolt never hit her. Instead, the old woman raised her own hand and sent it back to Ares. It hit him square in the chest and he fell against the wall. To Kyros' amazement, the old woman shifted shapes, turning into Thera's mother.

"Aphrodite!" yelled Ares. "I should have known you were involved. I thought I warned you to stay out of this."

"You did." She smiled and it lit up the room. She smoothed down her flowing white garment and it clung to her voluptuous curves. "That's why I disguised myself as the old weaver. No one had even known she'd died and I knew it would be the perfect way to get people to trust me."

"Yeah, well." Ares got to his feet. "You look much better now." He eyed up her body and Aphrodite glowed, obviously knowing the power she held over him.

"I'm glad to be out of that wreck of a body," she admitted. "It was really becoming disturbing."

"Thera is dead," Kyros interrupted. "And you two are rambling on about your appearances?"

"No!" said Chiron. "She can't be." He and Nemos rushed over to Kyros' side.

"Here," said Nemos, handing Kyros his father's sword. "I watched it well for you this time."

"Thank you." Kyros took the sword in one hand and used it to sever

the cord that connected the baby to Thera. He felt that action was so
final. That he'd severed Thera from his own life as well.

"May I hold the baby?" Nemos stood with hands outstretched. Kyros
handed it to him and Lippio calmed down and stopped his crying
immediately.

"Maybe Lippio likes Centaurs after all," smiled Kyros.

Kyros hunkered down and picked Thera up in his arms. Her head fell
back lifelessly. Blood dripped from her wounds. Her body was a mess
from birthing the baby.

He turned around and held her for Ares and Aphrodite to see. That's
when he noticed Harmonia, Thera's twin sister had joined them.

"No!" Harmonia rushed over to cradle Thera's head. "Father, do
something about this."

Aphrodite walked over to Thera's body and with a wave of her hand,
she'd cleaned and redressed her in a beautiful warm robe. Kyros looked
down to her and realized her wounds were gone as well.

"Bring her back to life," he said.

"I can't or I would," answered Aphrodite.

"Then *you* bring her back," he demanded of Ares.

"Don't you dare demand anything of a god!" He raised his hand to
throw another bolt, but Aphrodite stopped him.

"We haven't treated Thera all that well," she said to Ares.

"She wasn't the warrior I wanted her to be."

"And you weren't the father she wanted you to be either." Aphrodite
actually sounded sorry. "Just as I wasn't much of a mother."

"Is that why you took care of her in that old weaver's form?" asked
Ares.

"It's the least I could do for our daughter. Maybe she was foolish
enough to ask Zeus to take back her immortality and goddess powers,
but you were fool enough to try to start a war by getting her pregnant
with a Centaur's baby."

Ares looked over to the baby in Nemos' arms. "Even that didn't
work, of all the rotten luck. I guess it's just not meant to be."

Harmonia reached out and let the baby grab her finger. "He may be
human, but he sure is cute."

"One of you must be able to do something to bring her back to life,"
said Kyros. "Do it for your daughter; do it for your grandson."

"That's it?" asked Ares. "No one else?"

Kyros hated to admit it to the god of war, since he knew Ares hated him, but he admitted it for Thera's sake. "Do it ... for me."

"Never!" said Ares. "Or have you forgotten I don't like you? Must I remind you I'm the one that cursed you in the first place?"

"He can't do anything to bring her back," interrupted Aphrodite. "Neither can I. The only one that has that power is the god of the dead himself."

"Hades." Kyros wondered why he hadn't thought of it sooner. He brought Thera's body over to Chiron and put her across his back. "Chiron, take Thera's body to the hovel. Nemos, you watch Lippio. Follow the string from the shawl and it'll lead you out of here. Stay away from Pittheus' men; they may still give you trouble."

"And what about Pittheus?" asked Nemos

"He won't be giving you any trouble," Kyros said sadly looking over to the dead beast that lie not far from them. "My brother is dead as well." He picked up the golden bow of Artemis and the quiver of arrows. The bow and arrows had saved his life but sadly, it didn't save Pittheus or Thera.

"And what are you going to do?" asked Chiron.

"I'm going to go see Hades."

"But no mortal is allowed in Tartarus unless he's dead," stated Harmonia. "Uncle Hades doesn't like visitors."

Kyros looked at Ares and the god rolled his eyes and looked the other way. "Don't even ask me," Ares warned.

"What about you?" Kyros looked to Aphrodite. "Will you take me to Tartarus to see Hades?"

"It's the least we can do," Aphrodite said while looking at Ares. "And if we go pay him a visit, maybe you can convince him to give back your raven."

"I agree," piped in Harmonia. "Let's go see him, Dad. We'll all go together."

"Women!" snapped Ares and raised his hand above his head.

It all happened so fast, Kyros' thoughts spun. The room turned white and Chiron, Nemos, Thera's dead body and Lippio were gone. There was a fog around them and he couldn't even see Aphrodite, Ares or Harmonia. He clutched the bow in his hand and his side ached from the new wound he'd received from Demogorgan. He smelled the distinct odor of sulfur and the white light in the room suddenly turned red. The room stopped spinning with a jerk and he fell to his knees from the sudden force. When he focused on their surroundings, he realized he was no longer in the labyrinth.

It was dark and eerie in this place. Cold like a dank cave and yet hotter than the fires of summer. Torches were stuck into the cracks of the stone walls all around him and he heard the wailing of lost souls, trapped with nowhere to go. He lowered his head, not liking this place at all.

He saw a pair of sandaled feet in front of him and when he followed them upward he saw the tallest, eeriest man he'd ever seen. He was clad in a black cloak and was removing the hood from his face. His eyes were dark, yet burned with fire. His skin was pale, his lips very red.

"Who bothers me?" he ground out. A fog rolled in and covered the ground. Kyros got to his feet in order to answer.

"My name is Kyros," he answered, hoping to keep his voice steady.

"Ah, yes. Kyros," the man repeated. "I'm Hades, God of the Dead. Welcome to Tartarus."

THIRTY

Kyros didn't know if he liked the idea of being welcomed to the underworld. Hades wasn't the kind of friend he wanted. And now he wondered if coming here was such a good idea after all.

"He insisted on coming," came Ares' voice from behind Kyros.

"Since when do you cater to the whims of humans, brother?" Hades hissed out.

"I rather like having visitors," came a woman's voice. She stepped out from behind Hades and Kyros could see she was really beautiful. Red hair fell around her shoulders, her eyes were green like the trees of the earth. She was so full of life she glowed. And even her garments were cheery and vibrant. Not at all like the dead black that Hades wore. "Welcome, Aphrodite and Harmonia," she chirped out and went over to hug them. "It's been a long time."

"I don't usually like coming to this filthy place," said Harmonia. "But this time I made the exception."

"You're here to see Thera, I suppose?" asked the woman.

"Thera's here?" Kyros was shocked. "What is she doing in Tartarus? She deserves the Elysian fields!"

Smoke came from Hades' ears and fire blazed in his eyes. "Don't tell me where to put the dead. I ought to punish you for that." Kyros was sure he would have if Ares hadn't stopped him.

"Kyros is annoying, Hades; I can vouch for that. He tends to think he can order the gods around. But let's just ignore his ignorance and get this over with."

"What do you want?" Hades glared at Kyros.

"I want you to give Thera back her life."

"No." Hades word was so final. Kyros knew he could do nothing to change the mind of the god of the dead now.

"Why not?" asked Aphrodite. "You've brought people back before."

"This is different," said Hades. "She used the golden bow of Artemis. Artemis herself put the hex on that. If someone besides the king of the Centaurs uses it, they're eventually dead. Thera actually lived longer then I thought she would."

"But she's not the only one that used it," explained Kyros, clutching the bow in his hand. "Pittheus used it, and—"

"And he's dead," said Hades.

Kyros couldn't argue with that. Maybe the bow was cursed after all.

"But I used it also," said Kyros. "And I'm alive."

"Not for long," answered Hades. "You're due to join them shortly in the underworld."

"No, he won't." Everyone turned to see Thera stepping from the shadows. She was bedraggled and dirty. Her feet were bare and she only wore a coarse, torn dark tunic around her. Kyros' heart went out to her as he noticed the blood stains and the way she gripped her stomach. Also, the deep scratches across her face and chest were caked with blood.

"Thera!" He tried to run to her, but Hades held out his hand and an invisible wall with it. He wasn't going to allow him to touch her. He wouldn't let him near her—not while she was dead and he still lived.

"No mingling with the residents," announced Hades.

"Why did she go here?" Kyros demanded to know. "And why is she still in pain and not even cleaned up?"

"This is Tartarus," laughed Ares and his brother Hades joined him. "What did you expect to see? Hades serving Thera tea and crumpets?"

"She doesn't deserve this kind of treatment."

"She does," broke in Hades. "She not only used the bow but she killed. Anyone who kills another goes straight to Tartarus. Rule number 123 in *Hades' Book of the Dead*."

"Who'd she kill?" Ares' seemed interested and somewhat impressed. "You didn't count killing off those two goons I conjured up, did you?"

"Of course not," snapped Hades and paced the floor. "She killed Demogorgan, the offspring of my beloved pet. Not to mention she killed your raven."

"But they were animals, not humans," protested Kyros.

"Pets of the gods are considered sacred and more precious then humans in my book," retorted Hades.

"True," said Ares smoothing down his short beard. I hadn't thought of it like that."

"You two are acting like children," interrupted the beautiful woman. "That doesn't count and you know it. Now, I don't believe I've been properly introduced to Kyros." She walked up and smiled at him. "I'm Persephone, Hades' wife."

Kyros remembered Thera telling him about her. She was the only friend Thera ever had. Maybe Thera wouldn't be so lonely in Tartarus after all with Persephone with her. And then on the other hand, maybe she was just the ally Kyros needed in this dreadful place.

"Can you help her?" asked Kyros. "Can you bring her back to life?"

Persephone sadly shook her head.

There was silence for a moment and Kyros looked at Thera. Her eyes showed the anguish inside her. The sulfur was so strong now, it almost choked Kyros and he realized Thera must smell it even more, having her power of the senses. A bubbling noise came from the opposite side of the room and Kyros noticed a skeleton-type man sitting in a boat in the water. He wondered who he was and as if he'd spoken aloud, Hades answered.

"That's my ferryman of the river Styx. He's bored as you can see. I haven't had many dead lately. I have many vacancies down here. Ares was supposed to start a war and send me some business, but as you can see, he didn't keep his word."

"How do you think this all got started?" Ares asked Hades heatedly. "If you wouldn't have been hounding me, then Thera would still be alive."

"As if you care," said Kyros.

He was doing it once again. He was angering the god of war. Ares squinted his eyes. His mouth pursed in fury. That's when Aphrodite stepped in to interfere.

"We all want Thera back in the land of the living," she said.

"Why?" asked Hades flippantly. "She's a mortal now and Zeus won't give her back his gifts. He was angry at her in the first place when she told him she didn't want them."

"She's still my daughter," said Aphrodite. "And also the mother of my grandson."

"And she's my sister," added Harmonia. "And although we haven't been very nice to her, she doesn't deserve to die. Living as a mortal is punishment enough."

Kyros looked over to Thera and saw a smile flash across her face for an instant before it disappeared. She'd gotten the approval of her mother and sister. Something she'd never had before. Then Kyros noticed her looking at Ares. Ares folded his arms over his chest and looked away.

"This has to be unanimous before I'll even consider it," said Hades.

"Well, you know I want her back." Kyros was becoming a bit impatient. He wanted Thera out of there and he wanted it now.

"I vote to let her go back to her living form also," said Persephone. She walked over and laid a hand on Thera.

"And what about you?" Hades spoke to Ares and Ares pretended surprise.

"Me? What about me?"

"Do you want her back?"

The room was silent and all eyes were on him. It seemed the decision lay with him now.

"She's no good as a warrior," he complained. "But I suppose someone should take care of my grandson—someone more capable than a cursed man. Maybe someday I can train Lippio to be a warrior instead."

"So you agree?" Hades asked.

"I guess it wouldn't be all that bad. But does this mean I get back my raven as well?"

"My pet Demogorgan is dead," Hades reminded him. "You can do without that damned raven. We're talking about your daughter here. Now what's your answer?"

Ares looked over to Aphrodite who had her hands on her waist. He then looked over to Thera whose eyes begged him to cooperate.

"I agree," he said, looking at the ground.

"All right," answered Hades. Kyros felt his heart lighten. He'd have Thera after all. He'd have her back in his arms by nightfall. And even if he still was a damned cursed man, he'd do the best he could to be a good father for their baby and a husband to her.

"Thank you," said Kyros.

"Not so fast," snapped Hades. "I said I'd give her her life back, but things are a little more complicated than that down here."

"What do you mean?" asked Kyros, shifting the bow in his hand and letting his fingers rest against the hilt of his father's sword strapped to his waist. It felt good to have it back. Like it belonged there.

"What he means, is that there has to be a switch in order to let Thera live." Persephone came back to her husband's side. "It's the balance of nature. If Thera is to go back, then someone has to take her place."

Kyros felt his body tighten. "Are you trying to say that someone has to die in order for Thera to live?"

"That's exactly what he's saying," beamed Ares. "So who's it going to be? That new baby you two conceived?"

"No!" screamed Thera. "Never. Leave Lippio alone. Our baby deserves to live. I'll stay here rather than to switch places with him. Just leave me here, I no longer care about myself."

"Thera," said Kyros. "Are you saying you don't want to come back to me?"

Tears were in her eyes and Kyros felt her sadness and confusion in his own heart.

"Of course I do, Kyros. I love you. But I won't let Hades take our child."

"Neither will I," said Kyros. Then he looked at Hades head on. "Take my life. I'll switch places with Thera."

"Kyros, no!" Thera tried to run to him, but Hades still had up the invisible wall. "You can't give your life for me. Don't do it."

"Why not, Thera? I'm a cursed man. You could do better for yourself, not to mention our child. It'll be relief for me to no longer have to worry what Lippio will someday think of me."

"Oh, all this sentimental trash is so time wasting," blurted out Ares. "I've got better things to do." He raised his hand to disappear but Thera called out.

"Father, take the curse off of Kyros. Make him a man again."

"No, no, no," Ares muttered and shook his head. "Don't involve me in this deal. When I dished out that curse, I had no intention of taking it back. And I still don't. That's all I need is the reputation of being soft-hearted."

"It's all right, Thera. Just let me take your place. Our baby needs you," Kyros tried to convince her.

"I can't stand this anymore." Aphrodite stepped over to Ares. "You don't need to break the curse. And Hades, you'll get the switch you need. And everyone will still be happy."

"Mother, what are you talking about?" asked Harmonia. "How can that be?"

"Give Thera the bow, Kyros," said Aphrodite. "I'd take it to her myself, but as you know, a god can't touch it."

Kyros took the bow from his shoulder and the quiver of arrows. He handed it up to the wall and she tried to grab for it but couldn't take it.

"Hades," said Persephone. "Let the wall down so he can give it to her."

With a shake of Hades' fist, Kyros was able to hand Thera the bow. Her hand brushed against his and he felt his body tingle. He loved her. He wanted her to live, and as much as he wanted to live with her and Lippio, he'd give his life if it meant her freedom.

"I have to admit," said Aphrodite. "I'm surprised no one else has thought of this."

"Of what?" asked Harmonia.

"Of the fact that all Thera has to do is kill Kyros as he's transforming. That would take care of the death for a life. And it would also break Ares' curse."

"What!" Ares stood aghast. "No one breaks my curses."

"Just watch and see," smiled Aphrodite. "It's just about dusk. In a moment Kyros will be changing into his Centaur form."

Kyros felt a pain shoot through him and knew that what Aphrodite said was true. He was going to transform—and with an audience. An audience of gods, yet. Something even more humiliating.

"Is it true, Mother?" Thera's voice quavered. "If I shoot him as he's transforming, I'll break his curse?"

"You'll be killing his Centaur form," she explained. "It'll fill your void and you'll get to go back to the land of the living."

Thera fumbled with the golden bow. She knew it could work, but she also sensed there was something her mother wasn't telling her. She wanted nothing more than to come back to Kyros and the baby. She didn't like it in Tartarus. She hated the place and didn't know how Persephone could put up with it.

She watched Persephone go over to Hades and hold his hand. Even the god of the dead had someone to love. Something Thera wanted more than anything. She looked over to Kyros who was now doubled over in pain. It would be so good to see his curse broken. He would never have to go through this humiliation or pain again. He deserved to live a normal life and she had the power in her hands to make it happen.

"Shoot him, Thera," came her father's voice. "Do it just like I've shown you. You can kill. You know you can. Prove it to me, Daughter."

So once again, her father was instructing her to kill. But this time she had a reason for doing it. She raised the bow and cocked an arrow. One release and it would all be over. It would all be so easy. But yet, she couldn't help but feel something wasn't just right.

"There's something you're not telling me, Mother."

Aphrodite walked to her daughter's side. "And what may that be?"

Thera closed her eyes and took a deep breath. She felt the risk here. Knew this was more dangerous than her mother was letting on.

"What happens ... what happens if I miss?" Thera asked.

Hades answered. "Then you'll stay here, Kyros will remain cursed and the deal is off. This is the only chance you get."

Thera couldn't let that happen. She had to try for Kyros. She had to try for their baby.

"Do it, Thera," came Kyros' voice and she felt his body convulse with pain as he spoke. "Just do it."

She raised the bow again and held the arrow in place, trying to steady the shot. It didn't feel right, aiming at the man she loved. Her father's words when she was a goddess rang through her head. He'd told her she'd one day kill even those she loved. She gullibly thought he'd meant the animals of the forest. Never in all her life would she have thought he meant a person.

A thought suddenly hit Thera, and once more she lowered the bow. She looked at her mother who seemed almost as nervous as she felt at the moment.

"What if I don't hit him just as he's transforming?" Thera asked. "What if I hit him while he's still a man? Or what if I shoot him a bit too late and he's already turned into a Centaur?"

Thera knew this is what was making her mother so nervous. There was always a loophole in every plan, and she'd hit right on target with this one.

"Then he'll die, Thera. Your aim has to be true and the arrow has to pierce him right when he's in between the two worlds of being man and beast. A second sooner or later, and Kyros will join you in the underworld."

"And the curse will never be broken," added Hades. "He'll live with you here, but he'll still be cursed. And as you've already found out those who live in Tartarus feel the pain even more than when they were alive."

"I can't do it," said Thera, shaking her head.

Ares threw his hands up in the air. "Come on, Thera. I taught you how to kill. It's easy. Just pretend you're killing my raven again and you'll have no problem."

Thera wondered if her father almost cared what happened to Kyros. Then she wondered if he almost cared what happened to her. Even if he did, he'd never admit it. It would be weak for the god of war to admit to care for anyone or anything. She'd seen his fondness of his raven and used it against him. He'd learned from that mistake, she was sure. She'd never feel the fondness, approval or love of Ares. And in a way, she didn't really want it. He was the god of war, and she respected his position. He did what he had to, just as she was about to do what she had to, as well.

"Hurry, Thera," urged Persephone. "Kyros is starting to transform."

Thera knew Kyros could no longer talk. But if he'd been able to, he'd tell her again to shoot him. She raised the bow and told herself she was doing this for Kyros, for Lippio and for herself as well.

"Aim," came her father's words from somewhere in the dark room.

"Do it for Kyros and the baby," came her sister's voice.

"Hurry," urged her mother and Thera realized Kyros was now on the ground, his father's sword lying close to him. She remembered how much that sword meant to him and also his father's dying wish of peace between the Centaurs and the Trozens. Kyros was willing to sacrifice all that now. He was willing to give his life just so she could live again.

She pulled back the bowstring and tried to pretend Kyros was Ares' raven. It just didn't work. She couldn't help but see the man she loved, squirming with pain before her. His bones shifted and his Centaur legs started to emerge. His face twisted in pain and Thera knew it was now or never.

The bowstring creaked as she pulled it taut. She felt the unshed blood in her own mouth and felt Kyros' fear as well. Not unlike the fear of that little defenseless rabbit her father tried to get her to kill not long ago.

She felt herself weaken and the bow start to lower.

"Raise your bow and finish the job, you coward," came her father's bellow through the fog that now surrounded them.

He was goading her again; appealing to the war-like blood he'd spawned in her veins.

"I can't," she whispered.

"You will!" he called back.

Thera bit her lip and raised the bow. She had the shot all lined up. She swallowed deeply and closed her eyes. "I'm sorry, Kyros," she whispered. "I just can't do it."

But before she could lower the bow, something hit her elbow and her arm shot forward. Without meaning to, her fingers released the bowstring and the arrow split the air as it made its way towards Kyros. The fog was now so thick in the room, she couldn't see Kyros lying on the ground. She heard the arrow thud as it embedded itself into his flesh.

A wave of nausea swept through her and tears welled in her eyes. "Kyros?" she asked, but he didn't answer.

She dropped the bow and it went clattering to the floor. She ran to him and threw herself down into the fog where she'd last seen him. Kyros lay in Centaur form, his eyes closed and the golden arrow embedded in his chest.

"Right through the heart!" came Ares voice of approval. "I knew you could do it, Thera. Good job!"

Thera put her hand to her mouth to stop the scream that threatened to come forth. She was too late. He must have already been transformed when she let the arrow fly.

"I'm so sorry, Kyros," she whispered and reached a hand out to touch him. "I've killed you."

THIRTY-ONE

Kyros felt strange. Very strange. He was floating above himself looking down at his Centaur body. A golden arrow pierced his heart, his eyes were closed, his body still. He could see Thera kneeling over him, crying, and apologizing for something he didn't quite understand.

He willed himself down to the foggy floor and then to stand right behind Thera. He called her name, but she didn't even hear him. Then he tried to grab her shoulders, but he couldn't move his arms.

"You did it," he heard Ares' voice from somewhere in the darkness.

"No, Father. I killed him," came her sobbing reply.

Killed him? Kyros looked back at his Centaur body lying still on the ground. He did look dead, now that she'd mentioned it. If this was so, then was his curse broken? Or did she kill both his forms in the process?

His love for her was strong, and he didn't care either way. If he was truly dead, then it served a good purpose. Thera would return to the land of the living in exchange. She'd no longer feel her pain and the weariness of living in Tartarus. And if it was the curse she'd broken, then they'd return to Trozen together. There they'd live happily ever after as a family with Lippio. But either way, he had to know. Somehow, he had to find out the answer.

"Well, which is it Hades?" Kyros asked, searching for the god of the dead's tall form through the fog of Tartarus. "Am I dead and to spend an eternity with you, or is the curse broken and will I spend my eternity with Thera?"

Thera still didn't seem to hear him and this bothered him immensely. Then the fog parted and he saw the gods and goddesses standing before him as if they were a court judging his sentence. They could see him, so why couldn't Thera? They whispered among themselves, but didn't talk to him. He felt Thera's sadness as she wept over his Centaur body. He wanted nothing more than to reach out and comfort her, but didn't know how.

"I demand an answer, Hades. Tell me what happened." He no longer cared if he made demands of the gods. He no longer felt he had anything to lose. Not for himself, just for Thera.

"Demands again?" snapped Hades. "I couldn't put up with someone like you for the rest of eternity."

"I told you he was irritating, brother." Ares stroked his short beard and then crossed his muscled arms over his chest.

"Who are you talking to?" Thera jumped to her feet and turned a full circle. Kyros smiled at her, but her gaze went right through him. "Who are you two talking to?" she asked again.

"Tell her already." Aphrodite rolled her eyes and nodded toward him.

"Yes," added Harmonia. "I think Thera has suffered enough."

"Suffered enough?" Thera asked. "What does that mean? What are you trying to say?"

Persephone went to her, and because of this Kyros was happy. If he couldn't comfort Thera himself, then Persephone should be the one to do it.

"You did kill him," Persephone announced. Thera fell into her arms, shaking uncontrollably. "But only his Centaur form," she added. Thera stilled, and then pulled her wet face from Persephone's shoulder.

"Wh ...what do you mean?" She looked back at Kyros' dead Centaur body and then back to Persephone.

"Hades?" Persephone looked toward her husband. "Explain. Will you?"

"All right, all right," he grumbled. "Only because I want everyone out of here. Especially Kyros. That man is a trifle too irritating at times. I'll be glad to get rid of him."

"So he's still alive?" Thera perked up immediately.

"He is," Hades admitted. "Or at least, he's still alive in human form. Look." Hades pointed to Kyros' Centaur form lying on the floor. It faded from sight before their very eyes, until nothing was left but the golden arrow that had broken the curse.

"So I did it?" Thera asked feebly.

"You did," answered Hades.

"I didn't think she had it in her," grumbled Ares.

"Of course she did." Aphrodite came up and put her arm around her daughter.

Thera saw her mother wink and realized now how she'd been able to go through with the act. She, herself wasn't a warrior. She still wasn't able to kill anyone and never would be. She'd felt something or someone bump her elbow before it happened. The act caused her to release the bow. She knew now, her mother had something to do with it. Without Aphrodite's help, Kyros would still be a cursed man and Thera would have spent the rest of eternity in Tartarus with her uncle Hades.

"Thank you," she whispered, and honestly meant it.

"It was nothing," whispered her mother. "It was the same way I taught Eros to shoot his arrows of love."

"What's all the whispering about?" asked Ares. "If there's a secret, I want to know about it."

"No secret," said Aphrodite. "Just talk between a mother and her daughter."

Thera liked the way that sounded. A mother and her daughter. Maybe this whole experience wasn't so bad after all. Not if it brought them closer together. All the secrets were out now. She'd no longer have to keep secrets from Kyros. And Kyros' secret no longer existed.

"Where is he, Hades?" she asked.

He nodded his head but he didn't need to. Somehow, she'd known as soon as she'd asked that he was standing right behind her. She slowly turned around. He was there, in his man form. He smiled at her and her heart melted. He held out his arms for her, inviting her closer.

"Thera." His voice was the sweetest thing she'd ever heard. She ran to him and threw herself into his arms, but she went right through him.

She turned around and confronted her uncle. "I thought you said he was alive."

"He is."

"Then why can't I touch him?"

"You're forgetting, you're not back in your body yet, Thera," explained Hades. "It'll take a little while. These things don't happen overnight. Or actually, overnight is exactly how long it'll take."

"Hades," came Persephone's voice. "Just finish this up already, will you? The kids want to be together."

"All right, all right." Hades walked up to them both. Thera stood at Kyros' side. She felt an aching in her heart. A need to touch him. She wanted to be with him right now.

"I can't wait that long," said Thera, never taking her eyes off Kyros.

"Neither can I." Kyros interlocked eyes with her.

"Isn't love grand?" Aphrodite sighed, and put her arm around Harmonia.

"It is, Mother," Harmonia answered back.

"I've had enough of this absurd sentimental trash. I'm out of here." Ares raised his hands and was gone in an orange flash.

"He's just upset that his curse is broken," explained Aphrodite. "I'll go talk to him."

"I'll come too," said Harmonia.

In another flash they, too, had disappeared.

"It was good seeing you again, Thera." Persephone smiled. "I've missed you." She then walked back to Hades and snuggled into him.

Thera had missed Persephone too, since her friend had been claimed by Hades. But she looked happy with him. Thera couldn't understand it. She couldn't understand how Persephone could live underground and only see the sun and nature half a year—when Hades allowed it.

"Are you saying you actually like it here?" Thera was aghast to think anyone would like a place as horrifying as Tartarus.

"When you're with the right person, Thera—the person you love—it doesn't matter where you are. You can find happiness anywhere."

"I know you're right." Thera looked back at Kyros and smiled.

Persephone waved a finger and the golden bow rose from the ground and Kyros grabbed it along with the quiver of arrows. This made Thera wonder about Kyros' sword, and looking down, she saw it was already strapped to his waist. After all, Hades had been nice enough to clothe him, so why not give him the sword as well.

As if Kyros knew what she looked for, he put his hand on the hilt of his sword.

"You'll be my queen now, Thera. The people of Trozen will accept us, now that Pittheus is gone and I have my father's sword."

"We're not too late are we?" she asked. "I mean, did we miss the feast of Dionysus?"

"I don't know." Kyros' face turned solemn and he looked to Hades for the answer. "How long have we been down here? I've lost track of the time."

"Time is different in Tartarus," Hades said. "But when I send you back, I'll get you there in time for the feast."

Kyros nodded his head in thanks.

"How about you send them back refreshed and healed?" asked

Persephone. "And send them back in time for a wedding before Kyros is crowned king."

"Now Persephone," Hades warned. "You know I don't like to get involved in—"

"Do it for me, Uncle Hades. Please," begged Thera.

Hades shook his head and looked at his wife. He sighed and looked at Kyros. "Don't let the power of a woman ever be underestimated," he said.

"I won't," said Kyros with a smile.

"All right," said Hades. "I'll send you back now. You'll be in the great hall of your castle. The wedding will be in progress. Right afterwards you'll be crowned king. Any last requests?"

"Let the Centaurs be there too," said Kyros. "Let the Centaurs and the Trozens be united in peace."

"I do that," said Hades, "and my brother won't speak to me for a fortnight. Not to mention, Tartarus will be empty for a long time."

"Well, you asked," said Kyros. "And that's my wish."

"He deserves a wish or two after the curse your brother laid on him," interrupted Persephone.

"I suppose you're right," answered Hades. "I'll bring the Centaurs there, but I'll be no part of peace, that's up to you. And never let it be said I had anything to do with this."

"My lips are sealed," said Kyros.

"Mine too," added Thera.

"You may want to hold on to that golden bow," said Persephone. "It isn't welcome anywhere near any of the gods besides Artemis."

"I know exactly what to do with it," Kyros told her.

"Are you finally ready?" asked Hades.

"We are," answered Thera.

"Then close your eyes."

Thera thanked Persephone one last time and smiled at Hades. "Thank you, Uncle."

"You'll no longer be welcome on Mount Olympus," Hades told her. "Realize that the rest of the gods will have nothing to do with you since you're now human."

"I know," she answered. "But it'll be all right, as long as I'm with Kyros."

"We'd like to invite you and the other gods to the wedding," said Kyros.

"Can't." Hades seemed a bit touched if Thera wasn't mistaken. "I've got too much to do."

"I'll see what I can do," whispered Persephone.

Her whisper faded in Thera's ears and so did her surroundings. Her body felt light, then she felt a breeze against her face. She knew Kyros was with her, though she couldn't see him. But she felt his presence and it felt so reassuring, so comforting, so good. The flashes of light zipped by her and she felt a force pushing her through the space. Then everything stopped with a jarring halt. The room cleared and to her surprise she was right where Hades had said he would send her. She was standing on the steps to the dais in the great hall. She was dressed in white—the most beautiful gown she'd ever seen. Thin, wispy, material, shimmering and glistening like the sun. Around the neckline there were embroidered pink roses that trailed down the front, all the way to the floor. Her feet were clad in delicate sandals with golden straps that wound up her legs. She picked up the hem of the gown and marveled at the small live roses that climbed around the straps of her sandals.

She felt like a goddess even though she wasn't. She realized she clutched flowers in her hand, beautiful pink roses to match the ones on the gown. She heard Lippio's little baby voice babbling somewhere in the background. Then she turned her head and saw the most wonderful thing she'd ever seen in her life.

Kyros stood beside her dressed in a golden tunic wrap that touched his thighs. He had his father's sword strapped to his side and the gemstones glistened and winked at her. His hair was loose around him, and in his eyes she saw the spirit of Kaj as well as the man of Kyros. He was both the man and beast she had fallen in love with. He was her lover, her husband and the father of her child. He was her king and the man she would spend the rest of her living days with, and this pleased her more than anything.

"I do," she heard her own voice say the words.

"I do," repeated Kyros.

"I pronounce you man and wife," came another voice from somewhere. "You may kiss the bride."

Kyros leaned over and brought his arms around her. He touched her and it felt so wonderful she thought she would burst. Then he lowered his lips to hers and tasted her. She closed her eyes and reveled in their warmth and softness. She was his wife. He was her husband. Her dreams had come true. She would have thought it all a dream, hadn't Kyros voice pulled her back to reality.

"Thera," he said. "There's someone here to see you."

Ares stood across the hall, his raven perched upon his shoulder. Aphrodite graced his side as well as Harmonia. The women smiled, but Ares just gave a small nod. He held up her bow and quiver of arrows, now a bit more ornate then she remembered them.

"Kyros, they came to our wedding after all." In the second it took to speak to her husband, her family had disappeared. The bow and arrows leaned against a pillar—her wedding present from her father; also his little reminder that she was still the daughter of the god of war, and not to be without a weapon.

"They didn't all show up," said Kyros.

"No. But Hades has already bent his rules more than he ever has, just for us."

Lippio cried and Nemos handed the baby to Thera. She cuddled it to her breast and her son calmed instantly.

"It's time, Thera." Kyros led her to the seats at the top of the dais. He motioned for Nemos to join them, handing the boy Artemis' golden bow. The crowd quieted at the site of Kyros' raised sword.

"Today, as I raise my father's sword to Artemis, on the feast day of Dionysus," Kyros said to the crowd, "I will not only become king, but I will join together the Centaurs and the people of Trozen in peace."

The crowd gave a cheer of approval, and Thera noticed the Centaurs and the Trozens moving closer to one another.

"I will carry out my father's wish to maintain this peace between the two races. And when I'm someday gone from this world, my son Lippio will take my place and rule as I have ruled."

Nemos looked a bit nervous, and Kyros rested his hand on the boy's shoulder. "Nemos will become the king of the Centaurs today, at my side. He will rule as his father Phylo has ruled before him."

The sun shone brightly from the window overhead, the beam of light illuminating the dais. Kyros raised his sword up to Artemis, and Nemos did the same with the golden bow. There was a flash of light off the metal of the sword, and another strong flash off the golden bow.

"The fate has been sealed," announced Chiron, coming to their side. "The Centaurs and the people of Trozen will leave in peace for the next hundred years."

The crowd cheered and Thera felt the rush of excitement go through her own veins as the Trozens and the Centaurs came together slowly and started to interact.

"I now give you," said Chiron, "Kyros ... the new king of Trozen, and Thera, his queen."

The crowd cheered.

"And Prince Lippio," continued Chiron. He nodded toward Thera and she handed the baby to Kyros. Sword in one hand, baby in the other, Kyros rose them up for all to see. The crowd went wild and after a few moments, Kyros motioned with his hand to still them.

"And I give you the new king of the Centaurs," announced Kyros. "Nemos, the first boy-king of the race."

Nemos smiled and nodded and Kyros gave him a sour look. "You're a king now, Nemos," he whispered. "Let the people know it."

"I understand," said Nemos and raised his bow and arrows high, acknowledging both the Centaurs and the Trozen race. The crowd went wild and the sound in the hall was deafening. Little Lippio slept through it, and Thera was glad.

"Well, Thera," asked Kyros. "How does it feel to be queen?"

It was then she noticed the crowns on both hers and Kyros' head. Also, a crown on Nemos. She put her hand to her crown and thanked Artemis silently for the gift.

"It doesn't feel half as good as being your wife," she admitted.

"Well, now how would you know that?" asked Kyros. "You're not really my wife until the act is consummated."

"Well then, husband, perhaps we should ask Nemos and Chiron to watch Lippio so I can truly become your wife."

THIRTY-TWO

There was a warm fire burning in the fireplace and a decanter of wine and two goblets on a trunk near the foot of the bed when Kyros carried Thera into the bedchamber and closed the door behind them with his foot. Thera's senses were heightened, and she smelled the roasted foul and stuffed grape leaves set out on platters by the fire.

"Oh, that smells good, Kyros. I'm so hungry."

"And so am I, Thera." He unlatched the scabbard from his waist and tossed the sword on the foot of the bed. "But not for food."

Thera couldn't help but think of the night of intimacy she'd had with Kyros when he was in his Centaur form—when he was Kaj. Her body tingled and she felt herself wanting to do it all again. But this time she wanted more. So much more. She wanted to couple with Kyros in man form. She wanted to please him as he'd pleased her.

Thera noticed the steamy hot mist rising from a wooden tub on the far side of the room. "I'd like to go in there first," she said and couldn't help but feel the disappointment in Kyros' mind.

"Whatever you want, wife. But I'll not wait all night before I claim you. I'm not that patient of a man."

"Every mother has her needs to tend to. Do you realize I'm probably the only virgin mother in the history of Trozen?"

"I can remedy that."

She made her way to the tub, slipped the gown from her shoulders and let it fall to the floor at her feet. She kept her eyes focused on Kyros and was pleased when she realized he couldn't help himself from scanning her naked body.

"You ... you look quite different than the last time I saw you naked."

"Of course I do." She sat on the edge of the tub backwards and released her hair from it's imprisonment. It fell to her shoulders and she shook it loose around her. "I'm not pregnant anymore. And by the help of the gods in speeding up my healing I think we'll both find this to our liking."

"I've always found you to my liking, Thera." Kyros joined her by the tub.

She laughed and reached out and released the tie from his waist. She ran her hands over his shoulders and let his own garment drop to the ground, exposing his naked body. She ran her hands over his bare chest, feeling every ripple of the muscles beneath her fingers. He bent over again and kissed her on the lips. She took her fingers and ran them through his long, beautiful hair.

"You know, Kyros. I think in a way I'm going to miss Kaj."

"Really." It was more a statement than a question. He took her hands from him and put them on her lap. "Wait right here."

He slipped away toward the bed and took a hold of the rich purple curtains that surrounded it. He looked at her and then back to what he was doing. Thera shifted and put her feet in the water. With her back to him, she heard a ripping sound but didn't turn around. Instead, she lowered herself into the water and closed her eyes as the warmth enveloped her.

"Ohh, this feels so good," she exclaimed. "Care to join me?"

"Do you want me to?" Kyros' voice was soft and husky. A bit different than usual. It sounded familiar—like Kaj's voice. Her eyes sprung open and from her low position in the tub, over the edge she could only see from his waist up. He stood there with a purple mask around his eyes, his hair wild and tossed.

"Kaj?" She sat upright quickly and Kyros laughed as he came toward her. She had mistaken him for a moment for the Centaur she once knew and loved. But yet she hadn't mistaken him at all.

"You see, Thera. I can be any fantasy of yours you wish."

She slapped at him playfully and he grabbed her arms. She gave him a quick tug and he fell into the tub with her. Water splashed out over the sides, the smell of the crushed rosemary leaves used to sweeten the water tingled her nostrils.

She reached around his head and untied the mask. Then she stared deeply into his mahogany eyes as she spoke.

"You are my fantasy, Kyros. You are the only man I will ever want. I love you."

She brought her lips to his and they shared a kiss. Then Kyros pulled her atop his lap, facing her in a straddling position.

"Are you ready to consummate our marriage, wife? I've been dreaming of this moment for a long time."

"Yes. So have I. I'm ready and willing to become your wife."

Thera felt his hands spreading her legs a little farther. Then she felt him entering her and realized just what he was doing.

"Kyros. Is this the proper way to do it? And in the tub?"

"One thing you're going to have to realize, Thera. Being my wife may mean having to try all sorts of new ways to do it."

"I see." She closed her eyes as she felt him settling into her. It felt so right. It felt so real. "I think I'm going to like that part," she replied.

The next thing she knew he was rocking below her. He grabbed her hips and rocked hers to meet him in a wonderful kind of rhythm.

"Almost like a dance, isn't it?" she asked, and then realized no dance had ever made her feel this way before. The searing heat of the water was nothing compared to the heat that now consumed her. She was surprised the water didn't boil beneath them.

Her breathing deepened and she felt herself enliven. She rocked faster, and he matched her.

"Thera," he whispered, "let me know if I'm hurting you."

"Don't jest," she laughed and threw back her head. The ends of her long hair dipped in the water. "After birthing a baby, nothing can even be considered painful again."

Kyros chuckled, but never broke the rhythm. "Can't say I know how you feel."

She felt herself vibrating as her muscles grabbed him even closer. She wanted more of him. She wanted more of this.

"I … I feel the way I did when we were first joined by Ares' beam." She let loose with any restraints and inhibitions. This time she was going to feel it physically. This is the way it should have been the first time they were joined.

"I feel that way too, Thera. Only actually touching you is so much better." He caressed her body as he spoke.

"Yes!" Thera screamed as she inhaled his musky scent. She could hear his own breathing quicken and this excited her even more. He grabbed her head and kissed her, thrusting his tongue into her mouth as the action was imitated under the water. He tasted like wine, mountain and man. He tasted like freedom. He tasted like her husband.

Their movements quickened as she climbed to the peaks of her mind. She was alive, she was vibrating. For Zeus' sake, she was this man's wife. She liked how it felt and wanted to know the feeling even more. And she got to know it three more times all in a matter of minutes.

"That's it, Thera," Kyros whispered in her ear. "Let yourself go."

Then the scent of the roasted pheasant, stuffed grape leaves and wine drifted to her. She knew now that her hunger hadn't really been for food at all. It had been for this—for Kyros, all along. She couldn't stop herself from giving in to it and neither did she want to. She wanted to keep on going forever, but her body was beginning to tire.

"Done so soon, Thera?" Kyros laughed. "I thought you'd be happy to go on well into the night."

"I would if I could, Kyros. But I think I need to rest. But I'm not going to stop until I've pleased you as much as you've pleased me."

"That won't take long. I've only been waiting for you."

Kyros picked her hips up out of the water and had her kneel, holding on to the side of the tub. He then snuggled his body close behind her, using his knee in the water to part her legs.

"Something else I should learn?" she asked.

"I told you, you're going to learn all kinds of things." His hands moved around her, caressing her breasts as his body pressed up against her back.

He then entered from behind her, reminding her of the way an animal mates. Or possibly a Centaur. She didn't think she had an ounce of energy left but was proved a liar as she danced and released once again—and this time Kyros joined her. The breathing was heavy, the heat intense. The pleasure blissful, and the imminent joy was more than she could ever explain. Physical contact put the power of the gods to shame.

He pulled back from her and turned her around to face him. He kissed the top of her head and then behind her ear and down her neck. They were no longer joined, but she knew he was still a part of her. They would be a part of each other from this day on—as man and wife. Humans. Mortals. The power of love diminished forever the horrible curse of Kyros' Secret.

To my readers:

I hope you enjoyed Kyros and Thera's story. Greek mythology has always fascinated me, and I loved writing Kyros' Secret. *I also love writing medieval romance and chose to combine the two into a fantasy novel; hence, you'll find many medieval similarities along with the elements of ancient Greek myths and lore. I've chosen to create my characters with a bit of modern language or traits to help the reader identify and not feel hampered by too much authenticity. But then again, who really knows what ancient Greece three or four thousand years ago was really like?*

And who really knows if there was any basis behind the myths. I'd like to think there was. Fantasy has always intrigued me. I believe with a good imagination and a flair for creativity, anything is possible. Therefore, Kaj was born, a cursed man who maintains his individuality and quest for peace between the races even in his centaur form.

Let yourself get lost within the world of magic, centaurs, satyrs, mermaids, sirens and nymphs. Let your imagination believe in eternal youth and immortality. Let your beliefs extend to the world of shape-shifting, curses, the Elysian Fields and the Underworld of Tartarus. And always remember this world may not really be as you see it, but only an illusion in which we are lost.

I have many ideas for more Greek myth romances, one being probably the only myth that truly had a happy ending. Please write to me and let me know if you liked Kyros' Secret *and if you'd like to see more Greek myth fantasy romances in the future. My address is: Elizabeth Rose, P.O. Box 811, Downers Grove, IL 60515. Or you can reach me through my Web site at http://scribesworld.com/elizabethrose/.*

About the author

Romance novelist Elizabeth Rose lives in the suburbs of Chicago with her husband and two young sons. She is a free-lance artist as well as a cover photographer. Her photography can be seen on some Genesis Press releases including her own cover *Eden's Garden*. Her latest work can be seen on the cover of *Kyros' Secret*.

Elizabeth has taught preschool, practiced martial arts and taken a trip to the jungles of Peru where she traded goods with the native tribes. She loves tigers, crystals, myths, magic and anything out of the ordinary. Fantacy romance is her favorite genre.